MAN OR SPIRIT

His mission done, Wolf had one more thing to check on, so he returned to the front door of the trading post and entered. The Cheyenne woman made no move and no sound when the man in animal skins suddenly appeared in the doorway, a Winchester rifle in his hand. Wolf looked at her, then looked toward the corner where Boyd was just beginning to stir on the cot. Turning back to the woman then, he asked, "His name is Taggart?"

She shook her head slowly, then spoke. "His name Boyd Dawson."

Wolf nodded solemnly. "Then I got no quarrel with him."

He started to turn and leave, but Clem appeared in the doorway to the back room, holding a shotgun. When he looked into the eyes of the baleful avenger, the Winchester rifle ready to speak, he dropped the shotgun at once and held up his hands. Wolf fixed his gaze upon the frightened storekeeper for a moment before taking a step toward the door. "You're him, ain't you?" Clem asked hesitantly. "The one they call Wolf." Wolf didn't answer, but Clem was sure it was the man the Indians talked about, the one some of them were convinced was a spirit and not a man at all.

DAY OF THE WOLF

Charles G. West

BERKLEY
New York

BERKLEY
An imprint of Penguin Random House LLC
penguinrandomhouse.com

ISBN: 9780451414076

Signet mass-market edition / September 2012
Berkley mass-market edition / June 2021

Printed in the United States of America
10   9

For Ronda

Chapter 1

Wolf was as much a part of the violence of the forest and mountains as the savage beast for which he was named, and that name was almost a legend among the Lakota and Cheyenne bands that roamed the Powder River Valley. A ghostlike presence that haunted the rugged hills and valleys of the Big Horn Mountains and the Wind River Range, Wolf was seen on rare occasions by Indian hunting parties, but almost never by white men—soldiers or settlers. Even these infrequent sightings were only by his choice, such as a visit to a trading post or an unusual circumstance, like the time he suddenly appeared to warn two Lakota women and their children, who were picking berries, unaware that they had managed to come between a mama grizzly and her cubs. The women had never seen the lone hunter before, but they were sure that he was the one their people called the Wolf, for he appeared out of nowhere and advised them to take their children back the way they had come. He then distracted the bear until they were safely away.

Ernie Crockett, who traded with the Indians before tensions heated up to the point of open war with the Lakotas and the Cheyenne, said that Wolf was a man and no legend at all. It was likely a name the Indians had created, maybe from a rare sighting of the man disguised with a wolf hide over himself for the purpose of getting close enough to a buffalo to use his bow. It was a tactic used by the Indians themselves, since buffalo were accustomed to seeing wolves skulking around the herd. "Before I packed up my tradin' post and left," Ernie claimed, "the man came in and traded pelts for .44 cartridges on more than one occasion. He was real enough, just quiet and kinda edgy till he got his cartridges and left." Ernie chuckled when telling it. "Yep, he was real, all right, but I reckon the Injuns would rather have him be a spirit or somethin'."

On this day, however, man or spirit, Wolf was facing a situation he had never faced before. He had fought a cougar with no weapon but his skinning knife, and faced down an angry grizzly until the bear retreated. But he had never felt as uncertain and cautious as he did at this moment. His better judgment told him to back away carefully.

"Where you goin', darlin'? You ain't bashful, are ya?" Seated on a quilt draped over the tailgate of her wagon, her knees spread like the springs of a bear trap, Lorena Parker beckoned with an index finger, enticingly, she presumed. But her quarry seemed more intent upon retreating. "I said I'd pay you to take me to Fort Laramie," she went on. "What did you think I meant?

Money? Hell, I ain't got no money. That's the whole reason I'm goin' to Fort Laramie."

Wolf was distracted for a moment by the delighted giggles of the other two women who sat nearby as casual witnesses to Lorena's negotiations. He cast a wary glance in their direction before turning his gaze back to the buxom woman. His intimate experience with females was limited to a casual encounter with a young Crow maiden when he was little more than a boy. It was a time of innocence that bore no resemblance to the almost certain peril lurking within the jaws of the beckoning trap spread so easily before him. He took another step back.

"I swear," Lorena remarked, duly puzzled now by Wolf's reluctance. "What's the matter with you? Why don't you skin them buckskins off? You look like you oughta be a ragin' stud." Closing her knees then and sitting upright, she studied the wary young man. "Maybe I ain't the one you got your eye on. Maybe you'd rather take your trade out on Billie Jean or Rose. Is that it? I expect either one of 'em would be happy to accommodate you." The suggestion brought a new round of giggles from the two women, and finally caused him to find his voice.

"I'll take you to Fort Laramie," he stated flatly. "There ain't no charge."

"You don't know what you're missing," Rose teased.

"I bet he's got himself a little wife somewhere, and he's true-lovin' her," Billie Jean chimed in. "Is that it, stud?" Her question was answered with a blank stare of disbelief.

"As soon as your horses are rested up," he said, ignoring the question, "we'll start out for Fort Laramie.

They've been drove too hard." He paused before adding, "And in the wrong direction." He turned then and
walked away to tend to his horse, silently cursing the
luck that had caused him to come to the rescue of the
three prostitutes. It was the first time he had ever seen
a prostitute, as far as he knew, and he found it hard to
believe that a man would part with money to risk a
tussle with the two older women.

"Suit yourself. I wasn't hankerin' after it myself,"
Lorena called after him, although she could not deny a
certain fascination for a man who looked to be akin to
a cougar. When he made no reply, but kept walking
toward the bay gelding at the edge of the creek, she
attempted to excuse her erroneous sense of direction.
"That no-good son of a bitch we hired in Cheyenne
headed us out this way." If he heard her, he made no
indication of it. "How the hell do we know you're any
better'n he was?" she asked in a lowered voice, primarily for the benefit of her two companions, since she was
not willing to give him cause to change his mind.

"I reckon we oughta offer to feed him, since he ain't
lookin' to take it out in trade," Rose suggested. "There's
no telling where we woulda ended up if he hadn't
come along when he did."

"Most likely Medicine Bow is what he said," Billie
Jean recalled, "if we'da kept goin' west."

"Or nowhere a'tall after you drove my wagon into
that damn creek," Lorena reminded her.

"Well, I was wonderin' how long it was gonna be
before you started blaming me for that," Billie Jean
responded. "I wasn't the one who decided to cross
where we did. We all three thought it looked like a
good place to cross, so don't lay that blame on me."

"We shoulda known that darker water meant there was a hole there," Rose said. "Ain't nobody blaming you." She paused to recall the incident. "It was kinda scary the way he showed up, though, wasn't it? One minute we were stuck in that hole in the creek with nobody else in sight. The next minute we turn around and he was there, just sitting on his horse, watching us trying to get outta that hole." She turned her head then to gaze at the somber man leading his horse up from beside the creek.

Lorena didn't respond verbally, but it *had* been a little unnerving. All three women were startled to find the lone rider calmly watching their efforts to undo their mistake. She assumed they had been too absorbed in their predicament to notice his approach, but it did appear that he had simply popped up out of thin air. Her first thought upon seeing him was that they were about to be robbed at best, and maybe killed at worse. She didn't know which for a few long minutes, for he said nothing, his face absolutely devoid of expression. She had not been sure at first if he was white or Indian, for he was dressed in animal skins and carried both rifle and bow strapped in his saddle sling. When he finally spoke, it was to say, "You ain't never gonna get it out that way." Then he fixed his gaze upon Billie Jean, who had been flogging the horses in hopes of encouraging them to pull the wagon out of the hole that had trapped it. "Stop whippin' them horses," he calmly directed. She immediately dropped the reins. He nudged his horse out into the creek to check the extent of their problem and, after only a minute or two, took a coil of rope from the side of the wagon, stepped out of the saddle into the water, and tied the rope to the rear axle. In the saddle again, he took a couple of turns around the saddle horn and pulled the rope taut. "All right," he ordered as he nudged his horse, "haul back on the reins." The wagon backed out of the hole with very little strain. Letting the rope go slack, he rode back into the water to take hold of one of the horses' bridles, then turned the wagon upstream and led it out on the bank.

"Well, mister, I reckon we're beholden to you," Lorena had remarked, although she allowed that she might have come up with the same simple solution, given a little more time. Her main concern at that point had been to determine the strange man's intentions, now that the wagon was high and dry, although everybody was wet to some extent. His only reply to her comment was to suggest that they should build a fire to dry out. She couldn't argue with that, so she helped Billie Jean and Rose gather wood while he, without a word, unhitched her horses. *I reckon we're going to rest here a spell,* she had thought, somewhat chagrined.

Things had not gone according to Lorena's plans since she had decided to leave Cheyenne, where the competition in her line of employment had gotten too crowded for women of her age. One of her regular customers, Lige Ingram, had claimed to know the country like the back of his hand and for a price would take on the job as her guide. Her decision to accept his offer was not due to his claim to know how to go to Fort Laramie. There was a well-traveled trail between Cheyenne and the fort, but there had been recent trouble with the Sioux. Lige persuaded her that he knew shortcuts that would also lessen the danger of meeting an Indian war party. She looked upon it as insurance, for she felt responsible for Billie Jean and especially Rose. Billie Jean really needed no one to look out for her, but Rose was an unfortunate victim of fate who should not have found herself engaged in the ancient profession that Lorena and Billie Jean embraced. Her story was one of innocence betrayed by an unlucky encounter with a pair of rapists and the stigma the incident left on her in the tiny community where she was born. Although her abusers were caught and punished, she found she would be forever branded and ruined as far as young men who knew her were concerned. Feeling there was no future for her in her hometown, she left to try to make a new life for herself. Unfortunately she found that her only way to survive was to market her youthful body. Her story was not a great deal different from other soiled doves', but Lorena felt an obligation to watch over her. So when Lige lit out in the middle of the night, evidently content to settle for the half of the agreed-upon fee he already had in his pocket, Lorena was burdened with a feeling of increased responsibility.

As far as Lige was concerned, he was probably lost anyway, she figured, for he had led them away from the common road in a ruse to make them think he was taking a shortcut. Good riddance, she had thought, even though she hated the loss of the money, and had assumed that they should simply continue in the same direction he had been leading them. Now, with an agreement with this mysterious stranger, she couldn't help wondering if her situation was worse. She had not feared Lige Ingram, for she speculated that the three women could probably handle Lige if he chose to take advantage of them. But this wild-looking creature who had gotten their wagon out of the creek might be an entirely different kettle of fish.

On the other side of the fire, Wolf was no more comfortable with the unexpected partnership than Lorena. He still counted it as bad luck to have ridden this way. But after having come upon the three women, he had offered to lend a hand simply out of concern for the two horses that Billie Jean was flogging so relentlessly. Upon hearing their accounting of the unfortunate contract with Lige Ingram, he had not felt right about leaving them to find their way to Fort Laramie on their own—although the fort was easy enough to find. So he decided he would take them a little farther west until reaching Chugwater Creek. Then he could be done with them, for from that point, they could follow the Chugwater to its confluence with the Laramie River. Once they reached the Laramie, they could simply follow it to the fort.

Although eager to take his leave of the three women, he could not deny a measure of fascination for their unabashed lack of modesty. All three had removed their outer garments and hung them by the fire to dry while they proceeded to prepare a meal in the flimsiest of undergarments, seemingly oblivious of his curious eye. He found himself hoping that their clothes would dry quickly. There were other things about the women that he found interesting, however. He was especially curious about the coffee mill Rose used to grind the beans. It was a square wooden box with intricate carving on the sides and a cast-iron crank on the top. After pouring the coffee beans in the top, she turned the crank for a while, then pulled out a small drawer in the front of the box that held the ground coffee. He had heard of coffee mills before, but this was the first he had actually seen. If his mother had one when he was a small boy, he didn't remember it. He was impressed. It certainly was an improvement over his method of crushing the beans with a rock.

Lorena took note of his curious eye as he watched their every move and fixed his gaze on her preparation of pan bread. "Have to let it rise a little," she explained, although he had not asked why she had left the pan on the warm coals at the edge of the fire instead of cooking it closer to the center where the coals were hotter. "Then it'll be ready to bake," she said. He nodded in response, understanding then. A fleeting memory darted across his mind of his mother baking bread in an iron stove, but he quickly blinked it away, sending it back to the childhood that had been a prior life. Lorena glanced at Billie Jean, who was watching the two of them with a smile of amusement on her face. *He's like a child watching me,* Lorena thought. *He must have been living under a rock all his life.*

Lorena's thoughts were probably natural under the circumstances, but her mistake was in judging the man's fascination as a sign of innocence in all things. To the contrary, he knew the savage world he chose to live in better than any man, for he knew the ways of the red man and the mystery of the mountains and forests. More than anything else, his ability to survive in the isolation of the mountain wilderness to the northwest of this creek in the prairie was in great part due to his ability to observe and learn.

He was eleven years old when his parents were killed along with twenty-eight others as their wagon train traveled through South Pass. Eight men and their wives perished on that day, and all their children, save one, were murdered by an Indian war party. By which band, Wolf never knew, for none of the settlers could tell one Indian from another. With a shotgun taken from his dead father's hand and a sack of shotgun shells, the boy crawled nearly seventy-five yards up a narrow streambed to escape the scalping party that overran the wagon train to finish off the wounded. From a small stand of pines, the boy lay and watched the ransacking of the wagons and the mutilation of the dead. Tears had streamed down his face as he witnessed the desecration of his parents' bodies, and the agony he felt burning inside him almost caused him to rush to avenge them. But he knew that it would be useless to try. There were too many to fight. So he sat, helpless, and watched for what seemed an eternity while the savages darted from wagon to wagon, scattering furniture and belongings that had been hauled halfway across the continent, destined to be the seed for a new life in the Oregon country.

Finally, when the Indians had satisfied their lust for mayhem, and the sun dropped lower in the sky, they departed. So young Tom Logan left his hiding place and went back to stare at the inhumane carnage left by the warriors, temporarily paralyzed by the stark brutality and disregard for human life. He had not known such savagery existed in the world until this moment, but it was a lesson that would remain with him all his life.

After what seemed forever, he forced his mind to focus on what must be done to survive. The most important thing, he decided, was to bury his parents and perhaps to salvage anything that he might be able to use. The Indians had attempted to set the wagons on fire, but all but a few of the wagons survived with little more than scorched wagon beds and ruined wagon sheets. With no idea as to what he was going to do from this point forward, he occupied his mind with the task of giving his mother and father a decent burial. Pick and shovel were readily available on nearly every wagon, since the savages evidently had no regard for the tools.

It was close to dark by the time he had finished digging the grave and resolved himself to the task of dragging his parents' bodies into the shallow hole. He choked back a sob when he looked again at his mother's bloody body, her blouse soaked red from two bullet holes in her breast. But determined to save their remains from the wolves and buzzards, he pulled both bodies to the grave. Gently wrapping their bloody faces with the remains of a half-burned bedsheet, he then proceeded to shovel the dirt over them. It was the worst part of the ordeal for him, but when the grave was finally filled in, he felt more at peace with his parents safely settled in their eternal rest. That done, he sank down beside the grave, unable to think of what he should now do. The whole world seemed to be suddenly devoid of all sound—no birds, no rustling of night critters in the underbrush, no sounds of the horses. It was as if there was nothing left alive but him. Exhausted, he sat there for almost an hour, hardly moving, until at last he lay back on the ground and drifted off to sleep.

He was awakened early the next morning by the sound of an animal snuffling around the half-burned wagon behind him. Sitting upright, he discovered a pack of coyotes sniffing around the bodies strewn on the ground. A shadow flitted quickly across his face, and he looked up to see a circle of buzzards overhead. His first impulse was to fire his father's shotgun to frighten the scavengers away, so he quickly loaded a couple of shells in the double-barreled weapon and fired once in the air. The result was what he had hoped, for the coyotes immediately scattered in fright. But the success was short-lived, because within minutes the beasts began to slink back and the buzzards became even bolder, enticed by the abundance of food. It was then obvious to the eleven-year-old boy that he was not likely to win a battle with the law of nature. Even if successful in the endeavor, he was not willing to use up his precious shotgun shells in an attempt to kill all the coyotes and buzzards. Neither was he prepared to dig enough graves to bury all of the victims; so, accepting the fact that he was obliged to look out for his own existence, he joined in the scavenging of the wagons.

Knowing he was alone in the world, he searched for blankets and clothes to keep him warm, a pan to cook in, water sacks or a canteen, and anything else of use that the Indians might have overlooked. There was not much to find, for the war party had been pretty thorough. However, he was lucky to find a hatchet and a skinning knife in the storage compartment beneath the boards of a wagon bed. His fellow predators ignored him for the most part, having plenty of food sources to choose from, only challenging him once when a coyote contested a half side of bacon left in a barrel under a wagon. The contest was determined when Tom spent one of his shotgun shells to settle the debate, leaving one more meal for the other scavengers. When he had searched all the wagons and was satisfied there was nothing else of value for him to find, he looked around at the carnage still in progress. Then he turned and looked at the mountains to the north. It occurred to his young mind that there was safety for him in the mountains. He needed a place to hide, for he feared there would be other war parties riding through South Pass.

He was not sure of the exact date, but it was late August, and he knew that winter was already on its way. His father had been worried that they had started too late in the season to reach Oregon before the mountain passes would be closed with snow, and thoughts of the Donner party some ten years before had come to haunt him. Now similar thoughts came to trouble the boy's mind as he decided what to do. The possibility of continuing on to Oregon was out of the question with nothing awaiting him there. There was nothing for him at Fort Laramie, either, if he tried to return to that army post. Seeing no choice but to seek a place in the mountains where he could become invisible to the Indians, he turned his concentration toward finding the right spot to build his nest. Using twine from a ball he found in one of the wagons, he tied his blanket in a roll, with everything he could pack inside. With his hatchet and knife in his belt, his shotgun in one hand, and a sack containing the quarter side of bacon in the other, he started walking to the north.

With his sights set on the mountains, he continued to walk across the wide expanse of prairie and sagebrush until reaching the foothills that offered some protection from hostile eyes. With his father's flint and steel, he was able to build a fire to cook the bacon he had managed to save from the coyote. With hatchet and knife, he constructed a rough shelter to provide some protection from the cold mornings in this high elevation. With his first camp now established, he determined to hunt for food.

He had hunted many times with his father, and he was confident of his ability to use his father's shotgun, but he knew that he would soon be out of shells, so he assigned himself the task of making a bow for small game. With no one to teach him, he experimented with many failures, using limbs from various trees and twine for a bowstring, forcing him to rig traps for squirrels and other small animals to keep from starving. In time, he fashioned a crude bow that provided him with a weapon that worked after a fashion, but it would be some time yet before he learned to shape the proper wood and use animal gut for a bowstring. Through trial and error, he learned to survive.

Over the next several years, the boy found that he was at home in the mountains, and he moved from camp to camp, sometimes high up in the mountains, sometimes along the river that flowed through the valley, following the game that provided his food and clothing. Satisfied with the solitude he found, he had no desire for contact with other humans, and occasionally it was necessary to melt into the trees quickly to avoid an Indian hunting party. Isolation was not his intention in the beginning, but more a natural evolvement that made him at home in the forest, like the coyotes and wolves that hunted the prairie and mountain ridges. Before long, stories of a wild boy began to circulate among the different Shoshone villages when hunters caught a fleeting glimpse of him as he slipped away into the forest.

No one knew where the boy got the name of Wolf, but Wolf himself remembered the day he learned he was called that. It was an important day in the young man's life, for it marked the first time he had left the sanctuary of the mountains. And his first contact was not with Shoshone hunters but in a chance meeting with a group of Crow hunters in the eastern foothills of the Wind River Range. Now, on this day in June, he recalled those circumstances as he casually watched the three prostitutes prepare supper.

From a rocky ledge at the top of a cliff, he had watched the group of five Crow hunters following a wounded deer through the thick brush lining the stream below him. *They were lucky to find deer*, he thought, *for these hills are about hunted out*. Content to remain an observer, he remained kneeling on one knee, watching the event and thinking that if they did not find the deer, he would make use of their kill. A rustling among the willows on the opposite side of the stream caught his eye and he stared hard in that direction. A moment later, he glimpsed the head and shoulders of a Shoshone warrior as he pushed stealthily through the willow thicket. The first warrior was followed by a second, a third, and a fourth, all carrying rifles, and all advancing upon the unsuspecting Crows. Their intent was obvious, but Wolf felt no responsibility toward either faction, no more so than if it had been a fight between two beasts of the forest; so he remained hidden, content to watch the drama.

Possessing the element of surprise, the Shoshone hunters struck first, just as the Crows were about to find the deer, catching them completely off guard. The initial volley killed three of the Crows before they could respond. The remaining two, although one was wounded, reacted quickly enough to retaliate, killing two of their attackers. At that point, it became a duel between the four remaining combatants at point-blank range. After a series of shots were exchanged, all went quiet, and Wolf moved closer to the edge of the ledge in an effort to see what had happened. After a lengthy pause with no sound from below, he surmised that they had managed to kill each other, and as a result, it occurred to him that fate had provided him the opportunity to acquire weapons and possibly a horse, not to mention a fresh supply of meat. The thought of it caused a rush of excitement in his body. He had been without shells for his shotgun for several years, and he had never owned a horse.

Jumping from ledge to ledge like the goats he had observed in the high mountains, he descended the cliff to the stream below. He paused to take a look around the thicket before moving cautiously through it to the scene of the battle. The bodies lay close together, all apparently dead. He recognized the Shoshone hunters, because he had seen them many times. The others were not Indians he had seen before. Looking about him, he was excited to see rifles of several different makes, but the one that captured his attention was one with a lever-type action, lying next to one of the Shoshones. He immediately dropped the single-shot, bolt-action rifle he had first spotted and picked up the Henry. Turning it over and over, impressed by the cold, lethal beauty of the weapon, he was aware of a feeling of new confidence, for it gave him a powerful weapon for protection, far superior to his crude bow and arrows.

He rolled the body over to remove the cartridge belt. As he was strapping it around his waist, he sensed a possible danger, and he looked quickly at a body lying several feet away in time to catch the movement of the eyelids as they slammed shut. Immediately alert, he cocked the rifle and prepared to defend himself, but there was no threat from the wounded man, since Wolf could see the man's rifle lying several yards away. Having no animosity toward either side in the short, violent confrontation that had just taken place, Wolf went to the wounded man's side and knelt. When he rolled him over on his back, the Indian's eyes fluttered wide open and the two men stared at each other for a few moments—the white man in curiosity, the Indian in helpless fear that the scalping knife would come next.

Wolf looked at the hole in the Indian's upper chest and nodded solemnly. With no knowledge of any Indian dialects, he asked simply, "How bad?"

There was a flicker of hope in the wounded man's eyes, and he rasped a response in English. "Don't know. Hurt like hell."

"I'll try to help," Wolf said, almost startled when the Indian spoke. It was almost as strange to hear his own voice as well, for he had spoken very little over the past several years. "I'll be back," he said, and rose to his feet then to quickly check the other bodies to make sure they were dead. He wouldn't hesitate to help the wounded man, but he wanted to make sure he didn't get a bullet in the back while he was doing it. After he was satisfied that the other warriors offered no threat, he returned to the wounded man's side. "I don't know much about doctorin'," he said, "but I'll do what I can."

"Get horses first," the Indian said.

"All right," Wolf said. He had not thought about the horses, but he realized then that he should have. He immediately disappeared into the willows where he had seen four Indian ponies when he came down from the cliff. Knowing there should be five more close at hand, he continued to follow the stream until he came upon the other horses. He tied the reins together to a length of rawhide rope he found on one of the horses and led the five back to pick up the other four. When he returned to the scene of the fight, he tied his lead rope to a tree and left the horses to stand in a bunch.

While Wolf was fetching the horses, the wounded man had managed to pull himself up to a half-raised position with his back against a tree. Though obviously in great pain, the Indian gazed steadily at his white benefactor as he approached once again. "You're the one they call Wolf," he pronounced, for he was sure it could be no other.

Not understanding, Wolf responded with a blank stare at first, then asked, "Why do you say that? I don't know that name."

Certain that he was right, the Indian said, "That is what they call you. My name is Big Knife of the Absaroka people. I thank you for your kindness."

Remembering that Absaroka was how the Crows referred to themselves, he was somewhat surprised to find a Crow hunting party in this part of the Wind River Mountains. "My name is Tom Logan," he said. "I don't know this name you call me." It occurred to him then that he had had to pause to think for a moment before recalling his name. It had been years since it had been necessary. He turned his attention to the care of Big Knife's wound then. There was little more he could do for the wound than to fetch water from the stream and clean it as best he could. He had failed to notice earlier that, in addition to the chest wound, there was a long, shallow wound in Big Knife's scalp on the side of his head. Though not serious, this wound probably explained the unconscious state he was in when Wolf first arrived.

As his brain cleared somewhat from the grazing blow to his head, Big Knife realized that the wound in his chest was probably not as serious as he had at first thought. "I don't think bullet in too deep," he said. "Maybe you pull it out." Wolf nodded agreeably and drew his skinning knife, grateful for Big Knife's suggestion, having been undecided what he should do to help the wounded man. Proving the Crow's prognosis to be correct, Wolf was successful in probing for the lead slug and extracted it with a minimum of harm to the wound. At Big Knife's suggestion, Wolf built a fire for the purpose of cauterizing the wound. The treatment left Big Knife with limited use of his left arm and shoulder, but otherwise able to ride.

It was time then to decide what to do next. There was much to be done in order to return to his village, which was two full days' ride to the Sweetwater River. The bodies of his four brother tribesmen would have to be taken home, as well as extra horses that were too valuable to leave behind. Big Knife clearly needed help, and although Tom was reluctant to stray far from his familiar territory, he agreed to go with him. Although Big Knife felt an urgency to leave before encountering another Shoshone party, they decided to wait until morning to start. There was a deer to skin and butcher if they were to have food for the journey, so Wolf set about recovering the carcass at once. After he had meat roasting over the fire, he turned to the task of loading the bodies of Big Knife's friends on their ponies. Of the four Shoshone horses, Wolf took his pick, at Big Knife's insistence, and selected a stout bay with a substantial Indian saddle. Big Knife smiled, satisfied that Wolf had been rewarded with horse, rifle, and ammunition for his trouble. "Good pick," he said. "Pony strong. Make you good horse."

Big Knife watched his unlikely rescuer as Wolf finished the preparations to leave, fascinated by the young man known by several of the tribes as the seldom-seen spirit of the mountains. It was obvious by the crude workmanship of the deerskin garments and leggings that there was no woman's hand in the sewing. And there was an almost childlike air about the man's conduct. But there was no doubting the young man's strength, for he hefted the bodies of Big Knife's friends upon the backs of their horses with little more than an insignificant grunt. Now, the chores done, he sat down opposite Big Knife and examined his newly acquired rifle, again in a childlike manner. Big Knife was sure he was the one for whom the legend was created. "Wolf," he pronounced. "That good name for you."

The young man glanced up when Big Knife said it. He stopped to consider what the Crow warrior said. He had not been Tom Logan for many years now. "Wolf" suited him better. He decided to keep the name. It was what Big Knife was going to call him anyway.

What would have been a two-day ride turned into three because of Big Knife's injury. Although it was not a life-threatening wound, the bullet had torn into the muscles of his chest and shoulder, making it uncomfortable to ride for extended periods of time. During the times of rest, the Crow warrior sought to satisfy his curiosity for the seemingly guileless young white man who seemed as much a part of the frontier as the Indian. And yet there were many things that Crow boys learned at an early age that Wolf obviously did not know. The first lesson was to offer suggestions that would make the boy's butchering of the deer more efficient, saving time as well as some of the better parts of the carcass. He found Wolf to be receptive to his suggestions, and not offended at all. The butchering was the first of many lessons Wolf would learn from his new friend and mentor.

Eager to try out his new weapon, Wolf reluctantly waited until they had ridden farther from the Wind River Range where Big Knife felt they were closer to Crow country. On their last evening before reaching Big Knife's village, Wolf spent half a dozen cartridges to learn the rifle's tendencies. His marksmanship, with his having never fired the rifle before, was enough to impress his Crow friend. He nodded approvingly and said, "New rifle big medicine." Had it not been for the fact that the ride back to his village was in actuality a funeral procession for his four Crow brothers, Big Knife would have enjoyed the experience.

Arriving at the village in the afternoon of the third day, the party of two riders and nine horses was met with mourning for the slain warriors. Big Knife's new friend was well received and treated with gestures of welcome and gratitude for helping Big Knife return safely. Thinking his obligation to the wounded man complete, Wolf planned to return to the mountains the next day. However, Big Knife's entreaty to stay, as well as that from the rest of the village, was enough to persuade Wolf to prolong his visit for a few days. Those few days evolved into almost five years that taught the young man the ways of the Crow Indians. It was a happy time for Wolf as he became an accomplished hunter and trapper, with both rifle and a more efficient bow that Big Knife helped him make. He learned to steal horses from the Sioux and Blackfeet, and he counted his first coup soon after joining Big Knife's village when a war party rode west to avenge the four warriors who had lost their lives in the Shoshone fight.

The last traces of the innocence that had remained from his boyhood were destroyed in the twentieth year of his birth when the village was attacked by a large party of Lakota raiders while most of the Crow warriors were away hunting buffalo. The wanton slaughter of women and children was the catalyst that sealed the savage reality of the plains in Wolf's mind, and shattered his sense of a carefree existence with nature. The single most severe impact upon him was the death of his longtime mentor, Big Knife, who was killed trying to defend his wife and children from the Lakota attack. It was the second devastating loss in Wolf's life, and served to form a reluctance to let anyone else come that close to him in the future.

When he returned to the village with the other hunters, Wolf, along with most of the hunting party, immediately rode in pursuit of the Lakota. With horses already tired, the Crow party could not close the distance between themselves and the raiders. After two days, they gave up the chase when sign indicated they were getting farther and farther behind. On the morning of the third day, they talked among themselves and decided it was a useless endeavor to continue on into Sioux territory. There was the added concern over the safety of those survivors who remained in their village as well. So they decided to turn around and go back—all except one. So bitter was he over the loss of his friend, Wolf decided to continue on alone, determined to seek revenge for Big Knife's death. The others tried to persuade him to return with them, but he was confident that he could travel through enemy territory without being seen. He had spent most of his life remaining invisible to Shoshone warriors and hunters before he joined the Crow village, so he parted with his Crow friends on that morning, not realizing at the time that it would be a permanent separation.

As adept at reading sign as any Crow warrior, he followed the trail doggedly up through the Powder River country and into the Big Horn Valley. It was approaching dark when he came upon the Lakota village on the Big Horn River. When still some distance away, he could see the smoke from many campfires, so he left the trail he had been following and circled around a low ridge to the east of the river. Once he got to a point he guessed might be adjacent to the center of the village, he dismounted and left his horse while he climbed to the top of the ridge on foot to get a look at the camp.

From his position at the top, he got a good view of the sizable Lakota camp on the other side of the river, spread among the cottonwoods and brush that lined the banks. A pony herd of maybe twenty-five hundred grazed just beyond the village. Wolf lay there for quite some time, wondering now what vengeance he could take against a village of that size. While he thought about the possibilities, the darkness deepened as night came on. The longer he hesitated, the more rest his horse received, so he purposely lingered on the ridge, thinking it of dire importance to have a fresh horse to make good his escape when his vengeance was taken. *How,* he wondered, *can I find the members of the village who were actually on the raid that took the lives of so many of my friends?* His question was answered within the next few minutes when some of the people began to build a great fire in the middle of the village. It occurred to him then. *They're going to have a victory dance.* Of course they would celebrate the successful raid against their enemies, the Crows. His plan was simple now, even though limited. Still, it would send a message that their warriors would not escape without casualties.

As he went back down the ridge to get his horse, he could hear the people of the village gathering as the flames of the fire leaped higher into the dark sky. Leading the bay, Wolf made his way down to the bank of the river. Walking along the bank, he stopped at a slight rise in the bluffs that gave him an unobstructed view through the trees of the circle of dancers already forming. He decided at once that he was not likely to get a better spot to make his vengeance known, so he stepped up on his horse and gave it his heels. The bay started at once at a gallop. Wolf headed him back toward the ridge, letting him run for fifty yards or more before reining him back to a walk. Then he dismounted and led the horse back to the bank. He wasn't sure how many shots he would be able to fire before the Lakota realized he was only one man and came after him, but he hoped they would be fooled into following his tracks back toward the ridge.

He was ready now. He checked his rifle to see that the magazine was loaded, then cranked a cartridge into the chamber. Kneeling next to a cottonwood tree to steady himself, he trained his sights on the growing circle of dancers, hesitating for a few seconds while he watched the Lakota warriors sing of their deeds of bravery and victory, most of them holding the fresh scalps taken in the raid. Still, he waited to select his first victim until one warrior, who was more demonstrative in his reenactment of his taking of a woman's scalp, screamed out his war cry. With his front sight on the warrior's chest, Wolf squeezed the trigger and sent a .44 slug to slam into the dancer's breastbone, knocking him backward into the fire.

The initial reaction to the shot was one of startled confusion, with most of the dancers and spectators not sure what had just happened. Wolf took advantage of their confusion, cranking out three more shots while he still had stationary targets. It was only after three more of the dancers fell that the Lakota realized they were under attack, and the crowd scattered, seeking cover, but not until one more warrior was knocked to the ground as he tried to get on the other side of the fire. Moving quickly now to a different position in case his muzzle flashes had been spotted, Wolf searched for targets among the terrified people, passing up women and children, seeking warriors. One more clear shot and he decided he had retaliated in part for the cowardly attack upon his adopted village, and now thought it best to make his escape. Already he could hear sounds of a counterattack organizing. Calmer heads were bound to determine that their attacker was but one man firing a repeating rifle, and a furious mob of warriors would come charging across the river. Wolf did not plan to be there to greet them. He climbed on his horse and urged the bay into the water. Holding his rifle high in one hand, he turned the horse's head downstream and followed the current away from the Lakota village.

In the darkness behind him, he could hear the warriors as they splashed across the river to the point where his muzzle flashes had been spotted. With the help of a flaming limb from the fire, one of them spotted the fresh tracks of a horse galloping toward the ridge to the east. Without hesitating, the warriors started out after it, never noticing the horse and rider swimming down the river under cover of the dark, moonless night.

The fact that his escape was taking him deeper into Lakota territory did not cause him to be overly concerned. He felt confident that he could avoid contact with the Lakota Sioux as well as the Blackfeet farther north. With Big Knife and his family gone, he had no real interest in returning to the Crow camp. Maybe he would in time, but for now he felt a stronger pull to the mountains around him, for he had always felt at home in the mountains. Without realizing it, all traces of his carefree, almost boyish enjoyment of life had disappeared, washed away with the flood of cruelty that swept through Big Knife's village. His game of hide-and-seek with the Shoshone hunters had been no more than that, a boy's game. The slaughter of innocent Crow women and children was the stark reality of the world in which he lived. He had coolly executed six Lakota warriors and there had been no sense of remorse or regret in his heart. His transformation to unyielding granite was now complete.

The next several years saw a restless odyssey through the mountains of Wyoming and Montana, hunting and trapping to buy the cartridges and supplies he needed, avoiding white settlements as well as most Indian villages. His contact with white men was restricted to the few trading posts he visited. This did not mean that he lived in a world apart from Indian and white man, for he knew where the Indians were, and he knew where the soldiers marched. Those facts were vital to his existence.

Even for a man with Wolf's disdain for civilization, however, the notion to travel back to a place in time could tempt him after a while to return to see what had become of those he once knew in better circumstances. This was what prompted him to travel back to the Sweetwater and the Powder to find Big Knife's old village. So he now sat, gazing into a campfire, earnestly regretting the decision. If he had not gone looking for the Crow village, he would not now be saddled with the responsibility of guiding three whores to Fort Laramie.

Deputy Marshal Ned Bull turned the red roan he rode toward the jail in Cheyenne, Wyoming Territory.

Riding along behind him on a lead rope sat the sullen murderer Arlo Taggart, his hands tied behind him. The Cheyenne jail was a welcome sight to Ned's eyes. He couldn't turn his prisoner over to the sheriff soon enough to suit him. Arlo was one of three brothers who had raised enough hell down in the Nations to warrant a posse of U.S. deputy marshals to chase them out of Indian Territory into Texas, where they had seemingly disappeared for the better part of a year. A month ago, Arlo, the middle brother, surfaced again, this time in Ned's jurisdiction when he robbed the Cheyenne bank, pistol-whipped one of the tellers, and shot the manager down when he bolted for the door. Although Arlo was alone on the bank job, Ned figured Beau and Mace were in the vicinity as well, but there was no way to tell for sure, because Arlo claimed they were still in Texas. If that was the case, then it would be the first time the boys worked on their own, so Ned felt sure the other two were close by. He was inclined to hunt for them, but the witnesses to the shooting said Arlo was alone, and when Ned trailed him to Clem Russell's trading post on the North Platte River, he didn't see any choice but to take him back to Cheyenne. The arrest was relatively simple, since he caught Arlo in bed with Clem's Indian wife, Jewel, who practiced the ancient profession of prostitution. Arlo had a knot on his head and his hands cuffed before he knew what happened.

Ned pulled up to the hitching post in front of the jail and stepped down from the saddle. "Well, here you are, Arlo," he said as he pulled the brooding outlaw from his horse, "safe and sound. I'll see if we can find you a nice room with a view."

"You go to hell," Arlo snarled. "I ain't gonna be in no jail for long."

The big lawman smiled patiently at his prisoner. "I expect you're right," he said. "They'll most likely hang you pretty quick."

Arlo sneered. "I feel sorry for you, Marshal. When my brothers find out about this, your life won't be worth two cents."

"Why, I swear, that sure 'nough hurts my feelin's. I thought you and me was gettin' along just fine." It was not the first time in a long career that the deputy marshal had been threatened. "Now, step up on the stoop there, and let's check you into the sheriff's hotel." He gave Arlo a nudge between the shoulder blades with the muzzle of his Winchester '73.

The door opened just as Arlo stepped up on the narrow stoop. Acting sheriff J. R. Richardson stood framed in the doorway. "Marshal," J.R. greeted Ned. "I see you caught up with the murderin' son of a bitch."

"Yep," Ned replied cheerfully. "And as much as I'll miss his delightful company, I'll gladly turn him over to you."

"Well . . ." J.R. hesitated. "There's been a little change in plan. We got a wire from Omaha yesterday and they want you to take your prisoner to Fort Laramie and turn him over to the provost marshal there."

This was not welcome news to Ned. "What in hell for?" he responded. "He robbed the bank here. Why ain't you folks gonna try him and hang him right here?"

"Seems like Arlo and his brothers are wanted on federal charges in Oklahoma Territory and Texas. So they figure the army can hold him till the other two are rounded up. They'll probably give 'em a big trial and then hang 'em." He looked at a snarling Arlo Taggart and smiled. Returning his gaze to Ned then, he said, "I expect it's later than you'd wanna start out again today, so you can leave him in my jail overnight."

Ned answered with a grimace as he digested the sheriff's statement. He had been looking forward to parting company with the conscienceless killer and enjoying a day or two of relaxation in the hotel. Ned enjoyed staying in hotels, especially those with a fine dining room. "Dammit, J.R., I've been nursemaidin' this piece of dung for a hundred and forty miles. I've had about all of his company one man can stand." He fumed for a few moments more, only to be met with a shrug from the sheriff. "Hell," he finally replied, "orders are orders, I reckon. I'll take you up on entertainin' my prisoner for the night."

"You'll never get me to Fort Laramie," Arlo snarled. "You're as good as dead."

Ned cocked his head to give J.R. a mock look of concern. "Did you hear that, Sheriff? Threatenin' an officer of the law, and right in front of a witness." He nudged Arlo with a hard jab of his rifle, causing him to step forward to keep from falling. "He's just funnin'. He ain't really threatenin' nobody. Are you, Arlo?"

"You go to hell," Arlo spat.

Ned chuckled. "Ain't he a pure delight? Come on, Sheriff, I'll help you put him away, and I'll pick him up in the mornin'."

It was well after sunup by the time Ned walked into the stable to saddle his and Arlo Taggart's horses. He picked up the packhorse he had left in the stable while he had tracked Arlo, a decision he had regretted, for he had figured on catching the outlaw a helluva lot sooner, and a helluva lot closer to Cheyenne. As a result, he had run critically short of supplies, prompting plenty of complaints from his prisoner. The thought made him smile as he led the three horses up to the jail to pick up his prisoner. With Arlo on board, he started out for Fort Laramie, a trip he figured on making in two days' time, barring any trouble, planning to camp at Horse Creek that night.

By the time they reached Lodgepole Creek, not quite halfway, Arlo began complaining that his arms were paining him from so long with his hands behind his back. "It ain't that I don't feel sorry for you, Arlo," Ned told him, "'cause I do. I really want you to be comfortable on our little ride together. But I know you wouldn't respect me much if I was dumb enough to let you have your hands free. In about another twenty miles, we'll stop for the night, and I'll let you loosen up for a bit. In the meantime, just think about somethin' besides your arms. Think about what a nice day we've got for a ride to Fort Laramie."

"You go to hell," Arlo snorted.

Ned chuckled. "You know, Arlo, you oughta spend some of your time on your vocabulary while you're waitin' to be hanged."

"You go to hell," Arlo repeated, not sure what his vocabulary was, causing Ned to chuckle again.

Ned Bull was a cautious man, but not without compassion, even in the case of a cold-blooded murderer like Arlo Taggart. So when they reached Horse Creek, he helped Arlo off his horse and let him put his stiffened arms in front of him to answer nature's call. Arlo complained that he couldn't get his business done with his hands still tied together. "I reckon you're gonna have to figure a way to do it," Ned told him, "'cause I don't plan on untyin' you. If you can't manage it, then I expect you'll just have to let her fly in your britches, 'cause I sure as hell ain't gonna do it for you." He took a few steps back and kept his rifle trained on the belligerent prisoner.

"Bastard," Arlo muttered as he unbuttoned his trousers with very little awkwardness, even with his hands bound together.

After feeding Arlo, Ned selected a cottonwood of suitable size and sat his prisoner down, facing the tree trunk, with his hands and feet tied around it. Arlo had spent three nights hugging a tree trunk till morning on the ride into Cheyenne. No amount of complaining had any effect on Ned. "You're gonna have plenty of time to sleep in the hoosegow," Ned told him.

Morning came earlier than Ned had planned, owing to the constant complaining coming from Arlo. Well aware that most of it was just to keep him from sleeping, Ned finally rolled out of his blanket and stirred up the fire. "Hey, get me to hell off this damn tree," Arlo yelled.

"Why, certainly, Arlo, but I think it's best if you stay right where you are while I'm fixin' us some coffee and bacon. I don't wanna have to keep an eye on you. I might burn the bacon." When he finished cooking the bacon, he divided it evenly and placed Arlo's portion on a tin plate. Then he poured him a cup of coffee and placed it beside the plate next to the tree.

"Hey, how 'bout untyin' my hands?" Arlo complained. "How the hell can I eat wrapped around this tree?"

"Just hold your horses," Ned said as he knelt down on the opposite side of the tree. He laid his rifle on the ground behind him while he untied Arlo's hands. He backed away to pick up his rifle and said, "All right, you can untie your feet and eat your breakfast."

Arlo was very deliberate in his motions to untie the knot that held his ankles around the trunk of the tree. When he was free, he pushed away from the tree, and instead of reaching for his coffee, he rolled away from it and lay on his side as if he was sick. Watching suspiciously, Ned commented, "Damn if that ain't a helluva way to eat. It don't go in that end, you know. It goes in the other end."

"I'm all stove up," Arlo complained. "I've been settin' around that tree too long. My arms and legs is gone stiff on me."

"Is that a fact?" Ned responded, not totally unsympathetic. It had been a chilly night, and he supposed Arlo might be stove up at that. He had to admit that he was a bit stiff himself when he first got up. "Well, lyin' on the ground like that ain't gonna help it any. Roll over and drink some of that coffee. That'll warm you up some." He stepped a little closer with the intention of prodding him into movement with the barrel of his rifle.

"I'll try," Arlo said, and slowly began to turn back toward Ned, seemingly in great discomfort. The younger man was a lot quicker than Ned had given him credit for, for he suddenly whipped over and lunged into Ned's legs, pulling the deputy's legs out from under him. Ned was a large man, and his heavy body hit the ground with a thud. Before he could recover, Arlo kicked the rifle out of his hand and they both dived for it. Arlo, being the quicker, got his hands on it first. Rolling over and over until he was clear of Ned's reach, he scrambled to his feet and leveled the rifle at him. "Now, you old son of a bitch, you can start sayin' your prayers. I told you you'd never take me to Fort Laramie. Somebody oughta told you you was gettin' too old to be a lawman. But I reckon you can still learn one last lesson—don't nobody get the best of the Taggart brothers." He cranked the lever, ejecting a cartridge just to be sure there was one in the chamber. Then he aimed it at the fallen deputy. "Say hello to the devil for me," Arlo said with a laugh. The grin froze on his face and his eyes opened wide in shocked surprise as a .44 slug smashed into his chest, causing him to stagger backward a couple of steps. He snatched the rifle up again to fire, but before he could pull the trigger, another bullet hammered his breastbone. Quicker than Arlo figured the big lawman to be capable of being, Ned lunged into the startled outlaw and wrenched the rifle from his hands. Arlo crumpled to the ground, conscious, but mortally wounded.

Ned leaned down to tell him, "I reckon *you* had one more lesson to learn. If you're fixin' to shoot somebody, don't stand around crowin' about it like a bantam rooster—especially if the other feller's carryin' a handgun tucked in his belt." He stood erect again and stared down at the wounded man. "You came mighty damn close to skinnin' my cat. Maybe I am gettin' too old for this job." He knelt down beside Arlo and said, "Well, let's see if we can get you to Fort Laramie before you cash in. Maybe they can do somethin' to stop that bleedin' at the hospital there."

He did what he could to ease Arlo's pain, but it was plain to see that the outlaw's prospects didn't look encouraging. Before he got the horses saddled and broke camp, Arlo took his last breath. Ned gave the matter a few minutes' consideration before deciding to take the body on in to Fort Laramie to let the army deal with it. "It'll sure take the strain offa the rest of the trip," he decided.

Chapter 2

"I was afraid of that," Billie Jean Gunter lamented as she stood beside the front left wheel of the wagon. "The damn wheels stood in that creek too long before we got the wagon out and they're already trying to swell up." Billie Jean's father had been a blacksmith back in Arkansas, so she knew what she was talking about. She squatted on her heels to get a closer look.

"Well, what does that mean?" Lorena asked, concerned. "Are we gonna break down?"

"Maybe, maybe not," Billie Jean answered. "They're sure as hell gonna warp, though." She ran her hand along the iron rim. "They may hold together till we get to Fort Laramie." She looked up at Lorena. "How far did he say it was to Fort Laramie?"

"About eight days, he said, once we strike the Chugwater." Lorena shrugged, uncertain. "He admitted that he don't know much about how far we can travel in a day, though."

"Well, I don't know if these wheels will make it that far, this one here in particular," she said, standing next to the left front wheel. "Maybe if the weather stays warm and dry, they'll shrink back down." She shook her head, perplexed. "If I was back home in Little Rock at my daddy's forge, I could fix 'em."

"Huh," Lorena grunted, "if I was back home in New Orleans, I'd be ridin' in a fancy carriage instead of a damn farm wagon." She shrugged then. "Well, what are we gonna do?"

"Drive it and hope for the best, I reckon," Rose answered, arriving just in time to hear the last of the conversation between her two companions. By far the most optimistic of the three, Rose always expected things to work out in her favor.

"I reckon she's right," Billie Jean said, "but if this wheel goes, we're gonna be riding horseback the rest of the way."

Rose nodded toward their somber guide, who was in the process of leading the horses back from the creek, preparing to hitch them up to the wagon. "What about him?" she asked. "Do you think he can fix the wheel?"

"I doubt it," Billie Jean said, "even if we had the stuff to fix it with. If this wheel breaks down, your wagon stops right where it is."

The concern was obvious on the faces of all three women when Wolf led the horses up and backed them into the traces. He didn't ask, but Lorena told him of their problem. Billie Jean was correct in her assertion that he would be unable to do anything to fix the wheel. When told of her doubts the wagon would make it through eight days of travel unless the wheels shrank in the meantime, he couldn't help a twinge of conscience. He had not told the women of his intention to guide them only as far as the Chugwater, then leave them to follow it to the Laramie, all the way to Fort Laramie. That route was one he figured they could follow with no chance of getting lost. When he had estimated the distance, he was allowing for the winding route of the Chugwater, as well as the many turns of the Laramie. In actual distance from where they now stood just south of Horse Creek, the journey was about half that by heading almost straight north. The route would take them over some pretty rough country, and he figured the chance of their getting lost in the process was definitely possible. So he could not in good conscience send them on alone. *Damn!* He scolded himself once again for coming back to visit the Crow village, for he knew he was going to have to lead them to Fort Laramie. He studied the situation silently for a few minutes, trying to find a way out of it, but there was nothing short of abandoning three women on the open prairie. He took a long look at the wheel before declaring, "Get ready to go."

They hurried to load up, as if trying to get moving before the wheel decided to break. Lorena took the reins and prepared to start the horses, but hesitated when Wolf turned his horse's head directly north. "I thought the Chugwater was that way," she called after him, pointing west.

"It is," he answered. "This way's a shortcut." Without looking back to see if she was following, he started out to the north, grumbling under his breath about the folly of offering assistance to the women. Behind him, Lorena could not help being reminded that the last guide who took them on a shortcut had abandoned them in this wilderness.

It took them until late afternoon to reach Horse Creek, a distance of perhaps eight or nine miles, because of the necessity to find a passable route for the wagon through a region of rough cuts and draws. Impatient with the slow progress of the wagon, Wolf reluctantly stopped for the night. The horses needed the rest, and from the weary faces of the women, he figured they would have protested if he suggested going farther. So they went about making camp. Wolf led the horses to water, then hobbled them on the bank where there was a sparse patch of grass. "I expect your horses need some grain if you've got any," he said to Lorena when he came up from the creek. "There ain't much grass for 'em here."

"There's a sack of oats in the wagon," Lorena told him. "Got a quilt spread over it. Rose has been using it for an easy chair."

Wolf found the sack of oats and fed the team of horses, then took a little extra for his pony. "Don't go gettin' used to this," he said, using his hat as a feedbag. Once the horses were cared for, and the women busy with the campfire and preparation of supper, Wolf decided to scout along the creek on the chance he might find something to eat other than the bacon the women had brought.

"Where's he off to?" Billie Jean asked when she returned from the creek with the coffeepot filled with water.

Poking at the fire to encourage it, Lorena glanced in Wolf's direction before commenting, "He said, and I quote, 'I got a need for some real meat.' I guess he don't like bacon."

"Ha," Billie Jean grunted. "Tell him we'll get him a lobster dinner first fancy restaurant we come to." She, like her two companions, was not sure their stoic guide was any more dependable than Lige Ingram had been.

"Hell," Rose said, finishing Billie Jean's thought, "at least Lige could make conversation."

"Yeah," Lorena offered, "he sure as hell talked me outta my money." She shook her head when recalling. She had tried to talk him into taking them to Fort Laramie before paying him a cent, but he protested, reminding her that she always made him pay in advance before servicing him. So she gave in and gave him half of the one hundred dollars they had agreed upon. Her thoughts returned again to the somber man now out of sight beyond a bend in the creek. He had not asked for any payment. *Maybe he's thinking he'll take everything we've got*, she thought. *It might not be as easy as he thinks*. She patted the single-action Colt revolver she carried in her skirt pocket as a precaution. The Colt was not the only weapon the ladies had. Lorena was not fool enough to set out across the prairie without some means of protection. In the wagon there were three Sharps carbines and a good supply of ammunition.

Wolf was gone for over an hour. When he returned, he had nothing to show for his hunt but about a good handful of serviceberries in his hat. He offered them to the women, but only Billie Jean sampled them. "You didn't have much of a huntin' trip, did you, stud?"

Lorena remarked, unable to resist teasing him. "I thought all you wild mountain men always came back with some kinda game."

"Can't kill anythin' where there ain't nothin'," Wolf said, drew his knife, and speared a thick piece of the salty meat left in the frying pan. He accepted the cup of coffee she offered.

"There's beans in that pot," Billie Jean said. "They're probably still warm. At least, they were hot about an hour ago."

"Much obliged," he said, and helped himself. He saw no need to tell them the real reason he was late for supper. Around the bend of the creek, he had discovered tracks where a dozen or more horses had crossed over, heading north. They were unshod horses, Indian ponies, and they had crossed only several hours before, by his estimation. Whether they were friends or hostile, there was no way to tell, but they were traveling in the same direction he planned to take. So he followed them across and up through a rocky draw that emerged to a ridge top. At the top of the ridge, he looked back to see if the wagon and camp were visible from that vantage point. Relieved to find they were not, he continued down the ridge for a mile or so with still no sight of the Indians. They were most likely Crow, he told himself, but there was no way to tell for sure. Since it appeared that the Indians were not aware of their presence, he thought it best not to mention them to the women. He wondered, however, if it might be best to swing over a couple of miles to the west in the morning, just to put a little more distance between their trail and that of the Indians. When they set out in the morning, it would only take them a few hours to clear this stretch of rough ridges. There was nothing but wide, flat prairie after that, country where a wagon could be seen for quite some distance. It was not the country he wanted to be caught in if the tracks he found were made by a Sioux war party, especially one of that size.

His supper finished, he walked over to the wagon where Billie Jean was taking a close inspection of the suspect wagon wheel. "Well, it doesn't look any worse than it did this morning," she told him. "I think it's shrunk back a little, but Lorena's sure gonna have to have it fixed when we get to Fort Laramie." His only response was a slight nod, but he was thankful that it seemed to be holding up. He turned then and walked up a slight rise where his horse was pulling up what little grass it could find. Using his saddle for a pillow, he wrapped his blanket around him and turned in for the night.

"He'd rather sleep with his horse than one of us," Rose commented to Lorena. "There's something wrong with a man who won't take a free tussle when it's offered to him."

"That might be so," Lorena said. "There might be somethin' wrong about him, but I believe there's a lot of things right about him." She had given much thought to their partnership with the strange young man, and she had come to the conclusion that she was wrongly suspicious of his intentions. For one thing, it didn't figure that, if he had something evil in mind, he would have bothered to lead them this far to make his move. She expressed as much to her two friends. "You know," she said, "I think he's just shy as hell when it comes to women. I don't think he knows anythin' about dealin' with anybody but Injuns."

"You may be right," Rose allowed. "He acts like he's been living in a cave for most of his life, I swear, but he wouldn't look so wild if he wasn't wearing clothes made outta animal skins." She laughed at her own remark. Finding humor in all but the most dire situations, she reminded them, "Course Lorena's already tried to get him outta those buckskin britches, and she couldn't do it."

"Huh," Billie Jean chuckled, "it'd be like skinning a wildcat."

"You do carry on, Rose," Lorena declared. "We'd best forget about skinnin' Mister . . ." She paused then. "Damn, I don't even know his name. Did he say?" Billie Jean and Rose both shook their heads. Lorena shrugged. "Well, anyway, we'd best get to bed. It might be a long day tomorrow."

Up on the rise above the creek bank, the subject of the women's conversation slept, much the way a deer slept, with his ears attuned to the sounds of the creek around him, and alert to any sound that did not belong. The tracks he had seen earlier in the evening had told him that the party of Indians were on their way somewhere to the north, and should be far ahead of them, leaving them no cause for concern. Still, he would remain alert. Indians, like everybody else, could, and often did, change their minds.

Up before first light, Wolf freshened the fire, knowing that the women would most likely want to make some coffee before starting out. He would suggest that they drink it fast and get under way, stopping for breakfast when it was time to rest the horses. "I figured I'd wait

till you got up before I started coffee," he told Lorena
when she climbed out of the wagon, wearing nothing
but a suit of long johns for protection from the chilly
morning air. "I ain't got the coffee beans, anyway."

"Uh," she grunted, trying to blink away the sleep
from her eyes. "If you'll go fill the coffeepot, I'll grind
some beans, after I go behind the wagon to pee."

"All right," he replied. "You'd best get them other
two outta their beds. We need to put some country
behind us before we stop to rest the horses and eat
breakfast."

"What's the big hurry?" Lorena asked, thinking
that she was hungry now.

"It's better for the horses," he told her. "We can give
'em a longer rest. Easier on 'em in the mornin' when it's
still cooler, too." His real concern was for the Indian
pony tracks he had seen and the fact that they were too
close to the prior line of travel he had at first planned.
"They can travel longer in a day that way," he added.

"Hell, I don't wanna travel longer days," Lorena
retorted. "My behind is already gettin' blisters from
settin' on that wagon seat so long."

Wolf ignored her complaining. "Best we get started
right away," he stated stoically, and left to fill the coffeepot with water.

She started to protest, but decided to let him have
his way. He was probably just eager to get the trip over
with, so he could go back to living with the Indians
and the animals, or whatever it was he wanted to do.
After all, he wasn't charging her anything for the job,
so she had no reason to complain. "Rose! You and Billie Jean crawl outta there! We're fixin' to get started

pretty soon, and if you want a cup of coffee before we go, you best shake a leg." She waited a moment to hear their groans of protest, then unbuttoned the flap on her long johns and proceeded to squat right where she stood. "Hell," she groused, "he can't see me from down by the creek." She paused a moment, then said, "I don't care if he can."

As Lorena expected, there were complaints from Rose and Billie Jean when she informed them that breakfast was going to have to wait until midmorning. "And we probably wouldn't stop then if it wasn't for the horses," she remarked.

"Don't we have any say in it?" Billie Jean questioned. Her protest was interrupted then when she had to grab a rag and pull the coffeepot off the hot coals when it started to boil over. "We aren't on any kind of schedule. Why don't you tell him we'll go when we're ready? We wanna eat breakfast first."

Lorena smiled and nodded in the direction of their guide, walking the horses up to the wagon. "You tell him."

Billie Jean sputtered and Rose giggled at her fluster. "Let's do what he says," Rose suggested. "There ain't anything keeping him from taking off any time he feels like he doesn't wanna put up with us anymore. He ain't much when it comes to charming entertainment, but I feel a whole lot better having him around."

"Amen," Lorena said.

Backing the team on either side of the wagon tongue, Wolf glanced up to find all three women staring at him, smiles on their faces. "Here," Billie Jean offered, "let me hitch 'em up. You can go saddle your horse."

"Much obliged," he said, and let her take the traces. She was better at it than he was, anyway. She did more of the driving than Lorena, and Wolf had no trouble picturing her working in her father's blacksmith shop. While he went to fetch his horse, he wondered what had led her to her present occupation. She hardly looked the type. She wasn't as tall a woman as Lorena, but she was solidly built, with no slimming of her waistline, even though she appeared to have a flat stomach. *Built more like a man,* he thought. *Good thing she's got that long yellow hair.* She was a sharp contrast to Rose, the youngest of the three. There was a hardness about Rose, probably as a result of the brothels and saloons she had in her past. And yet she was quick with a smile and usually found something to be cheerful about. A slender woman with shiny black hair, she looked to be of Creole descent.

His horse saddled, he led the bay up to the fire, where Lorena handed him a cup of coffee. He drank the strong black liquid in quick gulps, impatient to get started. Then he pulled the fire apart and kicked dirt over it, stepped up in the saddle, and sat waiting for the women to climb in the wagon.

They were waiting, twelve Lakota warriors, fresh from a successful raid on a homestead no more than forty miles southeast of Fort Laramie where they had killed a farmer, his wife, and three children. The brazen attack, right under the army's nose, was led by Iron Hand, feared warrior of the Oglala Lakota. Intent as they were upon returning to their village on the Tongue River before army troops were sent after them, they were nevertheless excited to spot a single wagon heading toward Fort Laramie. Iron Hand knew his medicine was strong, for they might not have been given this opportunity to attack the wagon if the deer had not been sent to delay his return. His warriors did not doubt his medicine when their journey had been interrupted by the small group of deer that had gathered conveniently by a little pond at the bottom of a narrow stream flowing from the hill above. Two of the deer were killed before the others escaped, but that was plenty of meat to supply the raiding party. They decided to remain in the valley to butcher and prepare the unexpected bounty.

As a precaution, scouts were sent out to make sure there was no sign of an army patrol. Iron Hand didn't expect the soldiers to receive word of their raid on the farm this soon, but he felt it wise to know that they were in no danger of surprise. One of the scouts, Red Blanket, had returned early in the afternoon to announce the sighting of a lone wagon heading north. "One man on a horse leads the wagon," Red Blanket reported excitedly. "It looked like a woman driving the wagon and maybe another or maybe a child beside her."

Iron Hand and the others were immediately eager to attack. "How far?" Iron Hand asked. He was told that if the wagon continued along in the same direction, the war party could head directly west and wait in ambush where a line of low hills stretched across the prairie. The plan was enthusiastically accepted by all in the war party, and they had started without delay to arrive at the point of ambush, where they now waited.

* * *

Wolf reined the bay to a stop while he looked at the hills some two miles in the distance. *Good place for an ambush*, he thought, although he really didn't anticipate the possibility of hostile activity so close to Fort Laramie. He was more concerned with the best route that would place the least strain on the horses to pull the wagon through the hills. He turned in the saddle to look back on the women, a quarter of a mile behind him. Billie Jean was driving the horses and Rose, being the more spritely of the three, was walking beside it. Lorena never walked. He returned his attention to the hills before him, letting his gaze skim along the tops until he settled upon a low draw that seemed to be the best bet for an easy passage. Urging the bay to resume a comfortable walk, he veered slightly to the west and headed straight for the draw. He looked back once again to make sure Billie Jean was following.

Making his way across the treeless flat, he rode through large patches of sagebrush that covered most of the hills he was now entering. The draw he had chosen was plenty wide enough for the wagon to pass, with steep sides rising up to the tops of the hills on each side. After riding a couple of dozen yards into the defile, he pulled up and looked around to see if there was anything that might do damage to wagon wheels that were already in need of repair. He saw nothing that would cause any trouble, so he decided to wait there for Billie Jean to catch up.

The afternoon was clear and warm on the open prairie as the sun began to sink closer to the distant mountains, and there was a stillness that could almost be heard, interrupted only by an occasional cry of a hawk wheeling high overhead. His first sense of something wrong was triggered when the bay's ears pricked up, usually a sign that the horse was aware of something. When the bay snorted softly, he became totally alert and he felt the muscles in his arms tense. There was no answering whinny from the hills on either side of him. Still, he suddenly sensed the presence of something that shouldn't be there. Maybe he was being overly cautious, but he preferred to err in that direction if he was wrong. Acting on the possibility that he was leading the wagon into an ambush, he wheeled his horse around casually and slow-walked the bay back out of the draw, hoping to look as if he was not suspicious.

While he rode toward the wagon, he glanced around on either side to pick a spot that might be best to defend against a war party. If he was right, and the party set up to ambush them was the same bunch of Indians that had crossed Horse Creek a day or two ago, he didn't like his odds of repelling them. One rifle against ten or fifteen Sioux warriors didn't stand much chance. But that was the only choice he had, so he would make it as costly for them as he could. One spot looked about as good as another, so he chose the closest one, a deep gully at the base of the hill to the west of the draw.

Reining his horse up to a stop beside the wagon seat, he wheeled the bay around and told Rose in a calm but forceful voice, "Get in the wagon." Surprised by his tone, she promptly did as she was told. Addressing Billie Jean then, he said, "You see that gully yonder?" She nodded and he continued. "I want you to drive like hell to that gully when I give you the signal, and I don't mean maybe."

"What is it?" Lorena demanded as she crawled up to join Billie Jean in the seat.

"I think we got some trouble," Wolf replied. "I might be wrong, but I got a feelin' I ain't. I got a powerful itch that says there's a bunch of Injuns waitin' for us to ride through that notch in those hills up ahead. So we'll keep on kinda peaceable till we get to that big clump of sagebrush on the right, and then we'll make a run for it and hope we get to that gully before they can cut us off."

"Why don't we just turn around and run the other way?" Rose asked fearfully.

Billie Jean answered for Wolf. "'Cause they'd run us down on the open prairie before we got a mile."

"I'm afraid that's a fact," Wolf said. He shook his head and grimaced apologetically. "If there's as many of 'em as I think, I ain't sure how long I can hold 'em off, but I'll sure as hell make 'em pay a price for it. When we get to the gully, get the horses unhitched as fast as you can and lead 'em back of the wagon." Again he tried to apologize. "I'll do what I can, at least as long as my cartridges hold out." He looked at Lorena then. "Maybe you can break out that little pistol you tote in your pocket."

"Hell, I can do better'n that," Lorena replied. "Rose, get back there and pull those carbines outta the box under the floorboards, and pull all that ammunition out. Those Injuns will play hell takin' this wagon."

Astonished, Wolf was speechless for a moment before asking, "How many do you have?"

"Three," Lorena replied, "one for each of us, three Sharps carbines, converted to fire metal cartridges. And we know how to use 'em, don't we, girls?" She was answered with two nods of determination. "We didn't come out here to be guests of honor at no damn Injun scalpin' party."

"Well, I'll be damned . . . ," Wolf responded, hardly able to believe what he was hearing. In those brief moments the outlook had gone from hopeless to promising. "Let 'em come, then," he said. Billie Jean slapped the horses on their rumps with the reins, and they drove on toward the clump of sagebrush Wolf had specified.

Moving at a leisurely pace, they continued on toward the hills until almost even with the large clump of sagebrush. "Go!" Wolf commanded, and Billie Jean was quick to respond. She drew the horses sharply to the left and laid into them with the reins across their backsides. The horses responded as best they could under Billie Jean's flailing and Lorena and Rose held on as the wagon bounced over the rough terrain, all three praying that the warped wheel held together. Wolf drew his rifle from the saddle sling and reined his horse back, watching for any reaction from the hills on either side of the draw. No more than a few moments elapsed before his suspicions were proven to be accurate and the ridges on both sides of the passage erupted.

Their ambush obviously discovered, the Lakota warriors rose from their cover below the crest of the hills and immediately started firing at the departing wagon. The range was too great to afford any real chance of hitting the target, a fact that was soon apparent to them, so they scrambled to get to their ponies to give chase. Wolf continued to hold the bay back until the first of the Indian riders streamed down the sides of the hills. He hesitated a moment longer, just enough to throw a few shots at the leading riders in the hope of slowing them down and buying as much time as he could for the women to reach the gully. When their return fire began to kick up dirt around the bay's hooves, he wheeled the horse and fled after the women.

Knowing he had no more than a minute or two before the war party would be upon them, he reached the gully only seconds behind the wagon. As he had directed, Billie Jean had stopped the wagon in the mouth of the narrow gully and was in the process of unhitching the horses when he came sliding to a stop beside her. With a quick look at Lorena and Rose, he saw that they needed no instruction on what to do. They were loading the magazines of their carbines and picking positions to fire from. When they were set, they rolled the canvas wagon sheets up enough to give them room to fire. "I didn't have time to count, but it looks like twelve or fourteen of 'em," he called to Lorena. She nodded as he jumped down from his horse and led it into the gully. Then he ran back to help Billie Jean secure the team. That done, they hurried to take defensive positions with the other two women. Rose handed a Sharps carbine to Billie Jean, telling her it was already fully loaded.

Billie Jean had barely gotten in place behind the large sack of oats when the line of charging warriors opened fire again at a distance of about one hundred and fifty yards. "Let 'em get a little closer," Wolf called out. "Then we'll let 'em know how much it's gonna cost 'em." It was difficult to do, once the bullets started knocking holes in the wagon sheet and chipping chunks of wood from the sides. "Now!" he yelled when the range had closed to less than one hundred yards. He had no idea whether or not the women really knew how to shoot, but he figured the odds were a lot better at a shorter range. Their initial volley resulted in the reduction of the attacking force by three; one by Wolf, one by Lorena, and one by the other two women. It might have been four had not Rose and Billie Jean both aimed at the same Indian. More importantly, the volley stopped the headlong charge, causing the warriors to scatter, having been surprised by the responding firepower. Two more warriors were knocked from their horses by Wolf's Henry rifle before riding out of range.

"By God!" Lorena exclaimed as the Indians drew back. "That'll teach you to attack respectable ladies, you red-skinned sons of bitches!" She turned to exchange victorious grins with Rose and Billie Jean.

"We showed 'em," Billie Jean crowed.

"Yeah, I reckon we did," Wolf allowed, considerably less excited. "Now they know it ain't one rifle they're workin' against, and that sure as hell didn't tickle 'em none. It just comes down to how bad they wanna come after us now that we've killed five of their war party."

"Won't that be enough to keep them from wanting to charge us again?" Rose asked. "They'd be fools to keep doing that."

"I expect so," Wolf said. "We most likely did break 'em from tryin' to overrun us again, but I doubt they've had enough yet. Like I said, it depends on how bad they want our scalps now. We can make it cost too much to charge us again, but they've got us pretty much bottled up here in this gully. They can lie back and plunk away at us from a distance. Probably figure they can wait us out, since there ain't no water in this hole we're in." He glanced up at the sky. "Couple of hours it'll be dark. Then they might try to slip up on us."

His reasoning was sufficient to deflate the air of exhilaration the three women had been enjoying after their apparent victory against the savage warriors. "I don't like the sound of that," Lorena said, speaking for all three, and an atmosphere of concern returned. The thought of Lakota warriors sneaking into their stronghold under cover of darkness brought images of a more sinister nature than the broad daylight charge.

"Whaddaya think we oughta do?" Lorena asked. "You got any ideas?"

"Well, for one thing," he answered while never turning his gaze away from the prairie, "I don't reckon we'd better plan on sleepin' tonight. We're gonna all have to keep a sharp lookout in case they try to slip in on us." He turned then to look behind them, beyond the three horses, to the top of the gully. "That looks like the way I'd try to sneak in here, if it was me. So I think I'll be climbin' up there to see if I can cut anybody off that's trying to come in from above us." Returning his gaze to the prairie again, he pointed to a small rise about a hundred yards off to one side, and then another a little closer on the other side. "I expect they'll leave their ponies back safe somewhere and crawl up to those two humps. That'll give 'em some cover to shoot from. Then we'll just have to wait till dark to see what they'll do."

After some thirty minutes had passed with all quiet on the prairie before them, Lorena moved over beside

Wolf from her position behind the front wheels of the wagon. "Reckon why they ain't been shootin' at us? You think they figured it ain't worth it?"

"I expect they're hopin' we think they've gone and hitch up the wagon," he said. "We oughta hear somethin' from 'em before long."

There was still no indication that the Indians were there until the sun finally sank into the far hills, leaving the prairie bathed in a soft half-light. It wasn't long before the first of many random shots came from the very spots Wolf had pointed out. Billie Jean prepared to return fire, but Wolf told her she'd just be wasting cartridges. "As long as they're lyin' low behind that rise, you ain't likely to do anythin' but kick up some dirt. They're gonna have to make a move to get at us, so save your cartridges till then. Just keep your head down and your eyes peeled. It frustrates Injuns when you don't pay no attention to 'em."

Though mere speculation, Wolf's assessment of the Lakota's frame of mind was right on the mark. Frustrated by the loss of five of his party, Iron Hand was seething, impatiently waiting for darkness to fall. A war chief was judged by the welfare of his warriors, and it appeared that his medicine was not strong. Five dead from a party of twelve did not inspire others to follow him into battle. Growing angrier by the moment, he felt compelled to prove the strength of his medicine, until finally he could hold it in no longer. "I will sit back here like a frightened woman no more!" he exclaimed. "Their bullets cannot hurt me!" He jumped to his feet and charged straight at the wagon, firing his

Spencer carbine as he ran. Two of the other warriors, inspired by his bravery, leaped up to follow.

Iron Hand made it to within thirty yards of the wagon before he fell as a result of four almost simultaneous shots that stopped his upper body cold while his feet ran out from under him. The other two warriors quickly retreated to the safety of the rise amid a hailstorm of lead around their feet. The remaining warriors looked then to Red Blanket for council. "I think we have seen enough of this white man's medicine to know this is not a good day for us to fight," Lone Buffalo said. "I think we should go and leave this white man alone."

Red Blanket could not disagree. Half of the twelve warriors that had left the village were dead. Still, it did not seem honorable to leave without some retaliation for their losses. "I say we should go back to our ponies," he said. "Then I, and anyone who wants to go with me, will climb up the hill behind them and catch them watching for us in front of them."

Back in the gully, Wolf and the three women waited, watching for any movement in the rapidly growing darkness. After a few scattered shots over fifteen minutes before, there was no more shooting from the prairie. "I expect I'd best climb up the back of this gully in case they're thinkin' about sneakin' up behind us now," he said. "Might not be a bad idea if one of you kinda keep an eye on the horses while the other two keep watchin' the prairie." He started to leave then, but paused to say, "Only thing is, I don't wanna get shot by one of you when I come back." He looked at Billie Jean, who had moved from her position to watch the horses. "Maybe I'd better give you a little birdcall, so you'll know it's me—like this." He whistled a couple of low notes.

"What kinda bird is that?" Billie Jean questioned. "I ain't ever heard a bird that sounds like that."

"It don't matter," Wolf said impatiently. "That's the signal I'll make."

"All right, then," Billie Jean said. As he disappeared into the darkness of the gully, she turned to Lorena and commented, "Ain't no bird makes a sound like that."

The gully became more and more narrow the farther up it he climbed until it was little more than a ditch at the top, where it opened out on a domelike hilltop. Wolf crouched in the darkness and strained to scan the many clumps of sagebrush that dotted the backside of the hill and the prairie beyond. There was nothing moving that he could see, but he continued his sweeping surveillance, back and forth across the area within range of his eyesight. *They'll come,* he told himself, although he was not sure that they would. They might decide their medicine was bad and call it an ill-advised raid. He didn't have to wait long for the answer, for suddenly his gaze stopped on a small clump of sagebrush that wasn't there before. As he stared at the dark form near the bottom of the low hill, it moved, making its way to stop again behind a larger bush. Wolf quickly scanned back and forth again in an effort to spot any more dark forms moving. There were none—one warrior alone, which made Wolf speculate that the remaining warriors were having doubts regarding the wisdom of persisting.

Red Blanket was less than halfway up the back of

the hill when the clump of sagebrush several yards above him suddenly exploded with a burst of Wolf's muzzle flash. The surprised Indian was knocked backward to roll over and over before settling at the foot of the hill. Wolf inched his way down a little farther to locate himself behind a thick bush about ten yards above the body. When they heard the gunshot, this warrior's companions would surely investigate, so he pushed the barrel of his rifle through the middle of the bush and trained it on Red Blanket's corpse. He would wait now to find out what the other warriors would do. If they decided to storm up the slope, he would be ready to eliminate more of their number. By his count during the Indians' initial charge on the wagon, there had been twelve warriors in the party. With the body now lying below him at the foot of the hill, that left only five to be accounted for. The high number of casualties should surely discourage further attacks, but he would have to wait to see. At least there had been no more sounds of gunfire from the gully where the women were watching.

Soon he spotted several dark forms moving toward the foot of the hill. As they came closer, he was able to make out individuals and take a count. There were five, all that remained of the original war party. Suddenly his situation changed, and he questioned his decision to hide behind a bush for cover. If they discovered him, he couldn't be sure of getting more than one, possibly two of them, before they got him. Darkness was a good cover, but it wasn't much when it came to stopping a bullet. It was too late to retreat now; they were about to find their dead brother. There was nothing he could do but remain stone still.

"Here!" Lone Buffalo whispered when he almost stumbled over the body. "It's Red Blanket!" He knelt beside the body to determine if he was alive. In a moment, he was joined by the other four. They stood around him, all peering up into the darkness, searching for any sign of Red Blanket's killer.

The one man squatting behind a bush a few yards above them remained still, hardly daring to breathe. Although they all seemed to look right at him, he knew they couldn't see him, and the thought went through his mind that he could possibly kill two or more of them while they stood bunched together over the body. *And then get the hell shot outta this bush,* he told himself, and decided it was not worth the risk.

"What should we do?" one of the warriors asked Lone Buffalo. "We should have all gone with him."

"And we might have all been killed," Lone Buffalo said. "This was surely bad medicine to attack the wagon. Seven of us have been killed. How many more of us have to die before we know that we should not have made war on this wagon?" He reached down to take Red Blanket's feet. "Help me carry him back to our horses. Then, if we can, we must pick up the others and take our dead back to our village, and leave these white demons alone."

Now, that sounds like a right sensible idea to me, the observer in the bush thought, knowing enough of their tongue to understand, and close enough to hear. The other four Lakota must have also agreed, for they immediately did Lone Buffalo's bidding. He gave them plenty of time to depart before he backed away from his bush and hurried up the hill, anxious to tell the women what was going to happen, so they wouldn't shoot at anyone attempting to recover their dead.

Scrambling back down the gully, he paused before reaching the horses, remembering to give Billie Jean the signal. He whistled and waited for a response. All he heard was the cocking of a carbine. Not sure she had heard him, he whistled again, this time a little louder, then a third time, even louder. Finally he heard Billie Jean say to Lorena, "That don't sound like what he said was a birdcall."

Losing his patience, he blurted, "Dammit, Billie Jean, it's me and I'm comin' in!"

"Oh," she reacted, startled, when he suddenly appeared beside her elbow. "You scared me." And she was reminded of the first time he had showed up to help them pull the wagon out of the creek—just popped out of nowhere. "You don't need to waste your time whistling a signal. A body can't see you comin' anyway."

"We heard the shot," Rose said. "We were worried."

"They're leavin'," Wolf said. "They're gonna pick up their dead and leave. We just need to keep an eye on 'em to make sure they don't change their minds. If you see one of 'em, don't shoot at him. Just let 'em go about their business."

They remained vigilant throughout the rest of the long night, but there was no sign of any movement on the wide expanse of prairie leading up to the hills that were their refuge. When the sun finally struggled up over the plains to the east to draw long shadows from the knobby clumps of sagebrush on the prairie, the bodies were gone. "Damn," Lorena marveled. "When did they do that? We were watchin' all night. Hell, that one crazy one that came runnin' at us wasn't but twenty-five or thirty yards right out in front of us." She seemed to aim her question at Wolf.

He shrugged and replied, "They're Injuns. They don't ever stomp around, makin' a lot of noise."

She stared at him for a long second, astonished by his seeming indifference to the fact that they had all escaped with their scalps against a war party three times their number. Suddenly a thought occurred to her. "What the hell is your name?" In the time they had been in partnership with this strange man, he had never volunteered his name. Her question caught the attention of Rose and Billie Jean, and they both paused to hear his answer.

"Wolf," he said.

"Wolf," she repeated. "Well, that's a good name for you, Mr. Wolf. Ain't it, girls?" *A strange name for a strange man*, she thought. "Somethin' Wolf, or Wolf Somethin'?" she asked.

"Just Wolf," he replied.

"I'd drink to it if I had something to drink with," Billie Jean offered. They were reminded then that they were bottled up in a dry gulch with no water and no wood to build a fire.

"Hitch up the horses," Wolf said, "and we'll pull outta here. On the other side of these hills, in about two hours, I'd say, we oughta strike Old Woman Creek. We can stop there and fix somethin' to eat and rest a little. There's wood for a fire and good water if the creek ain't run dry."

Once again, they set out for Fort Laramie. Although hungry and tired, all three women were in high spirits now that the danger had been met and overcome. When asked of the chances of encountering another Sioux war party, Wolf replied that the odds were long, since they were now only a little over a day's travel from the fort. "I was mighty surprised to see that bunch runnin' this close to Fort Laramie," he confessed. "I doubt we'll see any more." This was the news the women wanted to hear, so the rest of the trip was under much more cheerful skies.

Chapter 3

Early afternoon found them approaching the Laramie River just short of its confluence with the North Platte. Wolf pulled his horse to a complete stop to gawk at the steel structure across the North Platte. The bridge, completed the year before, was not there the last time he had been to Fort Laramie and it seemed an amazing accomplishment to his mind. "Ain't you ever seen a bridge before?" Lorena asked when she pulled the wagon up beside him.

"Ain't ever seen one like that," he confessed. "Reckon how they lifted all those steel pieces up there?"

"I don't know," Lorena replied, "but if you think that's somethin', you oughta see some of the bridges back east."

"I don't think I wanna see 'em," he decided without having to give it much thought. He had lived with the Indians long enough to know that the rivers were put here by God, or Man Above, and they were meant to be left alone, free of bulky hunks of steel and iron. Lorena looked at Rose and shook her head. "Yonder's the fort," he said, pointing across the Laramie River. "I don't know where you wanna go. I know where the post trader's store is. I never had any business anywhere else. There's a ferry a short piece down the river, a bridge, too, but it don't look like that one." Thinking his job was surely finished, since they were in sight of the post's buildings, Wolf did not plan to cross over the river with them. Lorena was of a different mind, however, and was reluctant to part company with him. She insisted that she would repay him for his time and certainly for the cartridges he had spent to protect them from attack. The thought of replenishing his supply of ammunition was enough to change his mind about leaving.

None of the three women had ever been to Fort Laramie before, so they weren't sure where to look for an establishment that might have need of their special qualities. "We'll try the post trader's store," Lorena decided. As luck would have it, they pulled onto the post's parade ground right after a changing of the guard, and the wagon with two women in the seat, with one more standing behind it, was spotted by the officer of the day. He came at once to intercept them. Thinking to address Wolf, who was leading the wagon, he signaled for him to stop.

"Where do you think you're going with that wagon?" the lieutenant wanted to know.

"I reckon you'd best talk to the women," Wolf replied, and turned his horse back toward the wagon.

Having heard the lieutenant's question, Lorena told

him that they were new to the fort and were seeking information. "We were figurin' on goin' to the sutler's store to find what we needed."

Needing no more than a brief look at the three women, the officer advised them that what they were looking for was probably not at the post trader's store. "I think the place you ladies are trying to find is the social center, about three miles down that road at the corner of the stables." He pointed toward the road, but refrained from referring to their destination by the popular name for it, the Three-Mile Hog Ranch. "That's more than likely the best place if you're looking for a place to camp. Otherwise, you'll have to park your wagon on the far side of the river with the other civilian wagons."

"Well, thank you kindly, Lieutenant," Lorena replied sweetly. "I guess we'll be on our way, then. Hope to see you again."

"Don't count on it," the lieutenant muttered.

Anxious to be on his way, and away from the busy army post, Wolf nevertheless resigned himself to three more miles with the women if he was to get the money Lorena promised. Without a word, he turned the bay toward the road that had been pointed out, and started again.

The hog ranch was not difficult to find. The raucous sounds of a piano, mixed with the loud talking and laughter, could be heard almost a quarter of a mile away. Upon rolling into the complex of several buildings, they discovered a saloon and store, as well as a hotel, operated by the Cheyenne and Black Hills Stage Company. Behind the saloon sat a barn and another building that resembled a barn, with loopholes apparently for defense. The center of activity was a U-shaped lime-grout building where the saloon was located, and accounted for most of the noise. The feature that interested Lorena and her two companions the most was a series of two-room cabins. There were eight of them, and they were obviously built to accommodate prostitutes. "Girls," Lorena announced, "I guess we're home."

After the wagon was parked and the horses unhitched and hobbled to graze, Wolf followed his three traveling companions into the saloon. All eyes in the crowded room turned immediately toward the strange foursome, which seemed to please Lorena. With the trials of the trail behind her, she was in her element now, and back in charge. The patrons, almost all of whom were soldiers, paused to look over the new *stock*. A half dozen professional ladies, already in residence, were the only unfriendly faces to greet the three newcomers. Lorena gave them all a syrupy smile, led her party up to the bar, and ordered a bottle of whiskey. The bartender, a grumpy-faced middle-aged man called Smiley, insisted upon seeing some money before he complied. With her smile still in place, she reached in the bosom of her blouse and fished around until she came up with a small purse. From it, she picked out the exact amount, placed it on the bar, replaced the purse, and patted her bosom when it settled comfortably. "I think we oughta have a little drink to celebrate us gettin' ourselves out here with our scalps still on. Barkeep, we're gonna need four glasses."

Leaving Billie Jean and Rose to pick up the glasses, she grabbed her bottle by the neck and looked for a table in the crowded saloon. There were none empty, so she paused a moment to survey the room before deciding on a table occupied by four soldiers, but no women. She sidled over to the table. "Evenin', boys. You look like four gentlemen. We've just arrived here after a hard and dangerous journey through hostile country. How about lettin' me and my tired companions sit down?"

There was a brief pause while the four soldiers exchanged perplexed glances. When none voiced objection, one of them spoke for his friends. "All right, ladies, I reckon you can have a seat—but not him." He frowned at Wolf. "I ain't giving up my chair so he can sit down."

Wolf did not respond, his expression remaining passive. Already feeling uncomfortable in the atmosphere of the crowded barroom, he had no desire to sit at the table while the women drank. He had no reason to drink the fiery liquid, anyway. The one time he had tried it, he seemed to lose control of his reflexes, and he got a terrible headache. He intended never to experience that feeling again. One of the other soldiers pushed his chair back and stood up. "Hell, I'm finished drinking, anyway. I've got stable duty in the morning." The other three followed his example and got up as well. None seemed inspired to make the acquaintance of any of the newly arrived *soiled doves*.

"Ladies." The soldier who had first spoken gestured politely as he stepped back from the table. Then he looked at Wolf and said, "You ain't supposed to come in here with that rifle. I'm surprised Smiley didn't notice and tell you to leave it at the door."

Wolf nodded slowly, the stoic expression still in place. "I won't shoot nobody with it unless I have reason." The look in his eyes prompted the soldier to leave it at that. When the soldiers departed, he sat down in the empty chair and settled his gaze upon Lorena, wondering if the money she used to buy the whiskey might have been intended to replace his cartridges. His thoughts were interrupted when Smiley, having heard the conversation between Wolf and the departing soldiers, came over to the table and explained the saloon's policy regarding weapons inside. "All right," Wolf said, "I'll take it outside."

"No need to do that," Smiley said. "I'll keep it for you behind the bar till you're ready to leave."

After Smiley left with his rifle, Lorena gestured for him to slide his glass over, but he declined and turned it upside down. Surprised, she hesitated before insisting, then shook her head as if amazed. "You don't diddle with women. Now you tell me you don't drink. You're the damnedest man I've ever met."

"He sure is," Rose seconded with a strong hint of admiration in her tone.

"I reckon you're itchin' to get the money I promised you so you can get the hell away from here," Lorena said.

"You told me you didn't have no money," he reminded her.

"That's right, I did," she said, grinning as she recalled their first meeting. "Well, I didn't know you then. But I'da been crazy to start out on a trip like this with no money a'tall."

He shrugged, grateful for any money she offered.

She was about to dive into her bosom again when

she was interrupted by a tap on the shoulder. She looked up to see Billie Jean nodding toward two of the resident prostitutes heading toward the table. "I was beginnin' to think they weren't gonna welcome us," Lorena remarked facetiously, and settled back in her chair. "Howdy," she greeted them. "Have a drink with us." Her greeting was met with a cold glare from both women.

The tall, skinny one did the talking for the two, and probably represented the feelings of the other women in the saloon. "I don't know where you three came from," she said, "but you can see that there's all the girls we need here already."

"That so?" Billie Jean asked. "How many girls are living here, counting you six?"

"That doesn't make any difference," the tall woman replied. "We don't need any more girls to horn in."

"Ain't but six of you, then?" Lorena asked.

"There's six of us, counting Flora and Lucille."

"Well, then," Lorena said, "there ain't no problem. I counted eight of them cribs out back, and we've got a whole army of prospects, so we oughta get along just fine." She paused to give them a wide smile before continuing. "Course, if we ain't welcome, I reckon we'll just do our business in my wagon, parked out front with a big sign that says 'All Services to Soldiers Free.'"

The tall, thin woman grinned, exhibiting a smile marred by the absence of one of her front teeth, no doubt lost in a similar altercation in the past. "So that's how it is, is it?" She smirked. "What if me and the other ladies decide to throw you and your two friends outta here on your asses?"

"God, I'd love that," Billie Jean exclaimed. "How soon can we get started?"

Her question caused the thin whore to glance quickly at the mousey-looking woman standing beside her before they both took a closer look at the newcomers. Lorena was a big woman, but Billie Jean was stockier and powerfully built. Thinking the threat might have been poor judgment on her part, the woman reconsidered. "Maybe we're not being fair about this. I reckon there's room for all of us. The two cabins on the end are empty. You're welcome to those if Smiley says it's okay. My name's Mae and this is Esther. Welcome to Three-Mile."

Wolf detected a genuine look of disappointment on Billie Jean's face. He suspected that she was looking forward to the part about "throwing them out on their asses." But she was as cheerful as Rose and Lorena when they introduced themselves to their new business associates. As for him, he had no experience when it came to dealing with women, especially prostitutes, but his instincts told him not to get involved if at all possible. Content to be a silent spectator, he was sure he had not been noticed until Mae asked, "What about him?"

Lorena turned to look at Wolf as if wondering herself. "Him? He's our guide—brought us from back south of Horse Creek, saved our scalps from flyin' on some Injun's lance."

"Is that a fact?" Esther spoke up then. "Maybe he's ready to try something new for a change." She flashed an impish smile in Wolf's direction. "How 'bout it, Slim?"

The proposition was overheard by a soldier seated at the table Mae and Esther had just come from. Feeling he had a prior claim, he was quick to express it. "Esther, get your ass back over here!"

"Keep your shirt on, Carl," Esther said. "I'm talking to somebody."

When the soldier started to get up from his chair, Rose, seeing trouble brewing, spoke on Wolf's behalf. "Tell your soldier there's no need to get upset. Wolf wouldn't be interested in partying. He doesn't do stuff like that. He doesn't even drink."

Her comment served to bring the attention of everyone within earshot to focus on this strange individual who didn't drink or carouse with women. The soldier whom Esther had called Carl was especially interested in such a man. "Well, what the hell's he doin' in here with us men?" he insisted, and looked around to appreciate the round of chuckles his question had sparked. On his feet now, he pointed a finger at Wolf and ordered, "Get your ass outta here before I decide to stomp you into the floor." Standing over six feet tall, and built big in the shoulders, the soldier presented a formidable problem. Already uncomfortable in the noisy smoke-filled room, Wolf did not understand why the soldier was threatening him. He remained silent, preferring to ignore the obviously drunken bully.

Seeing Wolf's confusion, Lorena sought to intercede. "Leave him alone, soldier. He's not lookin' for any trouble. Why don't you go back to your table and have another drink with Esther?"

Mistaking Wolf's lack of response for cowardice,

Carl would not be dissuaded. "Like hell I will," he ranted. "The son of a bitch tried to take my girl, and if he don't get up outta that chair and get outta here, I'm gonna throw him out myself." He walked up to the table and pointed at Wolf again. "Get up from there!"

Still perplexed, wondering what he had done to cause the soldier to become so violent, Wolf continued to sit there for a few moments more before answering. "I have no quarrel with you. I ain't done nothin' to you. I think it's best if you go back to your table and leave me alone."

"Oh, you do, do you?" Carl retorted. "Well, we'll see about that!" Thinking to pull Wolf up out of the chair, he reached across the table. It was a serious mistake in judgment. Wolf did not understand barroom bullies or drunken brawls. The only fighting he had ever been involved in was one enemy fighting another, and was a fight to the death. He didn't understand the provocation that caused the soldier to attack him, but he assumed that he meant to kill him, so it was a matter of who killed who. The soldier was not prepared for the fury he had unleashed upon himself, for the stoic figure in the faded buckskins exploded into action, clutching the arm that reached for him and forcing it backward until Carl screamed out in pain when the bone broke. Pulling the injured man over the top of the table, Wolf slammed him facedown to the floor and was immediately on top of him. Stunned by the pain, Carl was helpless as Wolf grabbed a fistful of his hair and smashed his face against the floor. He drew his knife then and pulled the soldier's head back, preparing to cut his throat.

"No!" Rose screamed, and grabbed his wrist. "Don't kill him! You've done enough!"

Wolf hesitated. "He woulda kilt me," he said.

"No," Rose pleaded, "he wasn't trying to kill you. He just wanted to fight, that's all."

Wolf looked around him. The saloon was dead quiet, and all around him were stunned faces. It had happened so fast that no one was prepared to take any action to come to the unfortunate soldier's aid. "Rose is right," Lorena said calmly. "He's just a bully lookin' for a fistfight. Let him go. You don't want the army after you for murder. They'll stand you in front of a firin' squad." Still filled with the rage that had overcome him, he tried to make sense of what had just happened, and realized that he had lived in a world of wild beasts and Indians far too long. He had lost all contact with the civilized world of his father and mother, remembering little of his childhood. Anytime he had fought before, it had been to purposefully take a life or to save his own.

He released the injured soldier and got to his feet. The shroud of shock that had paralyzed the astonished barroom slowly began to dissipate, and he heard a few mutterings of outrage from Carl's fellow soldiers. He walked quickly to the bar, reached over, and retrieved his rifle as some of the patrons went to help the wounded man. A voice in the middle of the spectators spoke. "There weren't no call for that. He broke his arm."

"He'da killed him if she hadn't stopped him," another declared.

"He should have left him alone," Rose argued. "He

didn't know if the man was out to kill him or not. He was just protecting himself."

Wolf glanced at the young woman. He was grateful for her attempt to plead for him, but there was a steady increase in the grumbling among the soldiers, and he was not going to hang around to see if she could convince them to leave him alone. He cranked a cartridge into the chamber and held the Henry ready in front of his chest. "I didn't come here to hurt nobody," he said, "but I ain't sorry about that feller's arm. He had no call to come after me. Now, you folks just go on with your drinkin' and whorin', and you won't see me no more." He backed slowly toward the door, his rifle ready to fire at the slightest provocation. Step after cautious step, he backed away from the unfriendly faces staring at him in angry silence. And then they disappeared—everything went black as his head felt as if it had been split open brief seconds before he crumpled to the floor unconscious.

Deputy U.S. marshal Ned Bull stood over the body sprawled half inside the saloon door, still holding the Colt .44 he had used as a club by the barrel. When the injured man showed no sign of life, he replaced the pistol in his holster. "Damn, Marshal," Smiley remarked, "you hit him pretty hard. You mighta killed him."

"Might have at that," Ned replied, unconcerned. "Hell, that gal that ran over to the hotel to interrupt my supper said there was a wild man fixin' to shoot up the place, so I didn't think about askin' him politely to hand over his rifle." He continued to stare down at the prone figure, just then beginning to show signs of coming to, and considered what he should do about him. "You say he broke that feller's arm?" He stepped aside to let a couple of Carl's friends pass as they helped the injured soldier out the door on their way to the post hospital.

"Sure as hell did," Smiley replied. "He jumped on him like some kinda wild animal."

"Is that a fact?" Ned replied. "Well, he ain't no responsibility of mine. I've got other business to attend to. I suppose some of you boys oughta tie him up before he wakes up good, then take him to the guardhouse. I expect the army will wanna hold him awhile for assaultin' that soldier."

Fearing another violent reaction when Wolf regained consciousness, Smiley went immediately to fetch some rope from the back room. When he returned, he placed Wolf's hands behind his back and tied his wrists together with plenty of volunteer help from some of the soldiers. "We oughta hang the son of a bitch," one of them remarked.

"Nah," Ned Bull drawled. "You boys take him back on the post to the guardhouse. That's the best thing to do. Let the authorities handle it. Take his weapons and his horse, if he rode in on one, and turn 'em in to the officer of the day. I'd do it for you, but my supper's gettin' cold, and I ain't got no jurisdiction on this army post anyway." Ready to take action now that the danger was over, several volunteers were willing to step forward.

"Hold on there a minute, Marshal." Lorena Parker spoke up then. She had been no more than an interested observer to that point, but she wanted to do something to help the man who had led her and her two friends through Indian Territory. "The horse he was ridin' belongs to me. It's tied up to my wagon out front, and I was just lettin' him ride it while he was guidin' us."

Ned smiled. "Is that a fact?"

"That's the truth," Billie Jean piped up. "That ain't his horse."

"Well, I reckon we wouldn't wanna confiscate somethin' that belonged to you," Ned said, the smile still in place. He didn't care whether the prostitutes just stole themselves a horse or not. Amused by their claim, he commented further, "I don't suppose he was carryin' your Henry rifle, was he?"

"Well . . . ," Lorena started, then thought better of it, thinking she might lose the horse if she asked for everything. She shrugged indifferently.

Ready to be done with the incident, Ned turned to go back to the hotel and his supper. He paused to watch several soldiers load Wolf in the back of an army freight wagon and head back to the post. Then he felt someone grab his arm and he turned to see the plaintive face of Rose Hutto looking up at him. "Can't you help him?" she asked. "What happened here wasn't his fault. That soldier attacked him, and Wolf thought he was trying to kill him."

"Wolf?" Ned repeated. "Is that his name?" Rose nodded. "Where'd he come from? Has he been livin' with a pack of wolves or somethin'? How do you and your friends happen to know him?" Rose hurriedly told him of their chance meeting with Wolf and their association with him after that. "Well, that's mighty interestin'," Ned commented. "But like I said, I got supper settin' on the table that's most likely stone cold by now." He left her then, but after walking a dozen paces or so, he called back over his shoulder, "I'm gonna be here for a couple of days. I'll look in on him if I get a chance." Without looking back, he held up a hand to acknowledge her thank-you.

"Well, now, that was something, wasn't it?" Billie Jean said, her hands on her hips while she remained staring at the door. Thinking of the event she had just witnessed, she said, "I knew he was half wild, but I didn't think he could go plumb loco like that. I guess that's the last we'll ever see of him."

"Maybe, maybe not," Lorena said. "But if they do let him out again, he'll still have his horse. I'da asked for his rifle, too, but I figured I was lucky to get the horse."

"Is that what you were thinkin'?" Billie Jean asked. "Hell, I figured you were just quick enough to get yourself a horse."

"I ain't a complete bitch," Lorena said with a laugh.

"We should go talk to the army and tell them that he's not as bad as they're making him out to be," Rose said. "It's not fair to send him to jail for something he didn't start."

Lorena paused to take a hard look at her young friend. "If I didn't think you had better sense, I'd think you're gettin' soft in the head over that white Injun. Tell me I'm wrong, please, 'cause if you are, you're lettin' yourself in for a helluva lot of trouble."

Rose attempted to shrug the comment off. "I just think he's not being treated fairly, that's all. He certainly saved our lives, and hasn't asked for a penny for doing it."

"He was just waitin' around for money to buy more cartridges with," Lorena responded.

"You volunteered the money," Rose countered. "He didn't ask for it."

"Lorena's right," Billie Jean said. "You ought not get a soft spot for that wildcat. We most likely won't ever see him again."

Signaling an end to the discussion, Lorena walked away to the bar to confront Smiley, who was busy rinsing shot glasses now that the atmosphere in the saloon had returned to normal. With no intention of asking politely if the three of them could occupy the empty cabins at the end of the row, she informed him instead, "Me and Billie Jean and Rose will be movin' into those empty cribs you got. We'll pay the same rent as the other girls, so I'll need the door keys." She held out her hand expectantly.

Slightly taken aback, Smiley paused to consider his response. Finally he replied, "Well, it's mighty nice of you to let me know, seeing as how I'm the one who decides who lives here and who don't."

She gave him a big smile then and said, "You're gonna find that this is the best partnership you ever made. I've been workin' this trade long enough to know how to make 'em keep comin' back for more. Me and my two girls are gonna sell a lot of whiskey for you."

He shook his head and grinned. "You do beat all," he said, and went to get the keys.

Chapter 4

It was late morning the following day when Ned Bull finished his meeting with Lieutenant Colonel Luther Bradley, the post commanding officer. When he traveled, he liked to get an early start, so he decided to stay over one more night and start back to Omaha in the morning. With time on his hands, he decided to stop by the guardhouse to see how the "wild man" was doing. When he arrived, he found Captain Hartsuff, the post surgeon, on the lower floor where the prisoners were kept in one large area. He was applying a bandage to the back of Wolf's head. The patient submitted to treatment with no show of aggression, nor any indication that he was in pain. "Hello, Doc," Ned greeted the surgeon. "Is he gonna live?"

Hartsuff glanced back to see who had spoken to him. "It'd take a lot more than this, I think." He gave Ned a bit longer scrutiny then. "Are you the deputy marshal?" When Ned answered with a nod, Hartsuff said, "You're the one who hit him. A little bit harder and you might have cracked his skull for certain. You bring them in either dead or nearly dead, don't you?" he said, referring to Arlo Taggart. He then returned his attention to the wound, a two-inch split in Wolf's scalp, standing in sharp contrast to the white patch he had shaved to treat the cut.

"I reckon he's got a pretty hard head at that," Ned said, not really concerned, as he watched the captain wrap cloth around the bandage to hold it in place. "When they came to get me, they said he was a wild man, fixin' to shoot the place up. I reckon it ain't only Indians who can't handle their whiskey. A helluva lot of white men go crazy when they get drunk."

"This man wasn't drunk," the doctor said. "At least, I can't find any evidence of it in his breath or on his clothes. And it isn't usually hard to tell."

"Is that a fact?" Ned replied, genuinely surprised. "I reckon he's just plain crazy, then." He stepped to the side in order to look Wolf directly in the eye. The grim, sullen countenance that returned his gaze indicated a burning inferno inside the expressionless face. Although he was silent and motionless, the man's eyes were very much alert and studying the lawman intently. "Damn," Ned swore after a few moments of eye contact, "maybe he can't talk, but I swear, I can almost see the wheels turnin' in his mind." He turned back to the surgeon. "What's he got to say about why he attacked that soldier?"

"He hasn't said anything since I've been here," Hartsuff replied.

"He ain't said a word since they brought him in last night," a sergeant standing by to guard the prisoner said. "I just came on duty this morning, but that's what they told me. Said he didn't so much as look at the other prisoners, just stood staring out one of them little windows at the river till they got the straw pallets out. Then he laid down on the floor. He got blood all over that straw tick. That's why I called Captain Hartsuff."

"Maybe he just can't talk," Ned decided.

"There you go, fellow," the doctor said when he finished tying the knot on the bandage. "That oughta take care of it as long as you don't bump it and start it bleeding again."

"Much obliged," Wolf said. His comment brought a startled reaction from the three men standing nearby.

"Well, damn," Ned remarked, "he can talk." Then he asked, "How come you never said somethin' before this?"

"What good would it have done?" Wolf answered. "Nobody listens, especially soldiers. I told that soldier that came at me that I didn't want any trouble, and I was tryin' to leave when you knocked me in the head."

Ned took a moment to think about the prisoner's statement. He couldn't deny the possibility that he might have been able to handle the prior night's altercation more peacefully. But he had been a deputy marshal for a good many years, and one of the reasons for his longevity was the fact that he tried never to give a suspect any opportunity to react violently. "They tell me you rode in with a wagon with three whores in it. How'd you hook up with them?"

Wolf studied the big lawman for a few moments longer before deciding Ned was not being confrontational, merely wanting to know. So he told the deputy how he happened to come upon the three women in the middle of a creek, their encounter with Sioux hostiles, and how he happened to be in the saloon. "I never wanted to come into this army post," he said, "but Lorena wanted to pay me for some of the cartridges I spent. And that soldier jumped me. I didn't give him no cause."

Ned studied the man carefully while listening to his account of the incident that led to his arrest. The deputy marshal had met men like Wolf before, who for some reason or another were more accustomed to the Indian's world. The man who first came to mind was another white man raised by Indians, a man called Sunday. Judging by Wolf's mannerisms and the way he talked, as well as his buckskin attire, Ned guessed where it had all come from. "How old were you when you were took by Injuns?" he asked at one point. Wolf replied that he had never been taken by Indians, but Indians killed his folks when he was eleven. "But you spent some time with Injuns. Ain't that right?" Wolf told him about the years he had lived with the Crows. It was enough to give Ned a pretty good picture of Wolf's life up to that point, and to explain his savage reaction to a barroom bully.

"They took my rifle and my horse," Wolf said. "They've got no right to do that. What are they gonna do with me?"

"I don't know," Ned replied. "I'll see if I can find out, and I'll let you know." He smiled then, recalling his conversation with Lorena the night before. "That one whore, the big one that looks old enough to be your mother, said that bay was hers. She said she was just lettin' you use him while you were guidin' them. Couple of the boys upstairs in the guard quarters were lookin' at a Henry rifle when I came in—mighta been yours. I expect they'll keep it in a rack up there till they decide to let you go." The news did little to assure Wolf. He nodded and turned away.

As he closed up his bag, the doctor informed the sergeant, "I'm gonna want to take a look at that wound tomorrow afternoon. When I do, I want you to bring him upstairs out of this foul jail room. That place isn't fit to keep hogs in."

"Yessir," the sergeant replied, not really concerned, because he wouldn't be on duty after the guard mount in the morning. The captain could take it up with whoever took his place. The jail *was* in a pretty sad state, a stone building with overcrowded conditions and no furniture or beds, and nothing but a blanket for heat. There was no separation of prisoners. The murderers were mixed in with the poor bastards who got caught sleeping on guard duty. And now they had a "wild man" thrown into the stew. There was talk about building a new jail, but nobody complained but the doctor, the post commanding officer, and those who found themselves incarcerated.

Ned couldn't help feeling sorry for the poor caged animal as he watched Wolf go immediately to one of the small windows and remain standing there, looking out. He followed the sergeant back upstairs to the guards' quarters. "How long did they throw him in for?" he asked.

"Don't know," the sergeant replied. "I think the provost marshal is thinking about puttin' him on trial."

"Why?" Ned asked. "It wasn't much more'n a bar-room fight, same as they have every week. They don't put everybody that gets in a fight up for trial, do they?"

"No, but this fellow broke Sergeant Peterson's arm and was fixing to kill him. I think Colonel Bradley is cracking down on some of the trouble out at that hog ranch, and he's most likely gonna send a message to anybody else thinking about causing trouble down there."

"Well, there ain't nothin' I can do for the poor bastard," Ned concluded, although he kind of wished he hadn't caused him to be in the guardhouse.

Later on that afternoon, Wolf had another visitor. This one did not come inside to see him, however. He heard his name called outside the tiny window at the back of the jail room. When he reached that window, he looked down to see Rose Hutto standing alone beneath the window. "I had to see if you were all right," she said. "Are you? You looked like they had knocked you senseless."

"I'm all right now," he said. "Got a terrible headache, though. I'm hopin' they'll let me outta here pretty soon."

"That's something else I came to tell you. Lorena found out from a soldier that works in the provost marshal's office that they're gonna hold you for a military trial, and they might send you to prison."

"I can't do that," Wolf stated honestly. "I'm 'bout to go crazy shut up in this box. I've got to get out of here and get up in the mountains, somewhere I can breathe."

His obvious sense of panic caused her to fear for his

life. "Don't do something crazy and get yourself shot," she pleaded. "Don't do *anything* yet. Me and Lorena and Billie Jean are not gonna let them send you off to prison. Lorena's already thinking up a way to help you. Promise me you won't try anything until we have a chance to come up with a way to get you out."

"I'll wait a little while," he promised, "but I'm gonna get outta here one way or another, even if it's feetfirst on a slab. Dyin' is better'n livin' in a cage."

"You just hold on. We'll think of something." She started to leave but then remembered. "Oh, and we've got your horse. Lorena told them it was her horse, so they didn't take it."

"I know," he said. "That marshal told me. Tell Lorena I 'preciate it." *Now, if I can just figure out a way to get to it,* he thought, *I'll sure ride the hell away from here.* There were two things that were most precious to him, his horse and his rifle. And Ned Bull had said his Henry rifle was upstairs in a gun rack.

Captain Hartsuff returned the following day as he had said, but he was later than planned. The prisoners had been fed, and upstairs in the guard quarters the men on guard duty were going to, or returning from, the mess hall. Most of the men back from the mess hall were catching a few minutes of sleep before it was time for their tour. Some were playing cards or involved in a game of checkers. Two of the soldiers trying to sleep were unfortunate to have chosen cots closest to the sergeant's desk. These two were ordered to fetch the prisoner upstairs for treatment of his wound, because the surgeon was adamant that he was not going to give medical care in "that pigpen of filth."

"Ward and McPherson will bring your patient up," the sergeant told Hartsuff. "I'm gonna run over to the mess hall before they close it up." He turned to his two reluctant guards and said, "Keep on your toes. It's the wild man he's wantin' to attend to, so you two stay with him till the captain's finished." He left then while Ward and McPherson went downstairs to fetch the "wild man."

The two guards soon returned with the prisoner, who gave no indication of resistance, instead silently complying with their instructions to keep his hands clasped behind his head. "Well, mister," Captain Hartsuff said, "let's take a look at how that wound is healing." Wolf glanced at his guards to see if there were any objections to his moving his hands, since they were directly over the wound. Realizing the cause of his patient's hesitation, Hartsuff instructed impatiently, "Go ahead and take your arms down. I can't look at your wound with your hands in the way." Private McPherson nodded permission for Wolf to comply. "You two just sit down over at the table, and be careful with those rifles. You can see him over there and you've got plenty of time to shoot him if he runs for the door." This last remark was delivered with an ample helping of impatience. McPherson and Ward did as the captain ordered and withdrew to a table across the crowded room from the officer of the day's desk.

"Hey, McPherson," one of the checker players chided, "you better watch yourself. Make sure he don't go wild on you. He broke Sergeant Peterson's arm, you know."

Amid a smattering of chuckles from the other

soldiers who heard the remark, McPherson answered, "He doesn't look too wild right now. I reckon a night in the hoosegow mighta sobered him up."

In truth, Wolf did appear totally subdued as the surgeon unwrapped the binding that held his bandage in place. However, he was taking note of everything around him. One of the first things he noted was the gun rack near the center of the room where the guards stacked their rifles when waiting to go on duty. At the end of the rack, his glance was captured by the brass receiver plate and the lever action of a Henry rifle—his Henry rifle, he felt sure. He could not count on how many more times he would find himself outside the locked cell room downstairs, so he felt desperate to evaluate his chances of escape. The main problem confronting him at that moment was the discomforting fact that he was in a room with perhaps twenty soldiers. On the other hand, this might work in his favor, since he doubted the lounging guards gave any serious thought that the prisoner might try to escape, with odds so heavily in their favor. His eyes switched back to the two soldiers at the table. Their weapons were the only rifles out of the gun rack—better odds, he thought, but still not in his favor.

"I suspected as much," the doctor muttered to himself as he inspected Wolf's scalp. "I should have put a couple of stitches in this wound yesterday. I thought it had a chance of closing up without them, but it doesn't look like that's going to happen." He dabbed at the blood around the wound with the binding he had just removed, and continued to stare at it for a few moments more before declaring to the two guards, "I need to stitch him up, so I'm going to have to have him taken over to my surgery."

There was an immediate look of concern on the faces of both guards. "Beggin' your pardon, Captain," McPherson said, "we can't do that without Sergeant Wilson's or Lieutenant Davidson's permission. Can't you just sew him up right here?"

"I could," Hartsuff replied, "but I don't want to. These aren't the cleanest of conditions for closing a wound."

"Hell, sir," Private Ward interjected, "look at him. He's been livin' with Injuns most of his life, and they would most likely sew him up with the guts outta some animal. He ain't used to clean conditions."

Captain Albert Hartsuff was a compassionate man and he had little use for men who were not. "Just the same, Private, I think we'll take him to my surgery."

"Yessir," McPherson responded. "Can you wait for a minute or two, so one of us can run over to the mess hall and let Sergeant Wilson know what you're gonna do?"

"Make it quick," Hartsuff said. "I've got other things to do tonight."

Private Ward quickly placed his rifle in the gun rack and ran to the barracks mess hall to find Sergeant Wilson. When he returned, he was accompanied by Lieutenant Davidson, the officer of the day. Davidson was mounted on a bright chestnut Morgan gelding that he pulled up to the door of the guardhouse, then climbed down from the saddle and handed the reins to Private Ward to hold. "Hello, Albert," the lieutenant said when he saw the surgeon step out of the door of the guardhouse.

"Jim," Hartsuff returned.

"What is it you wanna do?" Davidson asked. When Hartsuff explained that he simply wanted to treat the prisoner in a more sanitary environment, Davidson expressed his concern. "I don't know if that's a good idea or not," he said. "My orders were to be especially watchful for any sign of trouble from this prisoner because of his violent nature. Are you sure you wanna take him all the way across the post to the hospital?"

"Like I've been trying to tell your men, I can't work on his wound here," Hartsuff repeated, growing more irritated by the moment.

Davidson shrugged indifferently. "Damn, Albert, what's so important about treating this fellow, anyway? To hell with his wound. It'll probably heal up all right on its own, and I'd rather not chance something happening while I'm O.D. So let's just put him back in lockup. He shouldn't have been let out in the first place."

"I believe I'm the one to decide what's best for the injured man, *Lieutenant*," Hartsuff stated emphatically, emphasizing Davidson's rank.

"Well, *Captain*," the lieutenant shot back, "I have a duty as officer of the day to see that my orders are carried out, and that includes not putting the men or the post in jeopardy."

The two officers were oblivious of the fact that their heated exchange had caught the rapt attention of the guard detail. This included that of Private McPherson, the only armed guard watching the prisoner at that point, as well as that of Private Ward, who was holding the lieutenant's reins. It was not often that the enlisted

men had the opportunity to witness a seemingly friv-
olous spat between two officers, as evidenced by the
grins of amusement on all their faces. While the officers stood toe-to-toe, glaring at each other, one among
the spectators was not smiling. Wolf, no longer the center of attention, focused on Private McPherson, who
was leaning forward in an effort to miss none of the
fun, his rifle propped casually against his leg. Wolf
shifted his gaze to Private Ward, standing just outside
the door, inching closer so as to hear every word of the
exchange. There was never going to be a better chance,
he decided as he took another look in McPherson's
direction. The private was totally absorbed in the altercation, and thoroughly enjoying it.

As quick as a cat, Wolf suddenly sprang out the
door, jerked the reins from Ward's hand, and leaped
into the saddle. His sudden move startled the horse,
causing it to jump sideways, almost stumbling down
the bluff behind the guardhouse before breaking into
a full gallop as Wolf flailed it with the reins. The reaction in the guardhouse was chaotic with troopers
scrambling to respond as they tried to draw weapons
from the rack and hurriedly fumbled to load them.
Trying his best to react, Private McPherson ran outside
and aimed his rifle at the fleeing prisoner, who was
already fifty yards away and getting farther by the second. "Don't hit my horse!" Davidson screamed, causing McPherson to raise his sights and send his shot
sailing over Wolf's head.

By the time McPherson could reload his single-shot
Springfield, Wolf was rapidly riding out of range in the
early evening light. The lieutenant's horse was not

only regal in appearance, but it could run as well, and Wolf held it to a full gallop as he raced along below the bluffs, giving the horse no rest until coming to a bridge crossing the Laramie. He drew back on the reins and guided the Morgan up the bluffs to cross over the road leading into the fort. Back down to the river's edge, he continued at a lope, promising the horse that he would haul him back to a walk before much longer. He had escaped for the time being, but he had been forced to leave his rifle behind, and he could only imagine the rush to form a posse to pursue him. *Got to get off of this sandy riverbank,* he thought, knowing his trail would be easy to follow, so when he came to a short road leading up from the river, he swung the horse up from the bluffs again. *At least I can mix my tracks with the tracks on the road,* he figured.

With still no sign of pursuit yet organized behind him, he reined the horse back to a walk as he passed a row of buildings that looked like houses, although there was no sign of anyone about. *Just as well,* he thought. When he passed the last of the buildings, he veered off the road and set out at an angle to intercept the road that led to the hog ranch. After striking the road, he followed it to a point he remembered to be a mile or so from the saloon where he had been arrested. He dismounted then and turned the horse back toward the fort. With a little encouragement in the form of a couple of sharp swats across its rump, the chestnut Morgan started back down the road at a trot. He didn't plan to add horse-stealing to whatever charges the army was already piling up on him, and he counted heavily on the reports that Lorena was keeping his horse for him. On foot now, he broke into a trot himself, a way of travel that he had ample experience with when he was a boy in the Wind River Mountains.

It was approaching darkness when he reached the Three-Mile Hog Ranch, a fact he was thankful for, and he hesitated a few moments when he didn't see Lorena's wagon. Then he spotted it parked beyond the last in the row of eight cabins. With the evening just beginning, he figured the women would all be working their trade in the saloon, so he didn't waste time in an effort to be stealthy. The soldiers would surely come to this place to look for him, especially since he had left tracks that pointed in this direction. So he went directly to the wagon and climbed into it, hoping his saddle and the rest of his possessions were stored there.

He had figured correctly, for in the back of the wagon he found his saddle and saddlebags. His spirits were dampened only by the empty saddle scabbard where his Henry once rode. In his mind, it was a heavy loss, for he could not survive without a rifle. He hopped back down from the wagon and was in the process of pulling his saddle out when he heard the low warning: "You can stop right there, mister." He turned around to face the solid, square figure of Billie Jean, her Sharps carbine pointed at him. Before he could speak, she recognized him. "Wolf! How the hell did you get here?" Before he could answer, she got a better look at the back of his head. "Good Lord in heaven!" she exclaimed. "We need to do something about that cut on the back of your head." She stepped closer again. "That's a nasty-looking wound."

"I ain't got much time to fool with it," he replied.

"There'll be soldiers come lookin' for me. Where's my horse?"

"In the corral back of the barn," she said. "How'd you get out?"

"It's a long story. I'll tell you sometime when we can sit down by the fire and drink a cup of coffee. Right now I've got to get my possibles and get outta here."

She stepped back and watched him pull his saddle out and heft it up on his shoulder. Noticing the empty saddle sling, she asked, "Where's your rifle?"

"In a gun rack in that army jail," he answered. "There wasn't no way I could get it."

"You need a rifle," she said. "Here, take mine. You can't go off with nothing for protection or to hunt with. There's more cartridges for it in the cabin. I'll get 'em while you get your horse." She slipped the carbine into the saddle sling. "It's loaded."

He was grateful beyond his ability to express it, so he simply replied with a simple "'Preciate it. I'll try to pay you back for it, but it might be a while."

"We'll worry about that later," she said as she hurried off to get the cartridges, and he headed for the corral.

Certain that Lorena and Rose would be cross with her if they weren't told that Wolf was there, Billie Jean ran inside the saloon to get her two friends. It was early enough in the evening that Lorena was not engaged in any negotiations, so she found her standing at the bar, talking to Smiley. "Come on," Billie Jean called from just inside the door. "Hurry up!" she encouraged as she motioned.

"What is it?" Lorena responded, but Billie Jean didn't answer. Instead she simply increased her motioning until Lorena gave in and walked to the door. "What in the hell is eatin' you?" Lorena demanded.

"It's Wolf. He's done broke outta that army jail and he's saddling his horse right now. Where's Rose?"

Lorena's attention was captured right away. "She's in the cabin with an early customer, that young soldier that works in the administration center. I think he's fallen in love with her."

"Well, we ain't got time to wait for her," Billie Jean said. "I let him have my carbine, and I'm fixin' to get him some cartridges to go with it. I hope that's all right with you, since you're the one that really owns it. The soldiers took his rifle."

"Oh, hell yeah," Lorena said as the two prostitutes hurried back toward the corral. "I reckon we owe him that much. You go ahead and get the cartridges. I'll be at the barn."

The bay gelding, standing near the back of the corral, threw his head up alertly at the first sound of Wolf's low whistle, then trotted straight to his master, waiting at the gate. "You ready to travel, boy?" Wolf greeted him as he slipped the bridle over the horse's ears. The bay stood patiently while he threw the saddle blanket and saddle on him and tightened the girth strap. He was leading the horse out of the corral when Lorena showed up, followed a few moments later by Billie Jean, carrying a sack of ammunition and what looked like an old bedsheet. Like Billie Jean, Lorena was appalled to see the open wound on the back of Wolf's head. "Who did that piece of work?" she wanted to know.

"That marshal," Wolf replied.

"I don't mean that," Lorena snapped. "I know who

knocked you in the head. I mean who shaved that big patch outta your hair?" She stepped up behind him to get a closer look. "They put some kind of grease on it but didn't bother to bandage it up."

"The doctor did that," Wolf explained. "He was wantin' to stitch it up, but I had some other business to tend to, and there ain't no time to bother with it now. I've got to get on my way."

"The hell you are," Billie Jean insisted. "You can wait five minutes while I slap a bandage on your head. You'll be catching flies, and bugs, and everything else in that open cut." She started ripping the sheet into strips. He took a quick look in the direction of the road to the fort and decided to accept her doctoring. "Get down on your knees so I can see what I'm doin'," she ordered. "You're too damn tall." As she fashioned the bandage around his head, she and Lorena questioned him about the details that led up to his escape.

"Where are you headin' from here?" Lorena asked.

"I ain't sure, maybe the Black Hills," he said. "I spent a winter up there a few years ago. There were plenty of deer and elk up there and plenty of places where a man could lose himself. The Injuns call the hills Paha Sapa. They say it's a sacred place and they've got a treaty with the government that keeps white folks out, so I don't reckon the army will follow me there. It don't make much difference if they do, 'cause there's plenty of hills and woods to hide in."

"Which way would that be?" Lorena pressed.

"Yonder way," he said, pointing to the north.

"All right, I just want to make sure we send the soldiers off in some other direction when they get here." She reached into her skirt pocket and pulled out two coins. "There's forty dollars gold there. That'll help you a little. You take care of yourself, boy."

He didn't know what to say. He wanted to tell her how much he appreciated the gift. She interrupted him before he started. "Don't worry about it. I know you ain't good with words. Just don't lose your scalp."

"I'll try not to. Much obliged," he finally managed before he climbed into the saddle and turned the bay's head north.

"I know you are," Lorena muttered as they watched him until he faded into the darkness.

"What are you doing out here in the dark?" They turned to see Rose walking toward them. "I was looking all over for you."

"Sayin' good-bye to Wolf," Lorena replied. "He broke outta that army jailhouse." She observed her young friend's obvious distress. "He had to get away before an army patrol shows up lookin' for him," she explained. "There wasn't any time for long good-byes."

"You were busy, anyway," Billie Jean commented.

"That's right," Lorena said, knowing full well that Rose was overly disappointed to have missed a chance to see Wolf. "How is that little private you've been entertainin' gettin' along? I swear, I believe you'll have him proposin' to you before long." She winked at Billie Jean, although it was so dark by then that Billie Jean probably did not see it. "That'ud be a sight better'n pairin' up with a drifter like Wolf, wouldn't it?"

"There ain't no doubt about that," Billie Jean quickly agreed. "Men like him would just as likely strike out for someplace without telling anybody they're going and you never see 'em again."

"I'm not wanting to settle down with anybody,"

Rose insisted. "And I sure as hell don't wanna be a private's wife. I'm not any more interested in Wolf than you two. It's chilly out here," she said in closing. "I'm going in by the fire." She turned abruptly and started toward the door of the saloon. In the darkness, her two friends could not see the disappointment in her face.

Chapter 5

Lieutenant Colonel Bradley looked up when the big deputy marshal strode into his office. "Oh . . . Bull," he acknowledged, "glad we were able to catch you before you got away." He motioned toward a side chair across from his desk. "Sit down."

"Mornin', Colonel," Ned responded. "I was almost gone when your man caught me. What did you wanna see me about?"

"I'm sure you heard we had a prisoner escape last night—that Wolf fellow."

"Yeah, I heard," Ned remarked. "Heard he stole the O.D.'s horse."

"That's right, he did. We recovered the horse. It came trotting back to the stables this morning, but we don't know if the prisoner fell off or turned it loose."

Ned pictured Wolf as he said, "I'd bet he turned the horse loose, 'cause I doubt he fell off." He patiently waited for the colonel to get to the point of the meeting.

"Well," Bradley began, "the prisoner's still on the loose. We sent a patrol down to that hog ranch to see if he went back there, but they got there a little too late. He had been there and picked up his horse and was already gone by that time. Lieutenant Willis was leading the patrol and he talked to one of the prostitutes who's supposed to be a friend of Wolf's. She said he had come there that night and took his horse, and said he took off in a hurry along the North Platte, heading west. Lieutenant Willis followed the river for about four miles, but he said it was too dark to see any tracks to confirm that to be the fugitive's line of flight."

It wasn't difficult for Ned to see where this interview was heading. "So you're wantin' me to take over and try to track this fellow down. Is that it?"

"I don't have the time or the troops to waste on it right now," Bradley explained. "But I want that man caught and brought to justice. I figure that it's more in your line of work to track men like Wolf down."

"Well, I reckon I've had a heap of experience in that part of my job," Ned admitted. "But I'm kinda surprised you're makin' such a fuss over catchin' this fellow. He ain't done much but get in a fight with one of your soldiers, has he? Seems to me you wouldn't wanna waste time on a saddle tramp like that."

"It's a matter of principle," Bradley replied. "He escaped from army custody, and that doesn't look good on my—I mean, the post's record. More than a barroom fight, though, he's wanted for assault on one of my sergeants, escape from federal custody, and stealing a horse. I want to let him and every drifter like him know that they'll answer for that."

Ned listened patiently before responding. "I'm sure

you understand that I don't operate independently. I've been ordered back to Omaha as soon as my business here was finished—which it is."

"I appreciate that," Bradley remarked, "so I telegraphed your headquarters in Omaha last night and requested you to be reassigned to track down this fugitive. I received the federal marshal's change of orders this morning. So it looks like you'll be delayed in returning to Omaha."

Not surprised by the sudden change of assignment, Ned shrugged his indifference. He had no particular desire to return to Omaha right away, and it made little difference to him in what part of the territory he worked. He had no family to return to, and really no family at all except for a brother who lived in Denver and whom he had last seen four years ago. Besides, this fellow Wolf held a particular interest for him. Ned was sure the Indian-raised man would offer a genuine challenge to his skills as a tracker. "If I run this fellow to ground," he asked, "where am I supposed to take him? Back here?"

"Well, I assume so," Bradley replied, "since this is where he escaped from."

"Just wanted to be sure. A fellow like that could be hard to catch up with—might be chasin' him a long way. Could end up closer to some other military post where it'd be easier to turn him over to them."

Bradley thought about it for only a second before saying, "I guess it doesn't really matter where you take him, just as long as you catch him, although I would prefer it to be here if possible."

"I'll do my best," Ned responded as he got up to leave. They were not empty words. Ned Bull always strived to do his best, and in most cases that was better than anybody else's best. He had been employed in the U.S. Marshals Service for over fifteen years. During that time, he had seen many deputy marshals come and go, some of their own volition, many others feet-first in a pine box. He naturally credited good luck with his long tenure, but that was only part of it. Ned was a patient man, and not given to taking foolish chances. He was a skillful tracker and, not least of all, a dead shot with a '73 Winchester.

Outside, he untied the reins from the corner porch post and turned the red roan away from the porch before climbing aboard. "Well, Brownie," he addressed the horse, "I reckon we'd best go right back out to that hog ranch. We've got a job to do." He aimed Brownie's head at the corner of the parade ground and the road that led to Three-Mile Hog Ranch and started on the hunt for Wolf, his sorrel packhorse following on a lead rope tied to his saddle. The sorrel was already packing the supplies needed for a long trip, so there was no time lost to that chore.

"Wait a damn minute," Lorena yelled when her caller continued to knock on her door. Her request succeeded in giving her only a few moments of peace before the knocking began again, this time a bit louder.

"Lorena," a man's deep voice called, "open up."

"Dammit," she yelled again, angry to have a caller this early in the morning. "I'm on the damn chamber pot! Just hold your horses." The knocking stopped. After a few minutes, she opened the door to find Ned Bull standing there, a grin on his face. "Well, Marshal," she said, surprised to see the big deputy, "you musta got an early case of the itch to come around before I've even had breakfast."

"Afraid not," he replied. Even if he had the urge, the mental picture of the disheveled middle-aged woman seated on a chamber pot was more than enough to discourage any thoughts of a carnal nature. "I just wanna talk to you for a minute about your friend Wolf."

Already having guessed the purpose of the marshal's call on her, she sought to play coy. "Well, now," she teased, pulling her housecoat up tighter around her throat, "people have to pay me for my time, and that's for talkin', diddlin', or whatever."

"Like I said, this ain't a business call. I just wanna ask you a few questions."

"All the same," she began, still playing coy in spite of an aching head that was crying for black coffee to help lessen the effects of too much drinking the night before.

"Well, let me put it this way," Ned interrupted, tired already of the game. "I don't have time to fool around. I can just as easily haul your ass back to the guardhouse for aidin' and abettin' an escaped prisoner—and lock you up till the army gets through with you. So let's make this easier on both of us. All right?"

Lorena couldn't help grinning. "You wouldn't really do that, would you, Marshal? You look like a big ol' softie to me. Hell, I was just havin' you on a little." She paused to give him a wink. "Besides, I know they ain't got no place to hold women in that guardhouse." They both grinned then. "But for God's sake, let me put on a pot of coffee before I keel over dead."

"I could use a cup of coffee myself," he said, and

walked over to the small table by the window and sat down to wait for her.

"Wouldn't hurt if you stirred up that fire in the stove a little while I go get some water," she said. He picked a couple of sticks of wood out of a box behind the stove while she went outside to the pump. Using one of the sticks for a poker, he poked at the reluctant flames until they caught on again, then dropped the sticks onto the rekindled fire.

Lorena was back shortly with the coffeepot filled with water, and soon there was coffee bubbling on the stove. Never in a hurry when there was coffee working, Ned waited patiently while Lorena pulled herself together to face yet another day. She sat down at the table with him with two cups of the boiling hot liquid. "All right," she said. "Whaddaya wanna ask me about Wolf?"

Before he had a chance to open his mouth, there was a light tap on the door, and a male voice asked, "You up, Lorena?"

"Yeah," Lorena called out. "Come on in."

The door opened to reveal the owner of the male voice to be Billie Jean. She paused when the door was still only half-open. "You entertaining?"

"No, this is an official call from a U.S. deputy marshal," Lorena replied grandly. "Come on in." Then she looked quickly at Ned. "Is that all right, Marshal? I'm the official coffee maker around here. Rose will most likely show up in a minute or two." Ned shrugged his indifference. A moment later, Rose came in, right on cue, equally surprised to find the lawman there. Ned noted that, unlike Lorena and Billie Jean, Rose was at once nervous and seemingly fearful.

"I reckon we've got everybody now," Ned declared. "So I need to know what happened to your guide last night. One thing I know for sure is that he was here to get his horse." He looked askance at Lorena. "Or should I say *your* horse?" Lorena nodded soberly, and Ned went on. "Where'd he say he was headin' when he rode outta here?"

"I'll tell you the same as I told those soldiers last night," Lorena said. "He didn't say much of anythin' to the three of us—just showed up suddenly, grabbed the horse, and took off. Didn't none of us have time to ask him where he was headed." She looked around at the other two women for confirmation.

"That's the God's honest truth," Billie Jean swore solemnly, and gave Rose a confirming nod.

"Which way did he go when he left here?" Ned asked.

"West," all three answered, almost simultaneously. "He headed west to follow the North Platte River," Rose volunteered further, causing both Lorena and Billie Jean to frown in her direction.

"How do you know that?" Ned asked. "You just said he didn't say much of anything, just took your horse and took off."

"Well," Lorena answered for her, wishing at that moment that she had not told Rose anything. "I forgot. He did say he was headed that way, but I told those soldiers that last night."

Ned shifted his gaze back and forth among the three faces all trying to present an earnest facade. He finally let it settle upon Rose. "You know what? I've been thinkin' about what I'd do if I was in his shoes. I believe I'd head someplace like the Black Hills where there's a lot of room to hide—up there where the Indians don't want any white men to come. Now that they've found gold up there, there's so many miners slippin' in their sacred Paha Sapa that it'd be damn hard to find one more white man." He caught an immediate flush of panic come over Rose's face.

"He didn't go there!" she blurted. "He said he wasn't going there. He said he was heading west."

Ned smiled at the naive young woman. He couldn't help a feeling of compassion for her apparent concern for the fugitive, but she had told him what he wanted to know—unless she was smarter than he gave her credit for. He doubted that. The fact was, however, that he had no earthly idea where Wolf had in mind to run, but judging by her fearful reaction, he now at least had a place to start looking. The problem he faced was what he had said about the odds of finding a man in that territory of high mountains and steep passes. He wouldn't bet on any success. He'd be damn lucky to find Wolf. The man was more Indian than white, but that was what the government paid him to do, so he'd give it his best shot.

He stayed long enough to get another cup of coffee, asking the women about how they happened to know such a man as Wolf. They answered his questions freely, and all made it a point to convince him that the man he was assigned to arrest had done nothing wrong. "My job ain't decidin'," he finally told them. "My job is to bring 'em in and let the smart folks do the decidin'. Thank you for the coffee. I'll be on my way now. Your boy has already got a big enough head start."

The three of them watched from the back window

of Lorena's cabin as Ned walked toward the corral, leading his horses. "What's he heading there for?" Billie Jean wondered aloud.

"Maybe he's looking for feed for his horses," Rose suggested. But it was soon apparent what the big man was doing when he began studying the tracks around the stable and corral.

"He's looking for a trail to follow," Billie Jean said, "trying to find one horse that headed north." She snapped at Rose then. "You just as good as told him that Wolf was heading for the Black Hills."

At once alarmed, Rose pleaded, "No, I told him Wolf *wasn't* going there!"

Billie Jean and Lorena exchanged perplexed glances. "Never mind," Lorena said. "You never meant to give him any idea. He ain't likely to find him, anyway."

Ned spent the better part of the morning studying the different tracks that were in profusion around the stable and corral. Trying to think as Wolf might, he looked out over the prairie beyond the gathering of buildings that made up Three-Mile and picked out the way he would go if he was heading to the Black Hills. Following a path that led across a small stream, he urged Brownie forward. He stopped again before crossing over the stream and dismounted again when he noticed a hoofprint in the soft sandbank. Seeing at once that it was left by an unshod horse, he knelt down to examine it more closely, looking for anything unusual about it that would allow future identification. There was nothing out of the ordinary about the print, but still he felt that he might have hit upon some luck. There was nothing beyond his natural instincts that told him the print was left by the bay horse Wolf rode. On the other hand, it was from an Indian pony, only one pony, and it was a fresh track. He felt that put the odds in his favor and he decided to bet on it. *If I'm wrong, hell, it won't be the first time,* he thought. He rose to his feet again and looked ahead across an expanse of prairie toward a pair of hills in the distance. Then he walked for a while, leading his horses, following the hoofprints until satisfied they were going to continue in the same direction, toward the twin hills. It just made sense, he thought, that the man would guide on the hills, so he spent no more time studying tracks and started out directly toward them.

While he rode, he speculated on the thinking of the man he hunted, and why he picked the Black Hills for his escape. He wondered then if Wolf had any idea of what was happening in the Black Hills: the fact that gold had been discovered there, and prospectors were already sneaking into the territory in spite of the treaty that prohibited it. *Most likely,* he decided, *the poor bastard thinks he'll be safe in a place whites can't go.*

More than fifty miles ahead of the deputy marshal, Wolf sat beside a shallow creek while he let his horse have some well-deserved rest. He had pushed the bay hard during the night, up through Rawhide Buttes, and across the rough prairie. The willing horse had not failed to respond to his master's bidding, but Wolf was reluctant to push the animal farther. He had hoped to make it to the Cheyenne River that night, but he feared it was asking too much of the bay. There was deer sign all along the creek, and the temptation to stop there long enough to hunt was strong. Fresh meat would be welcome, so he climbed a short slope to study his back trail. As before, there was no sign of anyone trailing him. He didn't really expect to see anyone, feeling fairly certain that an army patrol could not travel as fast as he, but it never paid to be careless. His intent was to outlast the soldiers, thinking they would more than likely start out after him with rations drawn for only so many days. And when they were used up, they'd call off the search and go home. He had done nothing wrong, so surely they would not follow him long. It would be a waste of the army's time to continue looking for a man who had done no more than break a soldier's arm. *In fact,* he told himself, *they may not be after me at all.* Lorena had said she would send them off in another direction, and he believed she would do as she promised, so he decided he could afford to take time to hunt.

He pulled the saddle off his horse and prepared to camp by the creek for the rest of the day. Once his horse was taken care of, he took his bow from the saddle sling and set out along the creek bank. A thick tangle of bushes intertwined with a stand of trees looked to be a good place for a herd of deer to settle down in the middle of the day, so he worked his way cautiously toward it. Sharp instincts, honed by the years he had spent as a boy and a young man living in the wilderness, did not fail him as he worked his way silently through the brush, pausing often to listen to the wind in the leaves overhead. They were there. He didn't know how he knew it, but he was as aware of their presence as they were of his. When it became clear to his prey that they were in danger, they bolted. He reacted immediately, loosing an arrow that struck one of the five does as they jumped across the creek. There

would be fresh meat for his supper, and there had been
no gunshot to alert anyone who might be within hearing distance. The thought brought to mind the loss of
his treasured Henry rifle. He had had no occasion to
fire the Sharps carbine he now carried. He supposed it
was an excellent weapon. From what he had heard, it
was a more accurate weapon at longer range than his
Henry, but it just didn't give him the same sense of
confidence. Cartridges to fit it might be more difficult
to find—he wasn't sure. It made little difference, he
supposed, for cartridges of any caliber would be hard
to find where he planned to go.

The rest of the day was spent skinning, butchering,
and preparing the meat. The doe was young and
tender and he filled his belly with the fresh-roasted
meat, a welcome relief from the salt pork the prostitutes had served while he was with them. He could not
take the time to cure the hide, so he rolled it up to ride
behind his saddle until he established a more permanent camp in the mountains ahead. Already, he was
beginning to feel the release of pressure that had been
brought about by his recent exposure to what people
referred to as the civilized world. The soldiers, the
saloons, the world of prostitutes, was a life of which he
had very limited knowledge, and he was not favorably
impressed by what he had seen. Cautioning himself,
however, that he could not assume he was free of the
army's pursuit, he periodically climbed up the slope to
scan the horizon around him to make certain. The day
passed with no sign of an army patrol.

The next morning, his horse rested, he left his camp
on the creek and struck out for the Cheyenne River
and its confluence with the Lightning. Reaching the

fork where the two rivers joined a short time after noon, he stopped to rest his horse before pushing on to follow the river to its confluence with the Beaver. He made one final camp on the Beaver before varying his line of travel slightly east to head into the heart of the Black Hills. As he rode deeper into the foothills, he was aware of his understanding of the Indian's reverence for the mysterious region they called Paha Sapa, which was Lakota for "Hills That Are Black." Wolf could understand the reason for the name, for from a distance the thick stands of ponderosa pines appeared to be black. The Sioux especially considered Paha Sapa the very center of the world. It was a place of mystique and magic, where young men would go to seek visions that would provide their pathway of life. To Wolf, it was a place where he could hide from those who would imprison him. Even though it was a place the Sioux held sacred, he was confident that he could fade into its high peaks and lush valleys with flowing streams of clear, cold water, much as he had done as a boy in the Wind River Mountains.

"Looks like our boy stopped here awhile," Ned Bull announced to his horse. He dismounted and let Brownie drink from the creek while he poked around the campsite. "He went huntin'," he continued musing aloud, "got him a deer, looks like." The tracking had not been easy up to that point, although it did not appear that Wolf was taking great pains to try to hide his trail. But Ned was still confident that the tracks he had followed to this creek bank were those of the single Indian pony that had left Fort Laramie. *I'm going to feel like a damn fool if they ain't Wolf's tracks,* he thought.

By the time he discovered Wolf's camp on the Beaver, Ned was convinced that the fugitive was no longer worried about being tailed. There were no efforts to hide his campsite or cover his tracks at all. "I believe he's ridin' pretty easy, Brownie. He don't figure on ol' Ned doggin' his trail." Even as he said it, he stood looking out at the dark, tree-covered mountains ahead and wondered if it was worth it to continue. "If it was the other way around, and he was chasin' me, I'd feel pretty good about my chances of losin' him in those mountains. Whaddaya think, Brownie?" As usual, the horse made no comment. Ned paused, as if waiting for it anyway, before deciding. "Ah, what the hell . . . might as well . . . give me a chance to see how good a tracker I am."

Back in the saddle, he looked for a good place to ford, hoping the man he trailed might have selected the same crossing, or one close by, so he could find where he left the water on the other bank. He knew all too well that he had to find Wolf's tracks on the other side or he might as well turn around and go home. His luck was holding steady, because when he crossed to the other bank, he discovered a fresh set of tracks leading up from the water. He looked up to project the apparent line of travel. It led straight toward the highest mountain he could see, so he set out to follow it. Unknown to him, there were two trackers behind him following the same trail, but their interest was not in the half-wild Wolf. Ned Bull was the object of their hunt.

"Maybe that wasn't Arlo they were talkin' about back there at that hog ranch," Beau Taggart said. "You know, we don't know for sure—just takin' that ol' whore's word for it. What if Arlo's back there in the jail at Fort Laramie all this time, and we're chasin' through Injun Territory lookin' for somebody we don't even know?" Beau, the youngest of the Taggart boys, was also the least patient. Four hard days in the saddle with little relief, except for one night at a hog ranch, was about the limit of his determination.

"Maybe it *wasn't* Arlo that deputy shot," Mace allowed, "but he damn sure brought in a dead man from the Cheyenne jail. That tall, bony whore, the one named Mae, said a soldier told her he saw the body. That big deputy that Clem Russell said came to get Arlo was Ned Bull, and there ain't no doubt about that. That whore said there wasn't no other dead prisoner brought in that she heard about, so don't go gettin' no ideas about quittin' this trail. That son of a bitch shot Arlo, and he's gonna have to pay for it. I ain't about to go back home and tell Ma the bastard that shot Arlo is still livin'."

Mavis Taggart had raised her three boys by herself, since their father ran off and left her when Mace was only nine years old. A born scrapper, and the youngest of Lester Dawson's three offspring, she didn't hesitate to beg, borrow, or steal anything she needed to keep food on the table, and she raised her sons to do the same. It came natural to her to live outside the law. It was a way of life the Dawson clan had lived by since before the Civil War. They set their own rules and enforced them as well, and they were not prone to forgive easily. Consequently, Mavis's brother, Doc, set out to find her runaway husband, found him in a saloon near the Texas-Arkansas border, and dispensed his punishment in the form of four .44 slugs in his chest and stomach.

By the time Mace was fourteen and Beau, the youngest, was ten, the boys were stealing cattle, horses, and anything else of value. When the law began to put too much pressure on the young outlaws, Mavis left Arkansas and moved to Indian Territory, where a great many outlaws fled to avoid capture, including her brother, Doc, and his four boys. The move was hastened when Mace shot a deputy marshal who apprehended the boys after a stage holdup.

After the first killing, murder became much easier, and proved to be the best and quickest way to lessen the chances of pursuit. By the time her youngest was eighteen, Mavis could afford to retire and stay at home near Doc Dawson and his family while her sons carried on in the tradition of the clan. It was a good life until federal marshals out of Fort Smith decided to rid the Nations of all forms of outlaws and riffraff. The Taggarts fled to Texas, but things got too uncomfortable there after a while, so when they figured enough time had elapsed to let Oklahoma Territory cool down, the boys were back in business in their old haunts, including Wyoming Territory. In a short time, Doc and his wife moved to Oklahoma and built a cabin next to Mavis's. Like his sister, he retired from the family business of rustling, robbery, and murder, leaving it in the capable hands of his four sons.

"I should never have let Arlo run off my hisself," Mace lamented.

"Hell, there wasn't much you could do to stop him unless you shot him," Beau said. "Arlo never listened to anybody when he got the itch to get movin'. I never thought he'd try to pull off a bank job without us, though."

"If he'da waited for us, he wouldn't have got caught," Mace said. "Holin' up at Clem Russell's place was a dumb thing to do. He shoulda knowed that would be one of the first places a marshal would look."

"I still can't see how Arlo let a lawman get the jump on him," Beau said.

"He had to be fallin'-down drunk to begin with, to get caught in bed with that butt-ugly woman of Clem's," Mace remarked. "He'da most likely died of somethin' he caught from her, even if that deputy hadn't shot him." Remembering it was his brother he was talking about, he reminded Beau that their mission was one of vengeance. "We need to quit this jawin' and get back in the saddle, just like Arlo would be doin' if it was one of us that got shot. I'd like to catch this bastard before he gets too far up in the Black Hills and we lose his trail in those mountains."

Splashing through the water, the two brothers followed the tracks leading up from Hat Creek and headed toward a ridge of pine-clad brakes that separated the high plains from the valley beyond.

Chapter 6

Wolf pulled a strip of roasted venison from the spit he had fashioned over his campfire. He tossed it back and forth from hand to hand for a few seconds to cool it a little before tearing off a chunk with his teeth. This was his second night in this camp in a small clearing by a clear mountain stream, and he was giving a lot of thought to the possibility of making it his permanent home for at least the winter. The cold weather was coming on strong now, especially high up in the mountains, so he would have to pick a spot soon. This was a good place. There was plenty of game, good grass and water for his horse, and plenty of wood for his fire. There was little more he could wish for, except some coffee. He had learned to enjoy coffee while traveling with his three prostitute friends, and he regretted the lack of opportunity to buy some of the beans, now that he had some money.

He was about to reach for another strip of venison when he suddenly tensed, sensing something or someone. He strained to listen above the sound of the breeze stroking the pines. Then he heard a sound. It was the whinny of a horse, and his bay answered. Wolf grabbed his carbine and rolled away from the fire, ready to defend himself. Lying out of the firelight, he listened. There it was again, and he was sure that it was a whinny, this time closer. In a few minutes, a horse entered the clearing, walking slowly toward his fire. It was saddled, but there was no rider. He watched it intently for a few moments more before he got to his feet and walked cautiously toward it, peering into the darkness from which the horse had come. Then he heard the voice behind him.

"You can just drop that carbine on the ground. I've got my rifle aimed right square between your shoulder blades. You make one wrong move and I'll send you straight to hell."

Wolf was stunned, unable to believe he had been so easily trapped. He had heard the voice before, but he couldn't place it. With no other choice, he laid the weapon on the ground.

"Now step back away from it," the voice instructed. Wolf did as he was told. "Put your hands behind your back." Wolf hesitated. "Put 'em back there or I'll put a bullet in you."

Wolf obeyed the command. He knew now where he had heard the voice before. "The last time you sneaked up on me, you damn near split my head open," he said.

"I noticed you got your head bandaged up," Ned replied as he quickly locked a pair of handcuffs on him. "Looks like you need to put a fresh one on, though. That one's lookin' kinda dirty."

"Why did you come after me?" Wolf asked. "I never done you no harm."

"I'm just followin' orders. I'm a U.S. deputy marshal. I have to do what the government tells me to do, and they told me to go get you." With the fugitive cuffed, Ned motioned for him to sit down by the fire. "I might not have found you if it wasn't for the odor of that meat on the spit there. I swear that smells good. Mind if I help myself?" He reached over and pulled a strip of the venison from the fire, keeping a steady eye on his prisoner, studying his reaction. He was rewarded with a look of pure astonishment.

"S'pose you just set yourself down right here by the fire?" Ned said, and stepped back while Wolf sat down, cross-legged, Indian-style. "I'm damn glad I caught up with you tonight. Another day or two tryin' to follow your trail in these mountains and I mighta lost you for good. Too bad you decided to camp here, but lucky for me." Wolf did not answer, but his eyes told Ned that he regretted it more. Ned chewed up the last bite and reached for another strip. "I swear this is good meat. I didn't have no time to hunt. I had to keep on your trail." He looked around him then as if searching for something. "We need some coffee to wash this deer meat down. Ain't you got no coffeepot?" Wolf slowly shook his head, amazed by the big man's rambling. "Well, I need some coffee. Can't operate without coffee." All the while as the lawman went on, he continued to study Wolf and his reaction to the meaningless banter. He could see no real evil in the young man's eyes. Instead, he was reminded of an animal captured in a cage, unable to understand why.

"Well, I caught you. Now I gotta decide what to do with you," Ned finally declared. Wolf remained silent, his steady gaze directed at the flames in his fire. Ned went on. "I could take you back for trial, but, damn, that's a long ride back to have to keep an eye on a wild buck like you. I might get careless and let you get the best of me. That ain't ever happened before, although there was a close time or two, and I'd hate for you to be the first." There was still no reaction from the stoic figure seated before the fire. "Course, it'd be no trouble to me if I was to take you back dead. Then I wouldn't have to worry about you gettin' rowdy on me." Even that remark caused no reaction beyond the raising of Wolf's eyes to meet the deputy's gaze. The wild man had evidently accepted his fate. "Yep, that's the best solution to my problem." He paused to wipe the grease from his mouth with the back of his hand. "The law says you deserve a trial, and I always go by the law. So I'm gonna give you a trial right now. We'll see if you're guilty or not, and the penalty is execution by Winchester '73."

With the stark realization that the slow-talking lawman was about to take the law into his own hands, Wolf's brain became instantly aware of the hopelessness of his situation. All along he had anticipated a long trip back to Fort Laramie with the possibility of an opportunity for escape. But he now understood that his life had no value to the marshal. He must fight for his life, but how? With his hands manacled behind him, he couldn't even get to his feet quickly enough to attack the big lawman.

With a grand air of formality, Ned started the "trial." "Order in the court. The territory of Dakota will now try the defendant, Wolf, of unknown origin, for attempted murder, assault on a sergeant in the U.S. Army, horse thievin', and escape from federal custody. Will the council for the defense stand and be recognized—make that sit and be recognized." Ned paused and nodded toward a completely astonished Wolf. "That'd be you, son. How does the defendant plead? Guilty, or not guilty?" He waited for Wolf to speak.

"I didn't do anythin' wrong," the puzzled young man finally said.

"All right," Ned continued, obviously enjoying his mock trial. "The council for the defense has spoke, so we'll now turn it over to the prosecution. Did you attack Sergeant Carl What's-his-name in the saloon at the Three-Mile Hog Ranch?"

"No. He attacked me."

"But you broke his arm. Ain't that right?"

"He had no call to grab me with it."

"But the witnesses say you started to cut his throat. Ain't *that* right?"

"I started to, because I thought he was tryin' to kill me."

Ned shook his head as if confused. "Well, what kept you from goin' ahead and slittin' his throat?"

"Rose said to stop—said he wasn't really out to kill me; said he just wanted to fistfight me—so I let him go."

"Rose?" Ned questioned. "Rose Hutto, a known whore, and that's your story?"

"I reckon," Wolf replied, weary of the deputy's idea

of entertainment. "Get it over with. Go ahead and do what you're aimin' to."

"It don't pay to try to hurry justice up," Ned replied. "How about that horse you stole?"

"I didn't steal him. I turned him loose and headed him back toward the fort."

"So you're tellin' the court you just borrowed the horse?"

"It don't make much difference what I say, does it?" Wolf replied.

"Well, I reckon the defense rests, so we'll have to wait for the verdict." He shifted the Winchester to rest across his arms. "Hold on, the jury's already back. Do we have a verdict? We do? Well, what say you?" Wolf leaned forward, testing the strength in his legs. It was impossible, sitting cross-legged as he was, to generate enough force to spring up before Ned shot him. It all seemed so meaningless to end his life at the hand of an obviously demented maniac, but there was nothing he could do about it.

"What say you?" Ned repeated, then pretended to be listening to the make-believe foreman of his make-believe jury. With an expression of mock surprise, he read the verdict. "Not guilty!"

Astounded, in total confusion as to whether he was to live or die, Wolf was left to wonder if there were additional games the marshal wanted to play before he either killed him or took him back for trial. He was further baffled by the lawman's next move. Ned got up from his seat across the fire from Wolf and walked over to kneel behind his prisoner. Wolf stiffened, anticipating the feel of the cold steel rifle barrel against the back of his head. Instead, he felt the tug at his wrists as

Ned unlocked the manacles and removed them. "Now, let's make some coffee to wash down the rest of that meat you got on the fire," he said. "Let me get my pack-horse up here and we'll make us some. Jury trials always make me hungry."

Still unable to believe his life had been handed back to him, Wolf did not move right away. The reversal of fortune was hard to justify, and he could not help thoughts of a devious motive behind the lawman's charade. Ned paused to give him a hard look before bending over to pick up the carbine Wolf had dropped. "I know what you're thinkin'," he said. "Maybe the son of a bitch is waitin' for me to jump up and run, so he can shoot me in the back. And keep his conscience clean by sayin' the prisoner made a run for it, so he had to shoot me. Well, let me set you straight. I ain't got no conscience." That said, he tossed the carbine to him. "Where'd you get the Sharps? From one of those whores, I bet. It's a good weapon, especially for huntin' buffalo, but I'll bet you'll be glad to see an old friend I brought with me. I got somethin' on my packhorse we can use to change that bandage on the back of your head, too. I don't think you could get that one any dirt-ier. Then we could be drinkin' coffee while we're set-tin' here jawin'."

Ned got up again and started walking toward the darkness beyond the clearing, boldly presenting his back to the still-startled fugitive, confident in his assess-ment of the young man's conscience. Wolf turned to watch him, holding the carbine firmly, unable to figure out the trick, if there was one. Maybe, to play it safe, he should take the opportunity given him to put a bullet in the middle of the broad back now fading into the dark trees. He couldn't pull the trigger. A few moments passed, and then Ned reappeared, leading a packhorse and carrying Wolf's Henry rifle in one hand. "Here you go," he said, and casually handed the Henry to Wolf.

Unable to erase the look of bewilderment from his face, Wolf mumbled, "'Preciate it."

Understanding Wolf's confusion, Ned paused before untying his coffeepot from the pack. "Look, young feller, I've been huntin' outlaws and murderers for enough years now to tell the really bad ones from the others. And it's plain to me that you ain't one of the bad ones. I figured you were gettin' a sour deal after I talked to your lady friends and that bartender in the saloon. That soldier jumped you and you fought back. There wasn't no reason to throw you in prison for fightin'. To tell you the truth, the main reason I came after you was just to see if I could track you—that and the fact that I was ordered to do it. And I figured if I turned the job down, they'd just send somebody else. Then somebody would have ended up dead, either you or him, and there wasn't no sense in that." His coffeepot free then, he paused another moment before going to fill it with water. "So you can take off from here to wherever you had in mind. I'll tell 'em I lost you." He grinned. "And they'll pay me anyway."

Wolf stood by the campfire, scarcely believing the events of the past few minutes. He gave serious thought to whether or not he was witnessing the actions of a crazy man. Maybe Ned Bull's being too long on the trail of murderers and thieves had finally worn a soft spot on his brain. He looked down at his prized Henry rifle, then glanced at the bay gelding standing near the water, grazing quietly. Would Ned attempt to stop him if he suddenly made a move to saddle his horse and depart? He was genuinely perplexed, but with his rifle in hand, he felt he was now able to deal with whatever bizarre move the deputy marshal made next.

With a coffeepot full of water, Ned climbed back up the bank to find Wolf still standing where he had left him, and the look on the young man's face told him he was troubled over his unexpected not-guilty verdict. So he attempted to set his mind at ease. "Look here, partner, I know you're kinda wonderin' if I'm crazy as a tick, just 'cause I got the jump on you and let you go. Well, you can stop worryin'. I ain't crazy. I've just been at this business long enough to know the law—in your case, the army—doesn't always get the right of things. You don't deserve to be punished for kickin' that bully's ass, and I got no intention of arrestin' you for somethin' that I'da done in the same fix. I know you've been livin' on your own or with a tribe of Injuns most of your life, and I figure you'll make out all right as long as you stay away from the soldiers. So you go on back in these mountains where you belong. I'll be headin' back to Fort Laramie in the mornin' and I'm wishin' you good luck."

Wolf finally realized that Ned was sincere in his statement, and he immediately relaxed his guard. "I reckon I'm obliged," he said. "I'll slice some more meat off that hindquarter. I sure would like some coffee."

Ned chuckled. "Now, that's more like it. We'll have us some pretty quick."

Before the night was over, a mutual feeling of trust

was established between the two men, although they were as much opposites as two men could be. As Ned had suspected, Wolf was almost completely naive in regard to the sanctity of the Black Hills, and was unaware of the recent discovery of gold in the hills. In answer to Wolf's insistence that the Black Hills were protected from white infringement by treaty, Ned told him the true status of that sacred area. "I know it ain't right," he explained, "but the government sent an army regiment in here last year, and they brought back reports of findin' gold. And once the word got out about it, prospectors started sneakin' in, and a big strike was made over on French Creek, fifty or sixty miles north of here. Now, I know the Lakota and the Cheyenne think the Black Hills is where God lives. But the white man worships gold, and they now know for damn sure that the Black Hills is where gold lives, and there ain't no way the army is gonna be able to keep 'em outta here."

It was sobering news for Wolf and something that he was going to think hard on. It was difficult for him to believe that these rugged mountains might be consumed by gold-seeking intruders. "But there's a treaty, signed by the government," he protested again.

"Don't matter," Ned replied. "Gold is more powerful than the government or any treaty they signed. I heard talk back at Fort Laramie that a strike at a place called Deadwood Gulch has already brought in so many prospectors that the army has given up tryin' to run 'em out." Seeing the trouble his enlightenment had brought to Wolf, he felt compassion for the simple child of the forest. "I know it ain't right, but gold is

king, and I don't reckon that'll ever be any different."
He paused again, studying his new friend's reaction
for a few moments before asking, "So, what are you
gonna do?"

"I don't know," Wolf replied. "Keep movin', I reckon.
Maybe move on up into Montana, up in Blackfoot
country. There can't be gold everywhere."

Ned continued to study the disillusioned young
man for a while before deciding to ignore his principle
of minding his own business and give Wolf some
advice. He had already decided that he liked the free-
spirited young man, and he truly wanted to help him.
"Ain't none of my business," he began, "but are you
sure you want a life alone, till you get so feeble you
can't make it on your own anymore, and you just have
to lie down and wait for the wolves, or coyotes, to come
to start feedin' off your bones? Hell, if you find someplace where there ain't no white settlers, where you
gonna buy cartridges for that Henry rifle? You've
already been livin' by yourself too long. If you don't
like livin' with white folks, you'd be better off goin'
back to live with the Crows." He paused to judge the
effect his words were having, if any, before suggesting,
"Instead of makin' the army your enemy, you oughta
work for 'em. They ain't likely to find a scout that
knows the country better'n you do. At least you might
have enough money to keep you in cartridges and
other supplies."

"That don't make sense," Wolf said. "The army wants
to arrest me. Ain't that why they sent you after me?"

"I can take care of that," Ned replied.

"How?"

"I'll tell Colonel Bradley you're dead, tell him I had to shoot you. If you was to buy you some decent clothes, somethin' that didn't look like you sewed 'em yourself, and cut that long hair, maybe grow a mustache, that would help a lot. Hell, I bet ol' Bradley wouldn't know the difference. I doubt he has much to do with the scouts he's got now. We'd have to change your name, though. Wolf ain't a fittin' name for you, anyway. What is your real name? Do you remember?"

"Course I do," Wolf replied. "It's Tom Logan. I wasn't *that* young."

"Tom Logan," Ned echoed. "Nothin' wrong with that. Just to make sure, you could stay clear of Fort Laramie, ride on up to Fort Fetterman, and try to get hired up there. I'll bet you wouldn't have no trouble signin' on at Fetterman. They're always lookin' for good trackers, and most of the civilian scouts don't wanna work there because it's a hard-luck post. Seems like they're always short of supplies, ain't no place in the world where the wind blows colder in the winter, and there ain't nothin' to keep the soldiers from desertin' except a hog ranch on the south side of the river—which means a soldier has to swim the river if he wants to see any of the gals at that establishment, since the fort's on the north side. Whaddaya think?"

Wolf shook his head and frowned. "I don't know. That don't sound like the kind of life I could stand for very long. I've always worked best by myself."

"How do you know?" Ned insisted, even more enthusiastic about the plan the more he thought about it. If he had been inclined, he might have recognized the same trait in himself that prompted him to track

Wolf down just to see if he could. "You might like scoutin', and it'd give you a steady paycheck."

"I reckon I'll just go on up to Blackfoot country," he finally decided.

"Well, I'll be headin' on back to Fort Laramie in the mornin'," Ned declared. "You can always change your mind if you decide you're tired of livin' like a lone wolf. I'll tell the colonel you're dead, anyway. Maybe that'll make him forget about you."

True to his word, Ned saddled up the next morning and prepared to head back south. "You're lookin' pretty spry for a dead man," he commented to Wolf as the two of them finished the pot of coffee Ned had made. "I can leave you some of these coffee beans, so you'll have some for later on."

"Thanks just the same," Wolf replied, "but there ain't much sense in me gettin' used to havin' coffee. There ain't likely any place to get more where I'm goin'."

They sat in silence for a few long minutes with no sound save that of Ned's loud sipping of the hot liquid. Ned finally broke the silence. "Well, I expect I'd better get started back. You sure you don't wanna ride back with me? I'd be glad to swing by Fort Fetterman before I go to Laramie. I'd recommend you to the commanding officer there to hire you on as a scout."

Wolf could not help giving the idea some serious thought, but it still seemed so foreign to his nature that he had to decline. "I reckon not," he finally said. Ned nodded his understanding, downed the last drop from his cup, and got to his feet. Wolf followed him to the

edge of the water and stood there forming the words
he wanted to say while Ned rinsed out his cup. It was
not an easy thing for him, but the formidable lawman
had given him back his freedom, and he felt obliged to
say something to express his gratitude. When Ned
stood up from the water's edge and gave him a friendly
grin, Wolf finally blurted out his thanks. "I 'preciate
what you've done for me. I hope it ain't gonna get you
in any trouble with the army."

Ned's grin spread wider over his weathered face.
He knew the difficulty Wolf had in expressing his
feelings. "Don't give it a thought," he replied. "I don't
work for the army, so I don't have to prove anythin' to
that colonel back at Fort Laramie. If it's all the same to
you, I'll take that Sharps back to show him I actually
did catch up with you." Wolf nodded his approval.
"You watch yourself, young feller. You're liable to run
into white men and Sioux Injuns in these hills, and
they're all probably gonna have their fingers on the
trigger."

"I will," Wolf said. "You watch your back." He
remained standing by the river, watching until Ned
rode out of sight. The big lawman had made a definite
impression in the short time they had spent together.
Wolf could not recall anyone else whom he looked
upon with such respect other than Big Knife of the
Crows. He wondered anew if he should give more consideration to Ned's suggestion to seek a scouting job
with the soldiers. Could Ned be right? Could he learn
to live in the white man's world, the world of his birth?
Then he thought of his father and mother, something
he had not done in many years. And he wondered if

they would have wished for him the same as Ned had. He realized then that he had established Ned as more than a friend in his mind. He was more like an uncle— a wise uncle, maybe. *I'll think more on this*, he told himself.

Chapter 7

Figuring he had ridden about ten miles, Ned decided to rest his horses at the fork where the Lightning and Cheyenne rivers joined. "This looks like the best spot to take a little rest, Brownie," he told the red roan, and guided his horses over to a clearing in the brush that lined the river. "We ain't gonna be here long, just long enough to let you get a drink and maybe a little break from haulin' my big ass across this prairie." He left the saddle on while the horse started nibbling at the grass near the water. *Wouldn't mind a little something myself*, he thought, and went to his saddlebag to find a strip of jerky he had gotten from Wolf. The deer jerky made him think of the young man he had decided to befriend, and wondered if he was getting softhearted in his old age. *Probably should have taken him back like the army wanted me to*, he thought. "Nah," he decided aloud. "They were wrong about that boy. I done the right thing." Further thoughts were interrupted by a whinny from Brownie, echoed by his packhorse, alerting him to the possibility of company.

Walking up closer to the fork of the two rivers, he soon spotted his visitors. There were two of them, one riding a buckskin, the other on a spotted gray. He remained still, watching to see if they would continue toward him or turn and cross farther downstream. Judging by their gestures to each other, they had also detected his presence, no doubt alerted the same way he had been. It would have suited him just fine if they had made the crossing oblivious of him and continued on their way, but it was too late for that now. So he walked out of the shade of the cottonwoods and let himself be seen. They pulled up when they saw him standing there with his rifle in one hand.

"Howdy," Mace Taggart called out. "No need for that rifle. We're on our way north. Thought this looked like a good place to cross over."

"It's as good as any," Ned called back. "Didn't mean to alarm you with the rifle. Tell you the truth, I forgot I was totin' it. Just a habit, I reckon."

"Well, it ain't a bad habit in this country," Mace returned, "with the Injuns gettin' all riled up."

"What the hell are we waitin' for?" Beau whispered. "Shoot him."

"Keep your shirt on," Mace whispered back. "At this distance, we might miss, and I don't know how good he is with that rifle. Let's find out who he is first."

"That's a fact," Ned called out, responding to Mace's comment. "Where you fellers headin'?"

"Headin' up in the hills," Mace replied. "Doin' some prospectin'. Heard they've struck some gold up there."

They rode forward to the river's edge. "Mind if we come across here?"

"Why, no, come on across. I sure as hell don't own the river." Ned kept a cautious eye on the two men as they entered the water. He couldn't guess what they might be up to. Maybe they had someplace to go; maybe they were running from the law. He couldn't say, but he doubted they were prospectors. They had no packhorse and no prospecting tools that he could see. Whatever their story, he wasn't interested, just as long as they continued on their way.

"Look at him, Mace," Beau insisted anxiously while trying to keep his voice low. "He's a big'un, just like that whore said. I bet he's that damn deputy. We caught him, Mace! We caught the son of a bitch!"

"Easy, dammit!" Mace growled, afraid his younger brother was going to get them both shot if he didn't control his excitement. "He's got the drop on us right now. You just simmer down till we find out if he's the marshal or not. If he ain't, he mighta run into him up ahead somewhere, and he can tell us where he saw him." He paused to look at Ned again with a cautious eye before adding, "Then you can shoot him." The two brothers were as opposite as night and day, although both placed little value on a human life. Where Beau was fiery and hair-trigger quick to act, Mace was cool and calculating. Mavis Taggart said of her eldest, "Mace is like a panther, patient on the hunt till it's right to pounce. Then he's like a lightning strike on the kill." There had been a gleam of pride in the old woman's eyes when she said it.

Ned took a few paces back toward his horses when

the two strangers rode up from the riverbank. Walking their horses up before him, they both dismounted. Mace glanced behind Ned and, seeing no fire, remarked, "Looks like you musta just been fixin' to make camp."

"Nope," Ned replied. "It's a little too early in the day to make camp. I just stopped to rest my horses for a spell. I was just fixin' to ride on when you fellers showed up."

"Which way are you headin'?" Beau asked. "North or south?" He took a few steps off to his left, trying to appear casual as he did it.

Ned responded with a wry smile as he answered, "South, headin' to Fort Laramie." He brought his rifle up to waist height, holding it in both hands now. "How 'bout steppin' back over close to your partner there? I got a bad eye on that side and I can see you better when you're closer together."

Beau froze.

Mace smiled, suspecting that the big man's eyes were as sharp as his. "I don't blame you for being careful with strangers in this country," he said. "Me and my brother was thinkin' the same thing. It don't pay to take chances. You don't have to worry about me and my brother, though. Ain't that right, Beau?" It was too late. He hadn't meant to drop the name, and he caught the slight narrowing of Ned's eyes and knew he recognized it. He had no choice but to try to carry on with the charade. "Well, I reckon we'll be on our way. If you was headin' north, we coulda rode together, but you ain't, so good luck to you." He stepped back up in the saddle then. "Come on, brother. We'd best be gettin' started. We've got a piece to ride before sundown."

Beau hesitated, looking uncertain. When he looked up at his brother, he found Mace frowning at him. "Let's go," Mace repeated firmly. Although reluctant, Beau got on his horse, trusting that Mace had no intention of permitting the man to ride away.

"Well, now, you boys have a nice ride, and good luck with your prospectin'," Ned said. He had never laid eyes on Mace or Beau Taggart, but he was pretty sure that was who they were. Along with their late brother, they were wanted in Oklahoma, Wyoming, and Texas. The problem was that he was in no position to arrest them. If he tried to, one of them was bound to get off a shot before he could secure them both. He had no intention of letting them go free, but his chances were better if he let them ride on, then followed them and made his move while they were sleeping. It did not occur to him that they had been tracking him or that they had any idea he was a marshal. And it was unlikely that they knew of Arlo's death. Most likely they thought he was in jail in Cheyenne.

He remained there, watching the two Taggart brothers ride off through the cottonwoods that lined the river until he could see them no longer. Then he hurried to climb into the saddle and give Brownie a kick. In case they had stopped to watch him, he plunged his horses into the river and crossed to the other side, where he kept going, heading south. He figured, if they were suspicious and were now watching him, they might think he had no interest in them. It was not the best of situations for making an arrest, and certainly one he would never brag about, but it was the best he could come up with, given the circumstances. He didn't stop until he put a low line of hills between himself and the river. "We're gonna have to wait here a spell," he told Brownie, "and let 'em get a little head start." There was still no suspicion in his mind that they knew he had killed their brother. Leaving his horses below the brow of the hill, he crawled up to the top where he could see his back trail and make sure they didn't take a notion to follow him. He waited for over an hour before deciding it was safe to get on their trail again while there was still plenty of daylight left. He didn't want to take a chance on the two of them getting too far ahead, causing him to lose their trail in the darkness.

"There he is!" Beau exclaimed. "Just like you said."

Mace moved over from the other side of the ravine to join his brother. "There ain't no doubt he's that damn deputy now," he said, "or he wouldn't be tailin' us. What was his name? Mr. Ned Bull?" He snorted a short laugh. "Ridin' right into the little party we've got waitin' for him."

"Yeah," Beau said excitedly. "He can change his name to Mr. Dead Bull now." They both laughed, eager to complete the assassination.

"Don't get too anxious," Mace warned. "Let's let him ride on up in the mouth of this ravine, so there ain't no chance he can run." When Beau assured him that he would not be too quick to shoot, Mace returned to his position on the other side so they could have Ned in a cross fire between them. With their target moving in according to their plan, they waited. "This is for Arlo," Mace said.

Down on the floor of the valley, Ned approached the line of rugged brakes, cautiously scanning the terrain ahead as he followed a clear trail of the two horses. It occurred to him that the trail might be too obvious, so he paused to consider the narrow ravine that lay ahead. After a moment's concern, he decided he was probably getting a little too cautious in his old age and continued on. The closer he got to the mouth of the ravine, however, the more hesitant he became about riding between those narrow walls when he could not see the top of the defile. "I don't like the look of this," he finally told Brownie, and swung the roan's head to the side. "We'll go around and pick up the trail on the other side."

"Damn!" Mace swore. "He's onto us. Get him before he gets out of range!"

It was unnecessary to tell Beau a second time. The eager young outlaw squeezed off two rounds before Mace could take proper aim. The first shot missed by a short foot. The second caught Ned in the shoulder, causing him to turn to the side. Mace's shot slammed into the big deputy's back, and he fell forward on Brownie's neck. Startled, the horse bolted. The wounded man could not stay in the saddle and came off hard, the impact with the ground knocking the breath from his lungs.

"Hot damn!" Beau shouted, and ran down the slope of the ravine to finish the job. Mace was only a few steps behind him. "We got us a U.S. marshal!" Beau shouted in childish delight, moments before the .44 slug slammed into his back and sent him sprawling face-first on the gravel of the rocky defile. In a panic, Mace dived on the ground beside his brother. Dragging himself around on the loose gravel of the ravine, he lay flat, using Beau's body for a shield. He strained to make himself as flat as possible while he tried to figure out where the shot had come from. Looking back toward the top of the ravine, he saw a lone man standing there, but only for an instant before he disappeared. It was long enough to sear the image into his brain—an Indian, he thought, wearing animal skins and wielding a rifle. Although there only for a brief moment, the image of the hunter who had shot his brother would remain in Mace's mind from that moment on. Foremost in his mind now was to remove himself from danger. In his haste to save himself, he almost forgot about Beau, so he quickly shook Beau's body and blurted, "Are you gonna make it?" But there was no answer from the corpse, already on its way to wherever bushwhackers go. Certain now that his brother was dead, he forgot all thoughts about the deputy marshal, driven by the one desire to save himself from the fate Beau had just met. As fast as he could manage, he pushed away from the corpse and tried to drag himself to a gully formed at the bottom of the ravine. As soon as he was free of his brother's body, a series of shots kicked up dirt around him. Certain to be hit at any minute, he got to his hands and knees and scrambled to the gully as fast as he could. Luck was with him, for the only shot that found him tore through the sole of his boot as he went into the gully headfirst.

Wolf cranked another cartridge into the chamber of the Henry, then quickly made his way down from the top of the hill, ready to fire as soon as he caught sight of a target. He cursed himself for getting there too late to keep Ned from being shot, but now he was concentrating on settling with the second of the two bushwhackers. When he got to the bottom of the ravine, the man was gone, but he could see where he had crawled out of the other side of the gully and escaped through a notch that led to the open prairie. Hoofprints he found there told him that the men had left their horses there while they set up the ambush on Ned. Knowing there was not enough time for the second bushwhacker to have gotten very far, he ran up to the top of the hill. From there, he spotted the fleeing assassin hightailing it at a gallop on a spotted gray horse and leading a riderless buckskin. He wanted to go in immediate pursuit, but he had to first see about Ned.

He found the wounded lawman lying several yards from the mouth of the ravine. The red roan named Brownie was standing beside him, waiting for his master to get up, but Ned was not moving. Wolf knelt down to search for any sign of life. When he rolled the heavy body over, he was met with Ned's .44 pistol aimed squarely in his face. With instincts as fast as the beast he was named for, he grabbed the weapon and pushed it aside just as Ned pulled the trigger and sent a bullet whistling up toward the clouds. The wounded man was too weak to struggle further against the powerful hand that pinned his wrist to the ground. "Ned, it's me, Wolf. They've gone."

The fingers holding the pistol relaxed then, freeing the weapon. Ned's shirt was already soaked with blood. The wounds looked serious. "Wolf? What are you doin' here?" His words were slow and laboring, his breathing becoming more and more difficult as he tried to speak. "I'm sorry I almost shot you," he managed before he coughed several painful times, bringing blood up from his nose and mouth.

"Don't try to talk no more," Wolf said. "It's makin' you bleed too much. I'll try to fix you up."

A tired smile formed on the old deputy's face. "Ain't nothin' you can do to fix me up." Interrupted by a coughing spell, he then went on, forcing his words out: "Watch out them two don't come back," he warned. "Mace Taggart and Beau Taggart, they're as bad as they come."

"I'll see if I can get those bullets outta you," Wolf said, though not sure if he could or not. Ned needed a doctor, and he needed him right now, and the nearest doctor that Wolf knew of was in Fort Fetterman, a post he had never been to, but he knew it was closer than Fort Laramie. He wasn't sure Ned could make it that far.

Ned saved him the trouble. He laid his hand on Wolf's and, speaking barely above a whisper now, said, "I'm gettin' too old and tired to do this anymore. Take care of Brownie for me." He smiled then and seemed to relax.

Wolf gazed at him for a long moment, trying to think what to say to his friend of such a short time. Several more seconds passed before he realized that Ned was gone. He immediately sensed a great loss in his life, a loss he had experienced only twice before—when his parents were killed, and when Big Knife was slain. There had been a bonding between the young man and the older deputy marshal, and Wolf felt a great void with the passing of Ned Bull. He was especially regretful of the fact that he had not had the opportunity to tell him that he had come after him to let him know he had changed his mind. He had decided to take Ned's advice to go to Fort Fetterman and seek a job as a scout. Now that notion was out of the question, for he felt the world would not be right again if Ned Bull's killer was allowed to live. Even now, kneeling beside Ned's body, he could feel the anger warming the blood in his veins, and he knew he could not rest until the remaining Taggart brother paid for Ned's murder.

There were thoughts of Mace getting away while he lingered there, but he would not leave Ned lying there on the prairie to be feasted upon by buzzards or coyotes. Resigned to the fact that the hunt for Taggart would be completed no matter how long it took, he looked around him for a suitable burial spot. With his hand ax and a short-handled spade he found on Ned's packhorse, he set to work on a spot in the shade of a pine tree. The ground was hard, causing him to spend some time before Ned was at rest in his grave. The lost time was of little concern to Wolf, because he was determined to track the killer down, no matter how long it took.

With Ned in the ground, there were other matters to take care of. He stopped to take another look at the other body that had fallen that day. A smallish man, younger than himself, he wore a pair of hand-tooled boots with the name Beau etched out near the top. His reading and writing skills had not been tested since he was eleven, so he guessed that was the way "Beau" could be spelled. *So the one that got away was Mace,* Wolf thought. *Ned said Mace and Beau Taggart.* He at least knew now which Taggart he was going after. The next question was what to do about the horses. He had two more than he needed. Ordinarily he would welcome the gain of extra horses, but for the job he had before him, two extra horses would be too much trouble to manage. The decision as to which two he would keep was already made for him. He could not part with the bay gelding he was riding, and Ned had asked him to take care of Brownie, so he would use Ned's horse as his packhorse and set the other two free. There were other useful items he "inherited" from the big lawman, since he didn't know if there was any family waiting somewhere for Ned. Foremost among these was a Winchester '73, but not far behind in importance was Ned's coffeepot. He kept a few more useful items: a flint and steel for making a fire, a straight razor, and Ned's bearskin coat. It would be handy when the mountain passes filled with snow. He hated to leave Ned's saddle, but it was fairly well worn, so he left it in the gully along with the other discarded items. Then he turned and, said good-bye to Ned, climbed into the saddle, and, with Brownie following, started out westward on a quest that would end in death—either his or Mace Taggart's.

The trail of two horses at full gallop was not hard to follow at first, but within thirty minutes of starting the chase the sun sank below the hills on the horizon and all light fled from the prairie before him. Having started out straight toward the setting sun, the trail had veered off to the south within a distance of half a mile. The change in direction prompted Wolf to make a decision to wait until daylight before taking up the chase again. Taggart had made one change in his direction of flight. Was it just the first of many, hoping to shake anyone trailing him? If so, Wolf was reluctant to take a chance on losing the trail in the dark. *I've got plenty of time,* he told himself, *and nothing else to do.* So he made his camp by one of the tiny streams in the area. He was in the process of building a fire when two dark forms approaching from behind him indicated that the two horses he had set free were reluctant to part company with him. He was not surprised. Both had been packhorses and were accustomed to following the other two. When morning came, they were still there, noisily pulling grass near his blanket. "Sooner or later you're gonna realize you're free," he said to Ned's packhorse. "Then you can do what you damn well please." He did not linger over Ned's coffeepot and was in the saddle again before the sun cleared the eastern horizon.

The trail, still easy to follow, continued in a fairly straight line until striking the Lightning River. Then it followed the river for a day and a half. Taggart was pushing his horses hard, for Wolf could not make up any ground on him. He guessed that Mace was most likely changing from one horse to the other and resting them very little. As he rode, Wolf speculated on where Mace might be heading. Following the Lightning as he had been would indicate his intention of going to Fort Fetterman on the North Platte. But why would a wanted outlaw head for an army post? The question was answered when a point was reached about three miles north of the post, and Taggart had turned more to the west to circle around the fort, striking the North Platte a mile or so west of it.

It was early afternoon when Wolf reached the site of Mace's camp on the North Platte, suggesting to him that maybe he was gradually closing the distance between himself and his prey. Taggart's horses were tiring. Wolf was confident he would soon be forced to stop long enough to give them a good rest. Since he had bypassed Fort Fetterman, Wolf speculated that Taggart might be heading for old Platte Bridge Station, now called Fort Casper, although it was no longer an army post. Eight or nine years ago the army had pulled out of Fort Casper and sent the troops to Fort Fetterman. His Crow mentor, Big Knife, had told him that a man named Guinard had built a bridge across the river and a trading post on the spot many years before the army had established a post there. Wolf knew that there was a trading post still there, although now run by a man named Clem Russell. He had never done business with Russell, primarily because it had never been convenient, but he also had a natural tendency to avoid the trading post because it had a reputation for being a favorite hiding-out place for outlaws. It made sense that a man like Mace Taggart would be heading there. Since it was still early in the afternoon, he continued on to make camp within ten miles of Fort Casper. Looking back over the way he had come, he could see no sign of the two extra horses. It appeared that they had finally decided to accept their freedom. His packhorse would have no trouble living off the prairie grass. It was used to it. Ned's packhorse might take some time adjusting to the diet.

Boyd Dawson was having a drink of whiskey with Clem Russell when Mace Taggart rode down from the ridge to the log trading post perched on the edge of the bluffs. In a natural reflexive action, Boyd jumped to his

feet and pulled his pistol from his belt, almost upset-
ting his whiskey in the process. "Who the hell is that?"
he demanded, as if Clem would know. He hurried up
to stand just inside the door where he could get a good
look at the man approaching on horseback. "Well I'll
be . . . ," he said after a moment. "It's Mace." He
dropped his revolver back in its holster and walked
out on the porch to greet him. The second he stepped
out of the door, the man on horseback reacted much
the same way until he recognized him. Mace pulled
up right in front of the porch and stepped down.
"Damn, cousin," Boyd remarked, "from the looks of
them horses, you musta been doin' some hard ridin'.
Somebody chasin' you?" He took a long look back at
the trail before adding, "I hope to hell it ain't a posse."

"I swear, Boyd, what are you doin' here?" Having
ridden as if the devil himself were after him, Mace was
at once relieved to be greeted by a friendly face. He
had no way of knowing if he had been chased or not.
He had not waited around to see, but the image he had
seen at the top of that ravine looked like something out
of hell, and was a problem he didn't care to deal with.
Seeing his cousin here restored his courage to the point
where he could regain his calm.

In answer to Mace's question, Boyd said, "I'm on my
way to meet my brothers down near Medicine Bow.
I've been up here to visit a little Cheyenne gal in ol'
Red Wind's village." He gave Mace a little wink. "But
all those bucks are gettin' stirred up and talkin' about
goin' on the warpath. It wasn't too healthy to stay
around much longer, being the only white man there."
Clem Russell walked out on the porch then, and Boyd
went on. "I had to stop by and spend a little money

with ol' Clem here. I was afraid he wasn't stealin' enough to get by." He laughed at his joke.

"How ya doin', Mace?" Clem asked. "Ain't seen you in a good while. Arlo was here for a day or two, till Ned Bull jumped him and dragged him off to Cheyenne. Did they lock him up?"

"They killed him," Mace replied, causing Clem and Boyd both to react with shock. "That marshal shot him down on the trail to Fort Laramie." An immediate frown of anger took possession of Boyd's face. Mace continued. "Me and Beau went after Ned Bull. He ain't gonna be shootin' nobody else."

Boyd glanced at the empty saddle on the buckskin. "Ain't that a horse like Beau rides?"

Mace nodded solemnly. "That's Beau's horse," he answered, "but they shot Beau."

"Who did?" Boyd demanded. "That marshal?"

"No. I killed Ned Bull, but he musta had a posse with him, because they got in behind us on a ridge and they hit Beau. Killed him dead. There wasn't nothin' I could do for him, and there was too many of 'em for me to fight, so I had to run for it."

"Damn," Boyd swore, "Arlo and Beau both, I can't hardly believe it. What's poor Aunt Mavis gonna say when she hears that sorry news?"

"I know," Mace said. "It ain't gonna be easy to tell her. She's gonna want somebody to pay for it."

"Damn right," Boyd said, "and I feel the same way. Somebody's got to pay when it comes to family." Working himself up to a righteous wrath over the thought, he asked, "How many was there in that posse?"

"I can't say for sure," Mace replied. "They were hid back up behind the rocks at the top of a long ravine, so

I couldn't see all of 'em. But there was bullets flyin' all around me when I made a break for it."

That was enough to plant a worrisome thought in Boyd's mind. "You think they're on your trail?"

"Nah, I don't think so. I'da seen somethin' by now. I was pretty careful."

"Well, we ain't takin' this lyin' down," Boyd ranted. "We need to show the law it's gonna cost 'em when they come after the Dawsons and the Taggarts. This is family business. We'll go fetch the rest of the boys and we'll teach that bunch of farmers to mind who they're dealin' with."

Boyd's bravado seemed to bolster Mace's courage. The only one not inspired was Clem Russell, already picturing a bloody war taking place in his saloon. He hesitated to make any demands on behalf of himself or his store, however, and limited his participation to no more than a suggestion that they should all have a drink. That seemed to be the obvious first step in the counterattack on the murdering "posse," so the meeting moved inside. When Mace came back outside a couple of hours later to take his horses to Clem's stable behind the store, the plan had been settled to ride to Medicine Bow and enlist Buck, Skinner, and Nate into the vengeance committee.

The drinking went late into the night, which brought a fair profit to Clem. Mace even expressed intentions to avail himself of Clem's woman's special services, in spite of his disdain for her. But his overindulgence in Clem's whiskey rendered him incapable of completing that quest, which brought a fair amount of relief to the Indian woman. All except the woman were reluctant to rise from their beds the next morning, leaving her to breakfast alone while Clem slept in the small room in the back of the store and Boyd snored lustily on a cot in the corner of the store. If the sullen Cheyenne woman saw the silent figure that stopped by the one window on the side to survey the scene inside, she gave no indication. Seeing no threat from those inside the trading post, the figure moved silently along the wall of the store toward the barn in back, pausing briefly at the corral to observe the buckskin and spotted gray standing with the other horses. Inside the barn, Wolf found two stalls. The man he looked for was in the second, fast asleep in the hay.

He moved quickly to the sleeping man, knelt beside him, and shook him gently several times until he struggled to climb out of his alcohol-induced slumber. "What is it? Whaddaya want?" Mace slurred, still very much drunk. "Leave me alone."

"Mace," Wolf pronounced his name. "Is that you, Mace?" He had no desire to kill the wrong man.

"Yeah, it's me," Mace blurted angrily. "For Pete's sake, leave me alone. My head's about to bust."

"I can fix that," Wolf said softly. He grabbed a handful of Mace's hair, pulling his head sharply up. An instant later, his skinning knife opened Mace's throat. It was only then that Mace became fully aware of what had happened to him as the sound of his breath wheezed out of his gaping throat. "You should not have killed Ned Bull" were the last words he heard on this side of hell.

His mission done, Wolf had one more thing to check on, so he returned to the front door of the trading post and entered. The Cheyenne woman made no move and no sound when the man in animal skins suddenly appeared in the doorway, a Winchester rifle in his hand. Wolf looked at her, then looked toward the corner where Boyd was just beginning to stir on the cot. Turning back to the woman then, he asked, "His name is Taggart?"

She shook her head slowly, then spoke. "His name Boyd Dawson."

Wolf nodded solemnly. "Then I got no quarrel with him."

He started to turn and leave, but Clem appeared in the doorway to the back room, holding a shotgun. When he looked into the eyes of the baleful avenger, the Winchester rifle ready to speak, he dropped the shotgun at once and held up his hands. Wolf fixed his gaze upon the frightened storekeeper for a moment before taking a step toward the door. "You're him, ain't you?" Clem asked hesitantly. "The one they call Wolf." Wolf didn't answer, but Clem was sure it was the man the Indians talked about, the one some of them were convinced was a spirit and not a man at all.

Chapter 8

Left to stare at the open door in shocked silence, Clem Russell could not be certain if the man he had just seen was real or the remnants of a drunken dream. Looking at Jewel, he received no enlightenment until she finally spoke. "Wolf gone," she expressed unemotionally. "You want food?"

"Food?" Clem echoed. "Hell no. I need a drink." He felt himself trembling, still unable to think clearly. "Yeah," he said then, changing his mind. "I need food. Go ahead, make some coffee and cook some breakfast." He turned, startled, when Boyd separated himself from the cot in the corner of the room and headed for the door with the intention of answering nature's call. Clem had forgotten he was there and, seeing his hungover guest, was also reminded that there was another sleeping in the stable.

"What the hell's the matter with you?" Boyd asked,

noticing the startled expression on Clem's face. "You look like you've seen a ghost."

"Maybe I have," Clem answered honestly.

"No ghost—Wolf," the Cheyenne woman offered unemotionally, causing further confusion for Boyd.

"What the hell's wrong with you two?" Boyd demanded, thinking them both loco.

"We'd best go check on your cousin in the barn," Clem replied. "We had a visitor here in the store while you was still sleepin'." He started at once toward the door.

"What?" Boyd exclaimed. "I didn't hear nobody." Still confused, he followed Clem out the door.

"It's a good thing for you that you didn't," Clem told him as he walked briskly toward the stable. "And if we find what I think we're gonna find in the barn, you're damn lucky your name ain't Taggart."

As Clem had suspected, they found Mace Taggart's body sprawled on the hay, a gaping slash across his throat, and a death mask of wide-eyed horror eternally fixed on his face. In a fog of confusion to that point, Boyd was staggered to see the blood-soaked body of his cousin. "What the hell . . . ? What the hell . . . ?" was all he could manage at first. Then he grabbed Clem by the collar and demanded to know what had happened, for his initial reaction was that Clem or his sullen woman had for some reason murdered Mace.

"Take it easy!" Clem sputtered. "I ain't had no part in this." When Boyd calmed down enough to listen, Clem recounted the events of the past half hour or so.

Still dazed by what Clem told him, Boyd found it hard to believe all this had gone on while he was sleeping right there in the corner of the store. "And you didn't make no move to stop him?" he asked. "Let him walk right in here and kill Mace?" Recovering from his initial shock somewhat, he was now getting angry.

"Ain't no call to get riled at me," Clem said. "He'd already done for Mace when he walked in here. I went for my shotgun, but he had the drop on me. And the only reason you're still alive is that my woman told him your name wasn't Taggart."

It was still a lot for Boyd's aching head to assimilate, but he finally realized what Clem was trying to tell him. And it also registered in his mind that the "posse" that chased Mace to Clem's place was actually one man, according to Clem's story, and the audacity of that man riled him no end. His delayed reaction was to go after the man who had murdered his cousin, but it was delayed a few minutes more by the urgency that had caused him to wake up before. While he took care of nature's demands in a corner of the stall, he told Clem of his intention to track down this "Wolf" spirit and avenge his cousin, knowing that was what any of his brothers or his father would do. Clem shook his head, somewhat doubtful, for he had heard the stories about the spirit that haunted the mountains. "You don't reckon you'd best eat somethin' first?" he asked.

"No," Boyd replied quickly, then reconsidered. "Maybe some coffee, if she's got it done. The longer I lallygag around here, the farther he's gonna get."

The more Boyd thought about what Clem had said, the more he wished his brothers were with him. This fellow who killed Mace might be the cougar Clem described. He saddled his horse, but then went back in the store to drink a cup of coffee and eat some pan bread the woman had made, although his stomach was not really prone to accept anything substantial yet. When Clem asked if he still intended to go after Wolf, Boyd responded, "Hell yes, I'm goin' after the son of a bitch! Mace was family." He admitted to himself, however, that Mace was never an especially favorite cousin. *But dammit,* he thought, *he's still family!*

With no knowledge that Wolf had left his horses in a gully in the ridge above Clem's store and moved down to the bluffs on foot, Boyd spent a great deal of time scouting the clearing around the store, searching for fresh hoofprints. There were many, some he had created himself with his own horse. None looked fresher than two or three days old. "Well, what the hell?" he complained to Clem. "Did he fly in here like a damn bird?"

Clem shrugged. "Maybe—" he started, but Boyd cut him off.

"Don't start up with that shit," he warned. His warning did little to strengthen his resolve. "He had to leave some tracks on the trail in here. I'll go up on the ridge and look there." He got on his horse and rode up the trail leading away from the trading post. At the top of the ridge, he spent more time searching around the head of the trail. There were fresh tracks from two horses rising out of a gully some forty yards from the trailhead. Had he searched that far along the ridge, he would probably have found them. He would not admit, even to himself, that he was relieved not to have found any tracks. After two hours of wasted time, he returned to the trading post. "I don't know how he did it," he told Clem when he got back, "but there ain't no tracks a'tall, and I can't trail him if I can't find his tracks."

"I reckon not," Clem said, keeping his opinion to

himself. His Cheyenne wife grunted her opinion, causing Boyd to respond.

"Oh, he ain't got away with this," he insisted, "not by a long shot. He's done signed his death sentence, and that's a fact. I'm headin' down to Medicine Bow to get my brothers and we'll track him down. I don't care how good he is at hidin' his trail. My brother Skinner can track an owl at night."

Boyd didn't hang around long after filling his belly with fried bacon, beans, and pan bread. The alcohol he had consumed the night before was not through with him yet, however, and he promptly emptied the contents of his stomach beside the trading post. Afraid to tempt it again, he settled for one more cup of coffee before he departed, heading for Medicine Bow with a queasy gut and an aching head. Clem was content to see him go, and hoped he didn't show up at his store with the rest of his brothers. "If he knows what's good for him," Clem commented, "he'll leave Wolf the hell alone and count himself lucky to have got away without gettin' *his* throat cut." He dragged out a long sigh and turned toward the barn. "He sure as hell didn't offer to hang around to help me stick Mace's body in the ground, did he?"

By the time Boyd Dawson left Clem Russell's store, Wolf was nearly fifteen miles away from the North Platte, riding a course he thought would take him in the direction he needed to follow. He figured he had settled Ned's account with the Taggart brothers, and that was the end of it. Heading generally northeast, he hoped to strike the Cheyenne River in a couple of days. From there, he felt he could work back to intersect his original trail into the foothills to the Black Hills, where Ned had overtaken him. He had already decided to forget thoughts of signing on as a scout at Fort Fetterman. Without Ned to vouch for him, he was not confident that the army would take a chance on him, and there was the possibility that he would be recognized as the escaped prisoner from Fort Laramie. In spite of what Ned had told him about the trouble brewing between the army and the prospectors, and the possibility that the Sioux were going to come down on both of them, he decided he would see for himself if the hills were being overrun by white prospectors.

Visible for miles before reaching them, the odd mountain chain stood out as an island of hills and trees in the treeless prairie surrounding them. They at once looked out of place in the midst of the high prairie land, as if some spiritual hand had placed them there as a sacred refuge of tall mountains covered with pines, with clear, rushing streams. It was a place of mystery, and there was little wonder that the Sioux, Cheyenne, and Arapaho called it Paha Sapa, the center of the world. He understood their reverence for the mountains and felt that he shared it as well, feelings that were left over from his one visit a few years back. It made him wonder why he had left there.

He reached in his pocket and pulled out the two double eagles Lorena had given him, and examined them carefully. "Maybe I can learn to find gold," he said to Brownie, remembering that Ned used to talk to the horse all the time. He stroked the face of his horse then and said, "Maybe I need to start talkin' to you. You don't even have a name." He was not a deep thinker. If he had been, he might have realized that his mind was more at ease now with the prospect of returning to his lonely existence in the mountains. It was the only life he really knew.

As he had estimated, he struck the Cheyenne River after riding two full days. He decided to make camp there while he investigated some fresh deer sign on the riverbank. With no particular need to hurry, he also took some time to reconsider his planned route into the mountains. After some thought, he decided not to return to the fork with the Beaver River, instead continuing farther north, paralleling the mountain range for another day's ride before entering the foothills. There was no practical basis for his change of mind; it just struck his fancy at the moment. With his campsite selected, he took care of his horses. Once he was sure they were able to get to grass and water, he hobbled Brownie, but not his horse, satisfied that the bay would not stray from where he left him. Then he trotted off through the cottonwoods that lined the river in search of the deer that had recently passed that way, and eager to try his newly acquired Winchester. He had had no occasion to fire it before.

The hunting was successful, producing a fine young doe for butchering, killed with one well-placed shot behind the deer's front leg. He was pleased with the accuracy of the Winchester, and the balance of the weapon felt just right. He had expected as much, confident that Ned Bull would have settled for nothing less. Aware of a feeling of peace within himself, he remained at his camp on the river for two days, taking his time to prepare the meat for packing. With his horses well rested, and a good supply of meat, he departed from the Cheyenne River and headed north, thinking to see a part of Paha Sapa he had never seen before.

His feeling of serene contentment did not last, for on the second day after leaving the river, he encountered the first of several trails leading into the mountains. They were made by shod horses, and in a couple of cases, there were wagon tracks as well. Ned had been right and the knowledge of that had a devastating effect on Wolf, for he envisioned the sacred hills alive with activity, like ants swarming over an anthill. That was not the case, however, as he rode deeper into the mountains, looking for a campsite that suited him. He moved several times over the next couple of weeks when he discovered neighbors too close for his liking. The first of these sightings—they were not really encounters, for he felt sure the occupants of the camps never saw him—occurred after hearing a gunshot echoing across the valley below him. Knowing that it had to have come from the neighboring mountain, he left his horse at his camp and crossed over to investigate on foot.

A strong stream made its way down to the valley floor and offered the best route up the steep slope, so he started climbing. He had made his way not quite fifty yards up the stream when he was met by half a dozen deer that scattered when they saw him. His guess was that the gunshot he had heard was the cause of their flight down the mountain. Judging by the time it had taken for him to reach that point on the mountain, he assumed the shot had been fired a good bit farther up the slope. As he continued to climb, he cautioned himself to make sure he wasn't mistaken for a deer.

He heard their voices before he actually saw them. There was the sound of laughter, and as he drew closer, he identified them as white men. There were three of them, and one of them was being good-naturedly chastised for shooting at a deer and missing. "I reckon we ain't gonna be dinin' on fresh venison tonight after all," one of them said.

"Well, they come up on us so quick, I didn't have time to aim," the butt of the joke replied.

Wolf left the stream and circled up above them, where he knelt among the pines to observe their camp. They looked to be building a sluice box out of what appeared to be parts of a wagon bed that they had evidently packed in on a couple of mules that were tied on a rope line between two trees next to their horses. Wolf slowly shook his head when he thought how easily a Sioux war party could surround the three men. And he had no doubt that the Sioux would not tolerate the intrusion upon their sacred mountains. If the army could not keep the prospectors out, then men like these three were sure to die. He would not have believed it if someone had told him that the army had already given up on enforcing the treaty with the Indians, and that there were already small towns forming in other parts of the mountains. Feeling crowded, he withdrew quietly and made his way back down the mountain to return to his camp. The next day, he packed up his camp and moved farther north.

Boyd Dawson rode into the town of Medicine Bow on a late summer day. He knew where to find his three brothers, so he went straight to the Cattleman's Saloon. Operated by Barney Grimes, it was the usual hangout

for the Dawson boys whenever they were in this part
of the territory. Barney was well aware of the Dawson
gang's real line of business, which was far from the
cattle business they claimed to anyone who happened
to inquire. He was a direct beneficiary of their "business trips" along the railroad towns of the Union
Pacific, and knew the name of Smith they used when
occupying his two back rooms was an alias. In fact, it
was a standing joke between the saloon owner and the
gang that they holed up right there under the noses of
the soldiers stationed in Medicine Bow.

Boyd walked into the saloon to find two of his
brothers sitting at a table in the back corner of the
room, talking with Barney Grimes. "Well, lookee here
what just blowed in off the prairie," Buck Dawson
remarked, causing his brother Skinner and Barney
Grimes to turn in their chairs to see. "We didn't expect
to see you for a while. What happened? Did that little
ol' Cheyenne gal wear your ass out?" His comments
brought a chuckle from the other two seated at the
table.

Boyd didn't bother to respond to the ribbing. Instead,
he got right to the reason for his unexpected arrival. "I
got some bad news for Aunt Mavis," he replied.

"What might that be?" Skinner asked.

"Mace, Arlo, and Beau Taggart are all dead, gunned
down by a U.S. marshal and some half-wild gunman.
There ain't no menfolk left of the Taggarts."

This gained the immediate attention of the three at
the table. "What the hell are you talkin' about, Boyd?"
Buck demanded.

"Ned Bull brought Arlo right here in Medicine Bow
to put him in jail," Boyd told them.

"Arlo was here?" Skinner responded in honest surprise. "In jail here?"

"That's right," Boyd replied, "but only for one night. That marshal took him out the next mornin', headin' to Fort Laramie, only I reckon Ned Bull didn't wanna bother with cousin Arlo, 'cause he shot him before they ever got to Laramie. He rode into Fort Laramie with poor Arlo's body a-layin' across his saddle."

"I swear," Buck gasped, finding it hard to believe, "Arlo dead?"

Immediately riled, Skinner blurted, "We need to pay Ned Bull a little visit." He paused then, remembering what Boyd had said when he came in. "But you said Mace and Beau, too."

"That's right," Boyd said, "but there ain't no need to go lookin' for Ned Bull, 'cause Mace took care of him. He's dead." He went on then to tell them of Mace's arrival at Clem Russell's trading post with some wild man chasing him after he'd already done for Beau. "He walked right in there and slit Mace's throat while I was asleep in the store." Both of his brothers looked at him expectantly. "He was gone before I woke up," Boyd exclaimed in his defense. "I was goin' after him, but I couldn't find hide nor hair of which way he went, so I had to give up on it. I don't know how he did it, but he didn't leave no tracks."

Both men were properly incensed to hear that their three cousins had been slain and nobody had answered for the foul deed. "I bet I'll find his trail," Skinner claimed, "long as there ain't been no rain or nothin' to wipe it out."

"What was you talkin' about when you said a 'wild man' killed Beau and Mace?" Buck wanted to know.

"I don't know for sure," Boyd said. "He might be an Injun. Clem and his woman said his name was Wolf. She thinks he's some kinda spirit or somethin'."

"Huh," Buck scoffed. "Spirit—I'll make him a spirit if I catch up with him."

"We're goin' after him, ain't we, Buck?" Boyd asked anxiously. "I mean, them Taggarts was just cousins, but that's the same as family, ain't it?"

"Hell yeah, they're family," Skinner said, "and Pa always said you got to take care of family. Ain't that right, Buck?"

"That's right," Buck answered. "We'll get the son of a bitch. I'm tired of lyin' around here, anyway. I'm gettin' downright rusty, and we ain't doin' nothin' but makin' Barney here rich."

"Where's Nate?" Boyd asked.

"Lyin' up in the room," Buck said, "sleepin' off a drunk." He paused to think a moment. "We'll head out to Clem's place first thing in the mornin' and see if Skinner can pick up the trail. Somebody needs to ride down and let Aunt Mavis—and Ma and Pa—know that her three sons are dead, but we'll do the reckonin' for her. Nate can do that."

"He ain't gonna like that," Boyd said. "He thinks he's a wagonload of hell with that six-gun of his."

"He's the youngest," Buck said. "He might complain, but he'll be the best to do it."

Buck was right: Nate did complain when told of the brothers' plan to seek vengeance for a sin against the family. "Why do I have to ride back home?" he asked. "Why can't Boyd do it? He's the next youngest, and I can outshoot him."

"The hell you say," Boyd retorted. "I'll outshoot you any day of the week, and twice on Sunday."

"Ain't no use in arguin'," Buck told him. "You go on back and tell the folks what happened. Besides, Boyd's the one that knows where to start lookin' for this feller's tracks." He looked at Boyd then. "What did you say his name was? Wolf?"

"That's right, Wolf is what Clem said his name was," Boyd replied.

"Well, now," Skinner crowed, "he sounds like a real hellion, don't he? Let's see what he looks like on the inside when I open him up with my skinnin' knife." His comment brought an amused grin to Buck's face. Skinner had come by his nickname when little more than a toddler, because he took his father's knife and tried to skin a two-week-old puppy the family dog had given birth to.

They were in the saddle early the next morning, heading for Clem Russell's trading post on the North Platte, while a still-unhappy Nate rode in the opposite direction to take the news of the three Taggart brothers' demise to their mother on Lodgepole Creek. He would have complained more, but Buck was the eldest, and he was the boss when his pa wasn't around.

Clem Russell was slopping the hogs when the Dawson boys rode down the trail from the ridge above his store. He prodded the boar with a stout pole designed for that purpose to nudge the big hog to the side so that the old sow could get to the trough. When he stood back to watch them eat, he caught sight of the visitors. Shaking his head slowly, he mumbled, "Here comes a heap of trouble for somebody." He started for the store then, yelling as he walked, "Jewel, company's a-comin', and they'll sure as hell want somethin' to eat!" It was with mixed emotions that he greeted the gang's visit. It always meant extra money in his pocket for the grub and whiskey they consumed, plus some extra if some of the boys were a little bit rutty. So he shouldn't complain, but the Dawsons were as mean a bunch of conscienceless miscreants as he had ever met up with. The Taggarts were evil, too, but he had never feared them as much as the Dawsons. Sometimes he asked himself how he happened to be on their list of hideouts, and the only reason he could come up with was that the gang needed places where they could get supplies and ammunition without a lot of questions. Clem was smart enough to figure out that the only reason they didn't kill him and clean him out was simply that they would need him again. Consequently, they paid for everything they took, so he couldn't complain—at least, not too loudly.

Clem stood by the front porch of his store, waiting to greet his customers as they rode up and dismounted. "Howdy, boys," he said, trying to sound as gracious as he possibly could. "I see Boyd brung you back, like he said he would. I expect you're hungry. My woman's cookin'."

"Clem," Buck acknowledged. "Some decent grub would be welcome right now." He stepped up on the porch and stuck his head inside the door to look around, making sure there was no one else in the saloon. Satisfied, he turned back to his brothers. "Boyd, take Skinner up on that ridge and find me a trail to follow. I wanna leave out of here in the mornin'." His two brothers got back in the saddle and did as he said. Then he laid his big arm on Clem's shoulders and walked with him to the bar. "Tell me about this feller that had Boyd talkin' crazy stuff about a wild man or somethin'."

"I don't know if he's a wild man or not," Clem replied. "But I saw him when he walked into the store here, and he had a look like a crazy man, just itchin' to kill somebody. Boyd was asleep on that cot in the corner, and like I told him, he was lucky he didn't jump up. That man woulda cut him down before he could blink an eye."

"Is that a fact?" Buck responded. "I don't know, Boyd ain't exactly slow. If it'da been Nate, though, it mighta been a different story."

Clem looked around then, just realizing that the gang was one short. "Where is Nate?" he asked. "He ain't in no trouble, is he?"

"Nah," Buck said. "I sent him home to tell the folks the bad news about the Taggart boys. Now, what about this wild feller?"

"Well, like I told Boyd," Clem continued, "he wouldn'ta had much of a chance against this feller. Hell, Boyd was asleep, and still pretty drunk. He didn't know anythin' about it till after this Wolf feller was done and gone. He asked Jewel if Boyd was a Taggart, she told him he wasn't, and he turned and left. I reckon he was just lookin' to wipe out the Taggarts."

"That's what he did, all right," Buck stated, "and now he's gonna have to pay for killin' my cousins. The Dawsons don't take kindly to anybody bringin' harm to our family."

"Set down yonder at the table," Clem said, "and I'll

go see what Jewel's doin' 'bout fixin' you and your brothers somethin' to eat."

While Buck went to the table in the back corner of the saloon, Clem went out the back door to the kitchen, where he found the stoic Indian woman stirring a big pot of beans. She glanced up at him with weary eyes devoid of emotion. "Make sure there's plenty of ham in them beans," he told her, then paused to give her a closer look. "For Pete's sake, change that rag you're wearin'. Put on that dress you just finished makin', so you don't look like you been sleepin' with the hogs."

She turned those lifeless eyes up to him again and asked, "You stir beans?"

"No, hell no," he replied indignantly, "I ain't gonna stir the damn beans. I've got customers to attend to." He spun around to return to the saloon. "But you get yourself outta that dirty rag and into somethin' that might make you look a little more like a female."

She paused to stare at his back as he went through the door. He would never know the desperate thoughts that filled her mind, for he was incapable of understanding the hell he had created for her over their years together. In the beginning, he had courted her as a man would court a wife. But the relationship soon turned into something she had not counted on, when she became a commodity to be sold in his store and used like the hogs in the pen. She had run away once in an attempt to return to her Cheyenne people, but he had caught her and dragged her back to be severely beaten and threatened with death if she tried it again. After a while she became oblivious of the rough pawing of his drunken customers, and one day realized that it was too late for her to think about escaping. So she resigned herself to her fate as a white man's slave. Even so, she had a sick feeling in the pit of her stomach when she heard Boyd and Skinner coming in the front door.

Clem, on his way to the table with a full bottle of whiskey, turned when he heard them behind him. "Come on in, boys. We'll have somethin' for you to eat in a minute or two."

"Any luck?" Buck asked.

"I reckon," Skinner said. "Didn't need none, though. Found tracks where a couple of horses came up out of a gully 'bout thirty or forty yards the other side of that path leading down from the ridge. Boyd woulda seen 'em if he'da looked a little farther than the end of his nose."

"I was just in too big a hurry to get after him," Boyd attempted to alibi. "I musta missed that gully."

Skinner gave him a knowing grin and continued. "I can track the bastard—two horses, one of 'em shod, the other'n barefoot."

"Which way did he go?" Buck asked. "Follow the river?"

"Nah," Skinner said. "He didn't follow the river more'n a hundred yards before cuttin' away to head straight north. Long as we don't get no gully-washers or it don't snow, I can track him."

"Good," Buck said. "The son of a bitch has already lived too long to suit me."

The conversation was interrupted briefly then with the arrival of the sullen Indian woman with their food. She was still wearing the same soiled dress, but there was only one who took note of it. Clem glared angrily at her as she spooned beans out on each plate, then went back to the kitchen to get a platter of bread, baked fresh that morning.

The atmosphere around the table that night was not the usual loud and rough talking affair that the Dawsons normally indulged in. There was a fair amount of drinking, but Skinner and Boyd were both aware of their elder brother's somber mood. It was something they had seen before, when he made up his mind that someone had to be dealt with. There was no argument from either when Buck told them to put a cork on the bottle and get to their blankets, because he was planning to go hunting early in the morning. All the Dawson brothers enjoyed hunting, and it was especially exciting when it was human prey they stalked.

The sun rose the next day to find Buck already drinking coffee in the kitchen with Jewel while he waited for his brothers to rouse themselves. Bacon was sizzling in the Indian woman's big iron skillet, and corn cakes were waiting to fry in the leftover grease. She was happy to arise early to cook for the three men, anxious to see them on their way, and thankful that there had been no demand for her worn-out body the night before. Clem had attempted to generate some interest in her reluctant services, but the brothers had hunting on their minds. There was no delay in their departure. They were ready to ride by the time Clem staggered out to see them off. Riding up from the bluffs, Skinner showed Buck the tracks left in the gully where Wolf had left his horses while he murdered their cousin. "If the weather holds," Skinner predicted, "we oughta be able to follow his trail for a good while. So far, it don't look like he's worried about anybody followin' him."

Buck nodded solemnly. He knew that no matter

how plain the trail was, it was bound to disappear after a while, whenever their prey came to a river or a tree-covered mountain. So it was necessary to follow it as long as they could and hope to run him down before he had a chance to lose them—and he already had a good five-day start. "Let's go," Buck ordered, and the three started out on their deadly mission.

"Skinner's good at trackin'," Boyd said, "but if we don't catch up with this Wolf feller before he heads up into the Black Hills, if that's where he's headed, we ain't got much of a chance to find him. What are you thinkin' on doin' if we don't track him down in a week or two?" Of further concern was the fact that summer was already nearing an end, and an early snow could make tracking impossible.

The question was not something Buck had not already given a great deal of thought. "Have you got a good reason why you wanna hang around here, or Cheyenne, or Medicine Bow, or anywhere else where we've been pretty busy lately?" he asked pointedly. "We might not find this son of a bitch right away, but we're gonna keep on lookin' till we run across him somewhere. And while we're lookin', it might as well be up in the Black Hills. That country has opened up to the gold prospectors. There's gonna be more prospectors in them hills than there is pine trees, and that just means more gold for us. They dig it outta the ground and we'll dig it outta them."

A wide smile of enlightenment spread across Boyd's face. "Damn," he remarked, "I hadn't thought about that. All them miners workin' their sluice boxes back up in them gulches, that'd be mighty easy pickin's, wouldn't it?"

"That's what I'm thinkin'," Buck replied. "And sooner or later this Wolf feller is gonna show up somewhere. We might as well have ourselves a payday while we're waitin' for him to come out of his hole."

Listening to the conversation between his brothers, Skinner silently nodded his approval, and thought, *That's why Buck calls all the shots. He was probably thinking about hitting those miners up in the Black Hills all along. Our cousins getting killed just gave him an excuse to go up there right now.*

Behind them, Clem Russell stood at the edge of the clearing that surrounded his trading post, where he had been watching the outlaws as they departed. As usual, he had conflicting feelings about their visit, half of him glad to see them moving on, while the other half was wishing they had stayed long enough to spend a little more money. *At least, this time they didn't tear anything up,* he thought. Then he remembered a little issue he wanted to address concerning Jewel, and her downright disobedience over the changing of her dress. He should have given her a good beating last night, but unlike his guests, he stayed with the bottle too long and passed out at the table. By the time he woke up in the middle of the night, he was too tired to think about anything beyond falling in bed. This morning, she was already up and in the kitchen before he was awake. *But, by God, there ain't nothing to save her from a whipping now,* he thought, and turned back toward the store to tend to it.

He found her in the kitchen, her back to him as she stood gazing out the back window. "Turn your sorry ass around," he commanded. "I've got somethin' to settle with you." When she did as she was told, he took a step backward, startled when he saw his shotgun in her hands. "Whoa!" he blurted. "What the hell are you doin'?"

"No more beatings," she announced in her usual stoic manner. "No more whore."

"Gimme that damn gun," he demanded angrily, and stepped toward her, reaching for it. With the barrel no more than six inches from his stomach, she pulled both triggers, knocking him off his feet, the recoil from both barrels firing simultaneously almost knocking her down as well. Flat on his back, the mortally wounded man lay helpless as the life drained rapidly from his mangled body. "You've kilt me, you damn Injun bitch," he managed to gasp. With a savage desire to finish the job, she got her butcher knife from the table and took his scalp before leaving him to die in the middle of the kitchen floor she had come to despise.

With no change in her dispassionate demeanor, she went about packing her things, along with all the supplies she could load on Clem's two horses, as well as his shotgun and revolver. When she was satisfied that she had all she needed, she went out back and opened the gate to the hog pen. Taking a rope from the barn, she tied a loop around the necks of the two hogs and tied the other end to her packhorse. When all was ready, she returned to the house with one of the rails out of the hog pen. Using it as a lever, she turned the stove over, dumping flaming ashes on the floor, which she used to ignite the firewood and broken furniture she piled on top. Content with the result, she waited until the firewood was burning lustily. Then she pulled out a couple of pieces, went outside, and pitched them up on the shingle roof.

When it was all done, she climbed up in the saddle and started up the path, never once looking back at the blazing funeral pyre she had left. At the top of the ridge, she turned the horses toward the northwest and Powder River country, walking them slowly at the pace of the two hogs following along behind. Somewhere on the Powder, or the Tongue, maybe, she would find Crazy Horse or Sitting Bull and hopefully some of the Cheyenne people who had joined with him. It was time for her to return to her people and fight the white man.

Chapter 9

His first confrontation with a sizable gathering of gold seekers came after a couple of weeks near the base of a mountain that stood high above the neighboring peaks. A few days earlier, he had made his camp by a wide rushing stream, close up under a steep slope with rocky outcroppings jutting out from the forest of tall pines. Game was plentiful. The spot he had picked showed signs of a favorite watering place for deer, and proved to be just that. Hunting with his bow was a great deal more difficult than using his rifle, but he felt the need to conserve his cartridges. After a couple of days of hunting, he was able to thin out the deer population a little before they moved out of the valley.

Extending his range of hunting then, he rode to the far side of the mountain, where he found sign of elk, and immediately set in to stalk them. Their tracks led him beyond the next mountain to a narrow canyon bisected by a rapidly flowing stream. There were no elk, but it was obvious that they had been there. He had started to continue after them when he was stopped by the sudden report of a rifle. It sounded to be of small caliber, but he was at once concerned. He paused to listen, but no shots followed the first one. Although it had come from somewhere beyond the ridge west of him, and he was obviously not the target, it troubled him that he had once again come in contact with man. White or red, he could not say, but instead of retreating to his camp on the other side of the tall mountain, now to the east of him, he decided it best to find out who was crowding him.

Making his way up the slope, he let the bay find the easiest way to the top, skirting clusters of rugged rocks to weave his way through the pines. Upon gaining the top of the ridge, he was amazed to find a sizable settlement of prospectors, working away like busy insects over a carcass. His first reaction was one of despair, for the once beautiful stream was already looking very much like a carcass. He could see nothing that would explain the reason for the shot he had heard. Evidently someone had decided to take a shot at something, maybe a varmint of some kind. And the realization struck him then that there was no sacred place on the earth safe from the white man's search for gold. His sense of curiosity demanded that he take a closer look at the collection of miners, however, so he guided the bay down the east side of the slope and up to the top of a lower rise that stood between him and the settlement.

He sat on his horse and watched the activity below him for a few minutes, noting the little city of tents with a few rough shacks scattered among them. Then he realized that not all of them were dwellings.

Already, there were two tents that displayed rough signs advertising whiskey, and one of the shacks appeared to be a trading post. It was a town in the making, right in the center of ceded Indian lands. He knew at once that he would be moving his camp even farther north. He wheeled his horse to retreat, but then reconsidered. He was almost out of coffee beans, and he had become quite accustomed to drinking the black liquid, so why not see if the trading post had them? He felt in his pockets to make sure his two gold coins were still there. *And some flour, too, if they don't want too much for it*, he thought.

Reuben Little glanced up when something blocked the sunlight coming in the door of his shack. "Come in, stranger," he greeted Wolf cordially. "I thought you were an Injun when I first looked up."

Puzzled, Wolf asked, "Why?" He thought it should be fairly obvious that he was not. It never occurred to him that his clothes made from animal skins, and sewn by himself, gave him a rather primitive appearance.

"Because you look . . . ," Reuben started; then, aware of the expressionless eyes searching his face, he said, "No reason. What can I do for you"

"I need some coffee beans if your price is not too high, and maybe some flour if you have some," Wolf told him. It had been some time since he had flour to make bread.

"My partner just brought in a wagonload of goods this week," Reuben told him. "We got a load of both coffee and flour."

Wolf remarked that he was surprised to find

wagons up in the hills. "Ain't no problem," Reuben said. "Hell, this spot is gonna be a regular city before you know it. They've already got a name for it, Stonewall, after that general in the War Between the States. And they're scouting out a stage road between here and Fort Laramie—said it'll go on down to Cheyenne when they finish."

None of this was welcome news to the stoic child of the mountains. He was positive now that he would move his camp again. "How much for the flour?" Wolf asked.

"How are you thinking about paying?" Reuben wanted to know. "I don't do any trading for pelts. This is a store, not a trading post."

"I'll pay with gold," Wolf said. "How much is the flour?"

"Right, I didn't mean to insult you. I do all my business with the prospectors, and they don't have pelts to trade. Flour is hard to come by. I was damn lucky to get my hands on a barrel of it. Then you have to get it by the Injuns, and there's a big demand for it, so that makes it kinda expensive. I have to get a dollar a pound just to break even."

Wolf thought that over for a few seconds and decided he could do without bread. He settled for a twenty-pound bag of coffee beans, a purchase considerably cheaper than the flour. He waited patiently while Reuben weighed out his coffee and dumped it in a sack, then surprised the storekeeper with a double eagle to pay for it. "What's your name, mister?" Reuben asked. "You gonna try your hand at prospecting?"

"I'm called Wolf," he said. "I'm not a prospector."

"Well, if you're gonna be staying around for a spell,

I'll be getting in a lot of supplies that you don't see here yet, including shirts, boots, and trousers." He couldn't help wondering how many more double eagles Wolf had.

"I ain't gonna be stayin," Wolf said, took his sack of coffee beans and his change in the form of a small sack of gold dust, then walked out the door. In the saddle once more, he never intended to visit Stonewall again unless he became desperate for supplies.

Reuben walked to the door to watch him ride away. *He ain't the first one of his kind I've ever seen*, he thought. *But I'll sure remember him.* "Wolf," he repeated. "I wouldn't doubt he was born in a litter of pups by an old wolf bitch."

Back in his camp at the foot of the mountain, Wolf looked around at the progress he had already made to ready the camp for the winter, now rapidly approaching. He thought it over, trying to make up his mind to stay until spring or to move right away. He walked to the edge of the stream and stared at it, wondering if there was any gold in its rushing waters that might bring a storm of prospectors to search for it. In the end, he decided to move farther north. He felt crowded, and there was still time for him to build a winter camp. He could not waste any more time, however, for there was a lot of hunting and curing of meat to be done to prepare for the long months when the mountain passes would be clogged with snow. These were the only things that occupied his thoughts now, for he had no way of knowing that he himself was being hunted by three men sworn to kill him. And although they had long since lost his trail, they were in the Black

Hills, searching, working their lawless way from mining camp to mining camp, sometimes leaving a trail of murdered prospectors in isolated streams and lonely gulches, knowing that inevitably they would track him down.

Far behind them, another had joined the hunt. Nate, youngest of the Dawson brothers, was already on his way to find them and hopefully to find the man called Wolf. It had been as difficult as he had anticipated to bring his aunt Mavis the news that all three of her sons had been killed. Mavis Dawson Taggart was not a woman to accept injury to any of her family without bloody retribution. When he had ridden into the front yard of the tiny cabin on Lodgepole Creek, he had found his aunt sweeping the bare ground around the porch steps with a broom made from willow switches. As soon as she saw him, she stopped dead in her tracks, sensing bad news in some form. She propped her broom against a porch post, wiped her hands on her apron, and waited patiently for Nate to dismount.

"Nate" was all she said as she watched him step down.

"Howdy, Aunt Mavis," Nate returned. "I reckon I got some bad news." He told her then about the tragic ending of her sons. She didn't make a sound, nor shed a single tear, as he identified their killers. A clenching of her jaw and the slight narrowing of her eyes were the only emotions registered. It was not the reaction Nate expected, and he wondered if she realized what he was telling her until she finally spoke.

"Gimme their names," she said, her voice steady as a rock.

"Mace told Boyd that a marshal named Ned Bull

was the one that killed Arlo, and Mace killed the marshal. But the one that shot Beau and knifed Mace got away."

"His name?" Mavis asked, still with no emotion evident in her weathered face.

"I ain't sure if it's his real name or not, but Clem said he was called Wolf."

"Wolf?" Mavis questioned, not sure she had heard right.

"Yes, ma'am," Nate replied, still puzzled by his aunt's lack of emotion. "But don't you worry none. All three of my brothers are already on his trail, and I'm fixin' to head that way myself. Me being the youngest, Buck made me come give you the news, or I'd be with 'em. Don't you worry, we'll get that feller."

"If you don't, I will," she promised. Then, without a change of expression, she asked, "Are you hungry? Have you had your breakfast?"

"No, ma'am," he replied. "I ain't et no breakfast yet, but I expect I'd best get started after my brothers pretty quick. I ain't even been to the house to tell Ma and Pa the bad news yet—thought you oughta been the one to hear about it first. I expect they'll be comin' over as soon as they find out."

"Can't hardly do your best if you start out hungry," she insisted. "Come on in the house. I've got biscuits I baked this mornin'."

"Yessum, thank you, ma'am. I reckon I could eat a biscuit or two. Then I'll go see Ma and Pa before I go after my brothers. That murderin' dog ain't gonna get away with what he done."

She fed him coffee and biscuits, and then he was on his way. She waited until his horse dropped below the rise that stood between her cabin and that of her brother Doc's before she released the agony that his news had created. She raised her face to the cloudy sky and brought her grief up from deep inside her in a mournful howl, like that of a coyote. With nothing in her life that meant anything to her other than her three boys, she would have satisfaction from their killers if she had to do it herself. *I may be old*, she thought, *but I ain't feeble. Nobody gets away with harming my boys.* But she still had her nephews. They would avenge her sons. She would see to that.

Winter set in with bitter cold temperatures and heavy snowfalls, but Wolf's camp was well prepared, as he had coped with wintry camps since he was first on his own in the Wind River Mountains. He had pushed on only about a day's ride from the boomtown of Stonewall before he came upon an ideal setting for his winter home in the form of a deep gulch running back into the side of a mountain that provided cover for his two horses as well as himself. When he first discovered it, he hurried to fashion a roof over the narrow end of the gulch with a smoke hole for his fire. As soon as it was finished to suit him, he worked hard to stock up on firewood, and then he spent all his time hunting. He was content there with nothing to concern himself with except seeing that his horses were protected and fed. Though game was scarce, there would still be some to supplement his store of smoked jerky as the occasional herd of deer moved through the sheltered valleys. Of more concern was the feed for his horses, but they could make it on a great deal less, since they would be doing little more than waiting for spring.

* * *

As he had anticipated, the winter was long and bitterly cold, but as he also expected, he and both horses survived it, although the horses looked a little thin and ragged. He knew that would soon be improved, now that the valleys were becoming passable once again and the warmer weather brought new grass. He waited until spring showed definite signs that she was officially here. Then, eager to move again after being confined for months, he packed his belongings on Brownie and saddled the bay. It was time to see more of Paha Sapa, and well aware of Stonewall behind him, he was eager to put more distance between himself and that town of gold seekers. It was bound to become even more populated by prospectors hoping to strike it rich, so he set his horse's nose on the mountains to the north.

On one knee, Wolf bent low to examine the tracks beside a wide stream that was swollen with melted snow from the cliffs above him. There was nothing to figure out. The tracks told a simple story—Indians—for the hoofprints were left by unshod ponies, and there were also moccasin prints in the sandy bank. A war party had crossed here not more than a few hours earlier. With no desire to tangle with what he figured to be at least a dozen or more warriors, probably intent upon attacking isolated mining claims, he crossed over the stream to look for their tracks on the other side. They appeared to be heading in the same general direction as he, so he decided it best to alter his course so as to be sure to avoid them. Veering off more to the west, he continued on his way.

He had ridden no more than an hour when he came

upon another trail that cut across his, leading toward a wide stream. It was fed by a waterfall cascading from a rocky notch about halfway up an almost vertical mountainside. Out of habit, he dismounted to examine the tracks more closely. *Another raiding party*, he thought, *about the same size as the one back yonder*. Then it struck him that it was probably the same war party. They had changed their direction. The tracks, along with some droppings from the ponies, told him that he was still hours behind the Indians. "I reckon I can turn back more toward the north now," he commented to Brownie, "and let these fellers go about their business, whatever mischief they're into." With one foot in the stirrup, he paused a moment before throwing his other leg over. Once again, his natural curiosity prompted him to change his mind. *Maybe I'll see what these boys are up to*, he thought, and turned the bay's head to the west before settling in the saddle.

With thoughts of avoiding riding into an ambush, he rode across the valley toward the stream, his eyes constantly searching the slopes that formed the far side of the valley. *If they're lying around up there, waiting to ambush me*, he thought, *they're pretty well hidden*. Reaching the bank of the stream, he started following it toward the waterfall. It was then that he saw the smoke, causing him to pull his horses up sharply while he thought it over. Too spread out to be from a camp-fire, the thin wisps of smoke wafted lazily up from what appeared to be two or three different sources, hidden from him behind a low hogback. He pulled the Winchester from his saddle sling and cranked a cartridge into the chamber.

With no intention of riding straight in to investigate,

he wheeled the bay around and set out at a lope to circle around to the side of the rise. When he reached a
point roughly opposite the origin of the smoke, he
pulled back on the reins and dismounted, leaving the
two horses there while he made his way on foot
through the maze of trees that bordered the stream. At
the top of the rise, he paused to take in the scene of the
massacre. There was no sign of the raiders, only the
blatant evidence of their evil passage. Smoldering
slowly, a wagon sat, half-burned before the flames had
died. Beyond it, two tents were still smoking, a result
of the war party's efforts to set them ablaze, but the
canvas had seemed reluctant to burn. As his eyes
scanned slowly across the destroyed campsite, his
gaze finally lit upon one body and then, several yards
away, another body. He rose to his feet and walked
down the slope to the camp.

From all appearances, the two prospectors had been
caught completely by surprise. A pan was lying on a
flat rock at the edge of the stream, and the loose gravel
and sand told him that the body had either dragged
itself or been dragged away from the water to the spot
where it now lay. An older man, he had been scalped,
his body mutilated, probably with a hatchet or war
axe. The second body was that of a younger man. It
appeared he had been running toward one of the tents
when he was shot several times. Like his partner, he
had been chopped to pieces and scalped. Wolf was not
without compassion for the innocent victims, but he
was not shocked by what he saw. Since he was eleven,
he had lived in the violent world of the warriors of
the plains. In his many years living with the Crows, he
had learned to count the Sioux as the enemy, but he

understood their hatred for the white man. How could it not be a natural reaction when their hunting grounds, even their sacred hills, were rapidly being taken away by the white man? As for these unfortunate victims of a Sioux war party, he was sure there were grieving relatives who would never know what had happened to them. But they had no business here. Even so, he knew that, had he been here at the time of the attack, he would have helped the prospectors fight.

There was no thought of burying the bodies. Doing so would have told the Sioux war party that he had been there, if for some reason they happened to return. It mattered little, anyway, he believed, for the spirits of the two men had departed their bodies. A quick scout around the camp told him that the Sioux warriors had moved off toward a ravine near the pool at the bottom of the waterfall. Wolf had not noticed it upon first reaching the camp, but the Sioux must have known it was there, since their tracks led straight to it. It took only a moment's thought before he decided to follow them. It was a natural impulse on his part, for he had grown up from childhood keeping a vigilant eye upon those who might threaten him. It was better, he thought, to track them so that he would know where they were, instead of the other way around.

As he had suspected, the ravine led him down to a broad lower valley and the beginnings of a rough wagon road that ran straight up the middle. It was not necessary to dismount to inspect the tracks he saw. They were left by heavily loaded wagons—freighters, he guessed, probably pulled by four-horse teams, judging by the many hoofprints. He remembered then what Reuben Little had told him: there were many wagon roads reaching into the valleys. The party of warriors had turned back to follow the road. He guessed their intention was to look for more victims to murder. With that possibility in mind, he felt he had no choice but to follow. Feeling a small sense of urgency now, he nudged the bay to pick up the pace.

It was fully a mile and a quarter to the south end of the valley, and he followed the road through a narrow notch that led to a winding trail around the base of two mountains. It was his guess that the party of warriors was returning to a village somewhere on the plains, possibly as far as the Belle Fourche, since by his estimate, the trail he was following would soon be out of the mountains. As he came to a point where the trail took a sharp turn, he heard the first of a great many shots ring out somewhere beyond the turn of the trail a quarter of a mile ahead. Soon the sound of answering fire echoed back from the narrow canyon, and he assumed the war party had found another prospector. He gave the bay a slight kick and headed for the bend in the trail at a gallop.

When he reached the point where the trail swung wide to go around a tree-covered knoll that jutted out from the base of the mountain, he rode straight up the side of it, using the pines for cover. Just before emerging from the trees on the other side of the knoll, he saw the conflict taking place. It was not a mining claim that was under attack but a single wagon, stalled in the middle of a wide stream. Evidently, the Sioux had been as surprised by the encounter as those in the wagon. They had not divided to surround the wagon, but were bunched on one side of the stream and shooting wildly at the occupants, who were returning fire from

behind the wagon. Wolf counted twelve warriors in
the war party and three extra horses that no doubt
belonged to the two dead prospectors he had found
earlier. He double-checked his Winchester, then drew
his Henry from the pack Brownie was carrying. After
leading the horses a little farther up in the pines, he
made his way down the slope with a rifle in each hand,
working along the foot of the knoll until reaching a
wash that ran about forty feet down to the valley floor.

"Keep shootin' at the middle of that bunch," Billie Jean
shouted, "and give me some cover. I'm gonna try to
unhitch the horses and get 'em behind the wagon with
us. We're gonna be in a helluva fix if they shoot the
horses." She stuck Lorena's revolver in her waistband
and prepared to run.

"I think we're in a helluva fix already," Rose replied
fearfully. She waded carefully in the knee-deep water
to move up beside Lorena to send a volley toward the
Sioux warriors gathered some seventy-five yards
behind them.

"What good is it gonna do to bring the horses back
of the wagon if those devils decide to split up and surround us?" Lorena asked. "And it looks like that's
what they're thinkin' about doin'." Her comment was
enough to cause Billie Jean to hesitate.

As Lorena had said, the warriors spread out in one
straight line, talking excitedly among themselves as if
deciding how to attack the wagon. While the three
women paused to watch them, Rose continued to fire
her weapon. A warrior at the end of the line braced suddenly before falling from his horse. "Good girl, Rose!"
Billie Jean exclaimed. "You got one of 'em." A moment

later she had cause to cheer again, for the warrior next in line slid from his horse to crumple to the ground. "You got another one!"

Astonished, Rose looked hard at the carbine in her hands, as if it had a will of its own. "I didn't shoot but once," she said, unable to explain.

A third warrior fell from his pony before the others realized the deadly rifle fire was not from the wagon but had come from beside them at the foot of the knoll. They immediately scattered, whipping their ponies hard to get out of range. It was not soon enough, however, to prevent the death of another of their war party. Moving rapidly from one end of the wash to the other, Wolf fired as rapidly as he could, alternating between his two rifles, hoping that there would be a little difference in the sounds of the Henry and the Winchester. Hopefully, the Sioux warriors would think there was more than one man firing at them. Whether they did or not, his one-man volley was not only rapid but deadly accurate, and was effective in causing the war party to retreat, having already lost too many of their number.

When it was apparent that the Sioux had had all they wanted of the fight, Wolf watched them until they disappeared from the valley. Then he reloaded his rifles and walked back to his horses, where he returned the Henry to its scabbard on Brownie's pack. His inclination was to climb in the saddle and head back north again. He felt no desire to see the folks in the wagon. From where he had stood in the deep wash, there appeared to be no reason for the wagon to be stuck. The water was not that deep. But the wagon looked somehow familiar, enough to trigger his ever-present curiosity, so he rode down out of the pines and headed toward the wagon in the creek, thinking it no harm to see if they were all right.

Three totally astonished women stood knee-deep in the chilly water of the creek, watching their departing attackers until they were well out of sight. Expecting to see an army patrol come charging out of the low hills to their west, they were astounded to discover one lone rider emerge to come toward them at a comfortable lope. "Well, I'll be dipped in shit," Lorena uttered profoundly. "I ain't believin' my eyes." It was too great a coincidence to really be happening.

"It's him!" Rose squealed delightedly. "He always comes when we need him!"

"It's him, all right," Billie Jean said. "I don't know how in hell he knows to show up when he does, and I ain't about to ask any questions. I'm just damn glad to see him." She slapped the horses hard on their rumps, and the wagon lurched reluctantly toward the low bank.

He realized why the wagon looked familiar as soon as he saw Billie Jean climb up in the seat. At first, he thought he had to be mistaken, for at a distance Billie Jean could pass for a man. But then he saw Lorena climb over the seat to join her. He felt an impulse to turn around and ride away, because it seemed that every time he met up with them, he got into some kind of trouble. But he also had to admit that he wished them well, and felt a little ashamed for thinking to avoid them.

"You just can't seem to get the knack of crossin' a stream in a wagon, can you?" he joked in greeting when he reined his horses to a stop in front of them.

"You just can't seem to mind your own business,

can you?" Billie Jean fired back. They both had a laugh over it. "Besides, we weren't stuck this time. We just had a surprise visit that caught us in the middle of crossing."

"Why didn't you keep goin'," Wolf asked, "at least till you got out of the water?"

Billie Jean glanced at Lorena as if stuck for an answer. "Hell, I don't know. They started shooting at us, so we just went for our guns."

"Hello, Wolf," Rose called out cheerfully when she stuck her head out between Lorena and Billie Jean. "How did you know we were here?"

"I didn't," Wolf replied.

"I reckon it was just luck," Lorena said.

"Yeah, just luck," Wolf muttered under his breath. "There's just one thing I'm wonderin': What in the hell are you three doin' up here in the Black Hills by yourself? Didn't anybody tell you this is hostile Indian country? That wasn't no welcomin' party that just rode off down the valley." He was frankly amazed that they had managed to get this far.

"Well, we wasn't supposed to be all by ourselves," Lorena said. "I made arrangements to meet up with a string of freighters headin' for Deadwood Gulch. We were supposed to meet them at Hat Creek last Sunday noon. Well, we got there, but they never showed up—"

"So you just came on by yourself," Wolf finished for her, "three women right up through territory swarmin' with Sioux war parties."

Lorena shrugged. "Well, hell, we were already a good part of the way, and we hadn't seen any sign of Injuns, so we figured we'd just come on by ourselves. There's already a little bit of a road we were able to follow, and we've got our carbines and my pistol. Besides, I thought we'd catch up with those freight wagons, and they would lead us on into Deadwood Gulch." She favored him with a crooked little smile then and added, "I'm missin' one of my Sharpses."

"Well, I'll give it back, and thank you for the loan," he said without telling them that the carbine had temporarily been in Ned Bull's possession until he had been killed. Ned had intended to use it as proof that he had caught Wolf and killed him. Wolf shook his head then, still perplexed about finding the three of them without escort. "You sure as hell must have somebody watchin' over you, 'cause anybody else pullin' a fool stunt like that would have their hair hangin' on some Lakota warrior's lance right now."

"We've got *you* watching over us," Rose offered with a contented smile.

"I ain't gonna happen along every time you three do somethin' dumb like this," he retorted in exasperation with the naive young girl. "What are you goin' to Deadwood Gulch for, anyway? I thought you were settled at Fort Laramie."

Rose and Lorena both looked quickly at Billie Jean in response to the question. Billie Jean shrugged sheepishly. Then Lorena answered, "It's a long story, but to give you the short version of it, you remember that tall, lanky bitch named Mae? Well, Billie Jean was talkin' to a customer and Mae told her he was one of her regulars and to keep her hands off. Then Billie Jean told her . . ." She paused then and looked at her. "What was it you said?" Without waiting for an answer, she went on. "Anyway, it was somethin' that Mae didn't particularly appreciate, and she called Billie Jean a bowlegged buffalo cow." She laughed. "I remember that one. So Billie Jean flattened her. Laid her out cold right in the middle of the saloon floor."

Wolf wasn't surprised. He knew that Billie Jean liked a scrap as well as anyone, but it didn't seem like reason enough to leave. Seeing that it was puzzling to him, Billie Jean went on to explain, "Smiley kicked us out. He said the colonel at the fort was already looking to put him out of business on account of too much trouble at the saloon, especially since that little run-in you had with that sergeant. We told him that the army didn't have anything to do with his saloon, long as it wasn't on the post. But he said they could sure as hell keep the soldiers from coming. And he said there wasn't no trouble until the three of us showed up—"

"That ain't the real reason," Lorena interrupted. "Mae and her pals wanted us outta there, and that skinny bitch has been takin' care of ol' Smiley's needs with no charge. She musta threatened to shut off the pump if he didn't get rid of us. I'm bettin' that's the real reason."

"It doesn't matter, anyway," Billie Jean resumed, "'cause we heard about the big gold strike in Dead-wood Gulch, and it'll be better for us to set ourselves up for business right from the start. Up there, with all those rutty miners striking it rich, it'll be a helluva lot better than working our asses off for soldiers' pay."

"I expect you'd best move your asses away from this place before those warriors come back," Wolf said. "They might wait till dark before comin' back to get their dead, and they might not. If they find out there ain't but one of me, they might decide to try us again. Only, this time they'll hit us from both sides." He was of the opinion that the war party might have been low on ammunition after their raids on the mining camps in the mountains. This could account for the conservative attack upon the wagon instead of an all-out assault while it was vulnerable.

"Now that you're here," Rose suggested hopefully, "maybe you can lead us to Deadwood."

"I don't know where Deadwood is," Wolf replied.

His response seemed to surprise them all. They had come to believe that he knew everything there was to know about the territory. Disappointed, Lorena told him that it was a gulch in the northern end of the Black Hills, and that the freighter she had talked to said that he had made two trips up there with all manner of supplies. "I know there's a heap of people already up there, and we might as well be the first in our line of work to join them."

The frown on his face revealed his lack of enthusiasm for helping them find another in a long list of boomtowns that threatened to ruin the grandeur of the mountains. They waited expectantly for his decision while he battled with his conscience. Like it or not, he surrendered to his sense of what was right, knowing he couldn't abandon them to try to find the gulch by themselves. "If they've been drivin' wagons up there, I reckon I oughta be able to follow their tracks easy enough." He thought of the deep wagon tracks he had seen earlier, running up the valley, and figured they were probably the freighters the women were supposed to meet. He told Lorena as much.

"Why, those low-down lyin' bastards," she fumed when he told her how far ahead of them they were. "They told me they would wait till we got there.

Dammit, we waited for them when we thought we were early."

"Nothing we can do about that now," Rose chimed in, still cheerful about the prospect of having Wolf to look after them. "We don't need them anyway. Isn't that right, Wolf?"

He shifted his dark eyes toward her and commented dryly, "Don't ever hurt to have a few extra rifles handy when you're ridin' through this country. Let's get started. We've still got a few good hours of daylight left, and we need to find a good place to camp tonight. Those Lakota warriors ain't likely to go back to their village without the bodies of the ones we killed. They'll be back. Best we're not here when they come."

Billie Jean was the only one who thought to ask the question that no one had thought to ask when he first appeared. "Do you know Ned Bull is on your trail?"

"He was," Wolf answered. "He ain't no more." The noticeable void that followed told of the disappointment all three felt. Realizing this, he told them of the circumstances that had led to Ned's death, and the part he had played to ensure his revenge. "I didn't kill Ned, but I didn't get there soon enough to keep him from gettin' killed. He was my friend." His confession of innocence brought a welcome relief to the women. Even though they had tried to help him escape, they would never have condoned his killing of the deputy marshal.

Chapter 10

Joe French propped his shovel against the side of the sluice box and picked up his rifle from the bank of the stream. "Oscar!" he called out. "We got company."

At the other end of the box, Oscar Morris responded at once. "Where?" he asked, alert at once while wading ashore to fetch his own rifle.

"Comin' up the stream, 'bout halfway down to that tree lyin' over it," Joe replied, his eyes never leaving the figure on horseback, partially hidden by the leaves of the plum bushes that lined both sides of the stream.

"How many? Can you tell?" Oscar asked while straining to catch sight of them.

After a long moment, Joe answered, "Just one." He kept his eyes on the solitary figure making its way up toward their claim. "Keep your rifle handy." There had been reports of some Indian attacks upon small claims along this stream, but they were in the lower part of it, closer to the valley. "It ain't no Injun," he called out a few seconds later. Relieved but still cautious, he walked a few paces farther up on the bank to await the arrival of the visitor. In a couple of minutes he was joined by his partner. "Looks like a drifter," Joe remarked, "but he's comin' on in. That one you saw a-settin' up on the hill the other time just watched for a spell and moved on." He didn't have to remind Oscar how that had spooked both of them into staying awake all night to stand guard.

"Might be the same feller," Oscar said, even though it had been back before the winter set in, "but this'un ain't wearin' animal hides." Further speculation was interrupted when the visitor hailed the camp.

"Hello there," Buck Dawson yelled. "All right if I come on in?"

"If you've got peaceful intentions, come in, and welcome," Oscar replied.

"Well, my intentions are peaceful," Buck replied, and started his horse walking again toward the sluice box. "Havin' any luck?" he asked in greeting as he pulled up before the two miners.

"Not so much as a feller would dance a jig over," Joe replied. "We keep hopin', though." He wanted to brag about the discovery of gold in the wide stream, and the fact that they were sluicing at the rate of almost fifty cents a pan, but he decided he'd better keep their success quiet. As far as he had been able to determine, he and Oscar were the only ones to have found this rich little stream, at least for half a mile in both directions. "If we don't find some pay dirt pretty soon, I reckon we'll pack up and look somewhere else."

"There's a bunch of fellers in a gulch a couple of miles back that way," Buck said, pointing to the east. "They was all findin' a little color. Trouble is, there's too many of 'em goin' after it. Ain't enough to go around. Now, me, I'm more like you fellers. I'll find me a spot where ain't nobody else been."

"That's what we done," Oscar said. "Get it before somebody else finds out about it and turns it into a glory hole." A look from Joe caused him to add, "Course, we ain't found nothin' here, so we'll most likely move on up the mountain." Thinking it best to change the subject then, he said, "There was a feller that came by our claim a few months back, but he didn't come on down to the camp—just sat up there on the side of the hill and watched for a while. Then he up and left. That wasn't you, was it?"

"Course it weren't him," Joe interrupted before Buck could answer. "That feller looked like an Injun, wearin' skins for clothes and sneakin' around in the trees." He turned to Buck. "He didn't think we saw him, but we caught a glimpse when he crossed that little clearin' in the pines up there." He pointed to a small opening in the trees a few hundred feet up the mountain.

Buck's interest was captured right away. He remembered the description that Boyd had given of the half-wild man called Wolf. It would be one hell of a coincidence if the man just described by Joe French was the man he and his brothers hunted. There were a good many men wearing buckskins on this side of the Mississippi, but what if they had been lucky enough to have stumbled upon his trail—even after this length of time? "No," he said, "your partner's right. It weren't me, but it might be somebody I know. Was he on a horse?"

"Well, like Joe said," Oscar replied, "we didn't get a real good look at him, but he was leadin' two horses—least that's what it looked like to me."

"That's mighty interestin'," Buck said, and turned to look again at the small clearing in the trees above the stream. When he turned back to face them, he had his .44 pistol in his hand. Both men tensed at once, too surprised to react quickly enough, although Joe started to pull his rifle up closer to him. "I wouldn't even try it," Buck warned. "I'd cut you down before you raised it above your pecker. Now, suppose you just drop them rifles right there on the ground, and we'll make this as easy as we can?"

Though startled by the sudden change in the friendly stranger, Joe recovered enough of his nerve to protest, "Mister, we done told you we ain't hit no pay dirt, so there ain't no use to try to take somethin' that ain't here."

His words were met with a broad smile from Buck. "I don't believe you've been honest with me. I believe you boys have been pullin' a lot of gold outta this stream. All I said was that I wanted to see it. Hell, if you make it easy on me, I'll cut you in for a share of it. Now, I think that's fair enough."

"You must be plumb loco, mister," Oscar said, recovering some of his nerve as well. "As far apart as we're standin', you might get one of us with that pistol, but the other'n is bound to get off a shot. Did you think about that?"

"I did," Buck answered thoughtfully. "That's why my brothers are settin' on the slope behind you with their rifles sighted right on your backs. Now, you make the first move toward those rifles, I mean wiggle a finger, and they're gonna cut you down like winter wheat." He raised his voice a little. "Ain't that right, boys?"

"That's right, Buck." The words came back from the pines on either side of the stream, almost in unison.

The rifles fell to the ground at once. "That's playin' it smart," Buck said. Then he raised his voice once again. "Come on in, boys." In a few moments, Boyd and Skinner emerged from the trees above the stream, their rifles trained upon the unfortunate prospectors. "These two fine-lookin' fellers are my brothers," Buck continued, a broad smile on his face again.

"Damn you," Joe snarled. "We ain't got nothin' to steal—not enough to kill a man for."

"You've got the wrong idea, friend," Buck replied. "We're not murderers. We're just partners. We don't wanna kill anybody unless we have to. So you just dig out that gold dust—wherever you got it hid—and we'll just take our share and leave you the rest. And if you come out with all of it, and don't make us have to look for it, why, we'll be on our way. And you'll never lay eyes on us again. Ain't that right, boys?"

"That's right, Buck," Skinner replied, "we only want our share."

Joe and Oscar looked at each other helplessly. Both men knew that they had little choice but to comply. And both men also desperately hoped that the three outlaws were intent upon robbing them only. Perhaps, if they did as Buck instructed, they would be satisfied to take what gold they had and leave them with their lives.

Growing impatient with the miners' reluctance to give in, Buck demanded, "What's it gonna be? You takin' the easy way or the hard way?" Boyd and Skinner moved in a little closer to them.

"All right, dammit." Joe spoke for them both. "We'll give you the dust if you'll take it and leave us in peace."

"Fair enough," Buck said.

"Come on, Oscar, we'll get our pokes from under the rock, and let these *gentlemen* get the hell on their way." They picked up their shovels and walked back up the stream to a rock about the size of a full-grown cow. The three brothers followed close behind, their rifles trained on the two, and stood, watching eagerly, as Oscar and Joe began digging at the base of the rock.

After a sizable hole had been dug, they unearthed a canvas bag, and then another. When one more bag was exposed, they stood back and Oscar said, "That's all there is. That's all of it."

"Is that a fact?" Buck replied. "Tell you what, why don't you widen that hole a little bit? You mighta forgot a sack or two."

"That's right" Skinner said, "it's easy to forget how many sacks of gold you buried." His comment brought a chuckle from Boyd and Buck.

"All right"—Joe exhaled wearily—"but there ain't no more pokes under this rock." He and Oscar set in to widen the hole. After half an hour more, with the hole now a trench all the way around the rock, Buck let them stop digging.

"Looks like you boys were right," he said. "And you ain't hid none under no other rocks. Right?" Both men nodded enthusiastically. "And you swear on your mama's soul?"

"I swear," Oscar said.

Buck nodded in return, and the broad smile returned to his face. He looked at his brothers again and gave one final distinctive nod. It was the signal they expected, and both rifles barked suddenly, dropping Joe and Oscar to the ground. The firing did not stop until they were sure the two were dead. Buck stuck the toe of his boot in Oscar's chest and rolled him over to drop in the trench freshly dug. "You ought not swear to a lie on your mama's soul," he said. Then, directing his younger brothers, he said, "Let's get busy and find where they hid the rest of their dust." Boyd and Skinner each grabbed a shovel and began searching for likely places to hide gold dust, while Buck went to rummage through the prospectors' tents.

After a couple of hours of searching, another cache of gold dust was unearthed at the base of a tall, column-like rock that yielded three more sacks. At the end of the day, they called it quits, after having dug around every likely rock. Well satisfied with the treasure that had cost them a full day's digging, they celebrated their "strike" with the prospectors' coffee and grub. "I swear," Boyd declared, "this prospectin' is hard work."

"Yeah, but the pay is good," Skinner said. "How much you think we got, Buck?"

"I don't know. Those two fools ain't even got a balance scale. I don't know what gold's sellin' for right now, but I figure we got us all we're gonna need before we track that son of a bitch down." The comment caused them to refocus on the reason they were there.

"It ain't gonna be easy finding him in these mountains," Boyd declared. "He could be campin' in the next valley to this one, and we wouldn't know it."

"Maybe so," Buck responded, "but this feller said he just kept goin' along that ridge, headin' north—didn't even bother to stop and say howdy. I'm bettin' he was on his way to that gold strike up in Deadwood Gulch— most likely spent the winter there—so we need to quit lookin' around in these mountains and head up that way ourselves.

Like the man they hunted, they had never been to Deadwood Gulch, but also like him, they found a common trail that miners and freighters had already created. It was easy enough to follow, and it led them to a thriving mining community of tents and huts. As the Dawson brothers rode into the midst of the activity, they could readily see a town in the early stages of birth, and figured this was the place they were looking for. To verify it, they pulled up before a rough shack with a sign that proclaimed it to be a general store, operated by one Reuben Little. The paint on the sign had not completely dried.

Inside, they found Reuben opening a barrel of dried apples with a hatchet. "Evenin', gents," Reuben said. "How can I help you?"

"Is this here Deadwood Gulch?" Buck asked.

"Ah, no, sir," Reuben answered. "This is Stonewall. If you're looking for that gulch, it's about forty-five or fifty miles north of here, as the crow flies." Seeing the look of disappointment upon their faces, he was quick to suggest, "This is gonna be a fine little town right here, if you fellows are looking to find a claim for yourselves." They were as rough a lot as he had ever seen, but so was most everybody else who braved the dangers of looking for gold in Indian Territory.

"Well, that's a mighty temptin' idea, ain't it, boys?" Buck replied. "But I reckon we'll be passin' right on through. But we might buy a few supplies before we go."

"I'd like me some of them apples," Skinner sang out. "Ain't that what's in that barrel?"

"Sure is," Reuben replied. "Come to me by way of Denver."

"Yes, sir, we mighta stayed here awhile," Buck continued. "But you see, we're supposed to catch up with a friend of ours, and he said he's goin' to Deadwood Gulch. You ain't seen him come through here, have you?" Reuben shrugged. "He's a kinda wild-lookin' feller—name's Wolf."

Reuben's eyes lit up immediately. "Him, yes, sir, he was in here, all right. I knew I'd remember him. But it was back before winter, I reckon. I ain't sure exactly."

Skinner shot Buck a look of smug satisfaction. It appeared Buck's hunch on where Wolf was likely heading was right on the money. "Did he say he was goin' to Deadwood Gulch?" Skinner asked.

Reuben thought for a second before answering, "He may have. Tell you the truth, I don't remember if he did or not. The more I recollect, I don't believe he said anything about where he was heading." He shook his head thoughtfully as he recalled the somber man with the unblinking stare. "He was a strange fellow. Say he was a friend of yours? He didn't lose any time hanging around here. I think towns make him nervous."

"They might at that," Buck remarked. "That's the way he is, all right." With plenty of stolen gold dust to buy supplies, they threw a little business Reuben's way, with rifle cartridges accounting for the most part—although they did spend a little for a sack of dried apples at Skinner's request. Boyd argued in favor of staying overnight in Stonewall to take advantage of the availability of a saloon. But Buck said no to the idea, his reason being they were at least a two-day ride from Deadwood, so he wanted to get started as soon as possible. "This critter we're chasin' is a drifter, blowing in the wind. I don't know how long he'll stay in one place before he gets the itch to move on, but he mighta stayed there. And it'll be a helluva sight easier lookin' for him in a town, instead of havin' to comb these damn mountains."

The object of their search was at that moment getting his first look at Deadwood, and he didn't care much for what he saw. The canyon walls were covered with dead trees and looked as if a huge fire had ravaged the gulch years before. He had thought Stonewall a festering hill of termites, but Deadwood looked to be even busier, swarming with miners already. "You said this place was a new strike," he said to Lorena as he sat his horse beside the wagon seat while the four of them paused to gaze down toward the gulch below them.

"It is," Lorena replied. "It don't take long for word to get around about a new strike. Hell, next week, there'll be a heap more folks movin' in, and more the week after that. We've gotten over the real winter weather now. There'll be a lot more placer minin' goin' on in a week or two now that the creeks ain't frozen over, and all these miners will be lookin' for someplace to spend everything they dig up. That's why we want to get set up for business while we still might have a chance to find a good spot, so we can help these boys get rid of some of that gold dust."

"Why do you want to stay in that business?" Wolf could not help asking. Lorena was not a young woman anymore. "Why don't you forget about Deadwood Gulch and maybe settle down with one man on a farm or a ranch?"

Lorena threw her head back and let forth a lusty laugh. "Who let the preacher in here? Is that a proposal of marriage? If it is, I accept. When do you wanna tie the knot?"

Embarrassed by her response, he was too flustered to respond. Rose stepped in to save him. "Lorena, don't tease him. You know what he was trying to say, and it was sweet of him to think you could settle down somewhere." Turning to him then, she said, "That would be a really nice thing, to marry someone and have a home and family. I'd like to do that, but it's too late for me."

"You're still young," Wolf said. "It's not too late for you."

She smiled, but there was a look of regret in her eyes. "It's too late," she stated simply.

Not one to miss much, Lorena saw the wistful look in Rose's eyes, and knew that Wolf did not. She understood Rose's feelings, but was frankly at a loss as to why the young woman had set her sights upon Wolf. If there was ever a man less likely to settle down with a wife to homestead and raise a family, she would like to meet him. *Hell*, she thought, *he ain't even got a last name. Wolf—what kind of name is that?* She was fond of Wolf, too, but as she might be fond of a dog. *A big guard dog, one kept for protection,* she told herself with a smile. She didn't see any chance of taming the naive young man. He was destined to live among the creatures of the wild, and would more than likely meet with an untimely and violent death as a result. *It's too bad,* she thought, *but just like Rose, it's too late for him. And Rose? She should have married that lovesick soldier at Fort Laramie. It's sad to say, but she'll end up just like me.* She chuckled to herself then when she thought, *I hope she learns to be satisfied with it as much as I am.* "Let's get on down there and see what we can stir up," she suggested. Looking at Wolf then, she said, "Well, you got us through safe and sound. I reckon you'll be on your way again to wherever you've a mind to now."

"Looks like you woulda got here by yourself," he replied, "since we didn't run into any trouble and the weather wasn't too bad." The temptation to do as she said and leave them now was hard to resist, but he had unknowingly developed a sense of responsibility for their safety. So he hesitated for a few moments before deciding. "I reckon I'll go down there with you to help you get settled before I go." He was still gazing down the hill at the beehive that was Deadwood Gulch, so he didn't see the broad smiles that spread across all three of the women's faces.

His stay extended past the day or two he had anticipated. Billie Jean parked Lorena's wagon a little way

up the north side of the gulch where the rude beginnings of a street had been carved out of the hill. There
was room for only one main street down the length of
the gulch, and that was already staked off in forty
placer-mining claims. The particular variety of mining that the three prostitutes were interested in did not
need a site next to the creek. Ever resourceful and
never shy, Lorena soon made contact with an aspiring
entrepreneur named Marvin Sloan. Sloan had already
established a saloon but was looking for ways to claim
more of the miners' harvests. At Lorena's suggestion,
an extension was soon under construction on the back
to expand his building to accommodate the women. It
would be big enough to provide a room for each of
them. In the interim, Lorena, Billie Jean, and Rose
would camp in the wagon until their rooms were
ready. There was some concern for the women's safety
while camping in the wagon, but this was only on
Wolf's part. Billie Jean assured him that she could handle any unruly drunks who sought to take advantage
of them. The temporary quarters did not delay the
start of business, although it did make things awkward at times. However, the arrangement was enough
to hurry Wolf on his way. As soon as he saw they were
settled, he bade them farewell, saying he might stop
back to see them in the summer. The three women
stood by the wagon and watched him ride away, leading Brownie along behind him.

"I kinda liked having him around," Billie Jean commented. "Kinda like having a pet rattlesnake, but he
don't belong in a town like this. He might scalp somebody."

"He'll be back," Lorena said as he disappeared into the busy street below, heading for the other side of the gulch.

"You really think so?" Rose asked hopefully.

"Hell, I know he will," Lorena replied.

"How do you know?" Billie Jean pressed. She figured that this was the last they'd see of their strange guide and protector.

"'Cause he ain't got nobody else," Lorena said, confident in her logic. "Except for some Crow Injuns he lived with a few years ago, he ain't got nobody but three old whores. We're his family, even if he don't know it."

"But being alone is what he claims he wants," Billie Jean argued. "All he's talked about ever since we met up with him is about how bad he wants to get back in the mountains where there ain't nobody else around."

"He'll be back," Lorena insisted. She looked at Rose and smiled as she said it. *But not too soon, I hope.* She and Billie Jean could still bring in a few bucks, but not usually until the hour was late and the whiskey bottles were low. She needed Rose to land some of the early drinkers. Lorena was realistic enough to know that she had only a year or two left before she would be too old to perform. When that time came, she intended to have a business set up with more girls like Rose to service the customers. Billie Jean was younger than she, but Billie Jean had not been blessed with gentle feminine traits. Rose was the future, at least for Lorena Parker. Realizing then that Rose was gazing at her hopefully, she repeated, "He'll be back."

"I hope you're right," Rose said.

Seeing the wistful look in the young girl's eyes, Lorena felt a slight tinge of guilt for planning so heavily on her to generate business. *But hell,* she told herself, *I didn't start her out in this business. She was a whore when she first came to me.*

Chapter II

He looked around him. It was time to move his camp.
It had been a good winter camp, but it was truly summer now and it was time to follow the animals out of
the canyons and valleys and hunt while the meat was
plentiful and the grass was green with new growth.
Already, his bay and Ned's red roan were fattening up
from the winter just passed. There were other things
on his mind as well. He needed supplies, mainly flour
and coffee. They had helped to make the winter more
bearable and he had been out of both for quite a while.
And cartridges—he needed to keep a good supply of
rifle cartridges. There were plenty of reasons for him
to ride back to Deadwood without having to admit to
himself that the primary reason was to see how Lorena
and the girls were taking to the gold mining town. It
was strictly a matter of curiosity, he told himself, and
there was nothing wrong with that. He had spent a
large portion of his life in a Crow village, and Crows

were naturally curious. With that justification, he packed up his camp on this clear summer morning and headed back through the mountains to Deadwood.

It was early afternoon by the time he reached the gulch where he had escorted the three prostitutes, and he was amazed to discover the growth that had taken place in such a short time. Seeing the greater number of people and buildings, he considered turning around and beating a hasty retreat, his usual reaction to busy towns. *But,* he told himself, *I've come this close, I might as well look in on the ladies. Besides, I've brought them some fine cuts of smoked venison I know they'd be glad to get—Billie Jean, for sure.* So he prodded the bay with his heels and followed the winding road down into the gulch.

He didn't remember the man's name who owned the saloon where the women had planned to move in, but he remembered the building. Even so, he had to pause for a few moments when he reined his horses to a halt in front of it, for it now proclaimed itself to be THE STAR OF DEADWOOD. Before it had simply said SALOON. Though it was early afternoon, the saloons were doing plenty of business, and the Star was no exception, causing him to hesitate again. "I'll just have a quick look inside," he told Brownie as he tied him to the hitching rail. He turned then to pull his rifle out of his saddle sling and stepped up on the stoop.

Marvin Sloan was tending bar in his establishment when Wolf walked in the door and stood there for a few moments scanning the room and the early evening collection of customers. His first thought was *Here comes trouble,* certain that Wolf was one of the occasional uncivilized mountain men who wandered into town to get likkered up and raise a little hell after spending the winter in a snow cave somewhere. Something about this one looked familiar, however. Then he remembered. This was the one they called Wolf that Lorena Parker had rolled into town with. Recognizing Sloan's face, Wolf walked up to the bar. "You want a drink?" Sloan asked. "Or are you looking to find Lorena or one of the other two ladies?"

"Lorena," Wolf answered.

"I thought so," Sloan said. "Look here, I hope you ain't coming to talk her into moving on somewhere else, 'cause I spent a lot of money addin' those rooms on the back, and she guaranteed me she would bring in enough business to cover the cost."

"If she guaranteed it, then I expect she'll do it," Wolf replied. "She usually does what she sets out to do. I just came for a visit. Then I'll be on my way."

Relieved, Sloan pointed toward the back of the room. "Go through that door there to the hallway. Lorena's in room number one." Wolf nodded and promptly turned toward the door. Sloan wondered if he should have asked him if he could read numbers. It was hard to see him as anything other than a creature of the wild, maybe the one he was named for.

Lorena Parker opened her door to the light tapping that came only moments before she planned to leave the room to work the tables in the saloon. "Well, I'll be!" she exclaimed. "I figured that was Marvin knockin' on my door, wantin' me to get out there to help him sell more whiskey. I knew it wasn't a customer this early. How in the hell are you, Wolf? I'm glad to see the Injuns ain't caught up with you yet. You look mean as ever." She finally paused then, long enough for him to respond.

"I brought you some deer meat" was his simple response.

"What?" she replied, surprised by his choice of gifts, but she recovered quickly. "Deer meat—well, that'll come in mighty handy," she said, at once hoping that it was not in great quantity and wondering what she would do with it if it was. "I'll give it to Marvin's cook and see if he knows how to fix it." Changing the subject, she said, "Come on, we'll let Billie Jean and Rose know you're here. They'll be tickled. I know Rose will, especially." She took him by the arm and led him down the hall, but stopped abruptly when she saw a little sign that said COME BACK LATER hanging on each doorknob. "Well, looks like they're both busy. Never mind, we'll just go in the saloon and have us a little drink. They won't be long." She took his arm again and turned him back toward the door to the saloon.

"I'll just have a glass of beer," he told her as they walked into the half-filled saloon. "That hard likker makes me unsteady on my feet."

"Is that a fact?" she replied. "Most men think it makes 'em big and strong, and the best lovers in the territory." She led him to a table in a corner close to the back door. "We'll catch the girls as soon as they come back," she said, then went to the bar to get their drinks.

They had not sat there long when the back door opened and a gray-whiskered miner came into the saloon, still hitching up his trousers, followed closely behind by Billie Jean. "Come see me when you get it up again," she said to the man, who made straight for the front door. Billie Jean laughed and nudged Lorena on the shoulder. "That'll be in about six months," she giggled. Having paid no attention to the man drinking with Lorena, she glanced at him then and immediately took a step back. "As I live and breathe," she exclaimed. "I swear, I didn't think we'd ever see you again around this hellhole. What brings you out of those mountains you love so much?"

"I brought you some deer meat," Wolf said, repeating the same simple statement he had made to Lorena.

Billie Jean, however, reacted with much more enthusiasm for his offering. "Hot damn," she responded, "that'll be a treat. We've been eating so much pork till we're starting to look like hogs. I'd almost forgot how good that fresh venison tasted when we were driving that wagon from Hat Creek." He showed his appreciation for her response with a shy smile, which inspired Billie Jean to continue. "Look there, Lorena, right there. Did you see that? That's Wolf's version of a big grin." Turning back to Wolf, she gave him a playful punch on the shoulder. "Where is that meat?"

"On my packhorse out front," he said. "I'll go get it for you." He got to his feet.

"I'll help you," Billie Jean said, and they started toward the door.

Just shy of reaching the front door, they heard Rose scream across the noisy barroom. "Wolf!" she yelled. "Wait!"

The man following her into the room suddenly grabbed her by the front of her blouse and demanded, "What did you call him?"

"Wolf," she replied. "That's his name. Now let me go before you tear my blouse."

He cast her aside violently and drew the pistol from

the holster and gun belt he was carrying in his hand. "Wolf!" Boyd Dawson called out defiantly, and aimed the revolver at the startled man already turning around in response to Rose's outburst. Impassioned by his craving for vengeance and shaking uncontrollably at the chance meeting with his brother's killer, he fired twice. The first shot missed, smashing the window beside the front door. The second shot found Wolf in the side, causing him to stagger against the door frame and slide down on one knee, his rifle clattering to the floor. The next moments were filled with instant chaos. Rose screamed again, this time horrified; customers scrambled to take cover behind overturned tables; Billie Jean was stunned speechless. Boyd, his target seriously wounded, paused to take more careful aim. Lorena, always the quick thinker, was close enough to Boyd to launch her substantial body into him, knocking him sideways and spoiling his aim. Furious, Boyd regained his balance enough to keep from falling, and turned his gun on Lorena. Before he could pull the trigger, Rose grabbed his arm and sank her teeth into his wrist. By the time he managed to pull her off him, Billie Jean had snatched Wolf's rifle from the floor and handed it to him.

With blood already soaking his deerskin shirt, and his mind clouded with confusion over the sudden attack, Wolf nevertheless reacted instinctively. Even as the room began to spin around in his head, he automatically cranked a cartridge into the chamber and pulled the trigger. His shot slammed Boyd low on his breastbone, causing him to stagger backward against the door to the hall, where he stood staring in disbelief.

Wolf's next shot finished him and he slid down the doorjamb to sit slumped in death.

Billie Jean went quickly to Wolf's side, followed immediately by Rose and Lorena, and the three women tried to stop the blood pumping out of his wound. Lorena pulled up her skirt, ripped off a large piece of her petticoat, and stuffed it against the bullet hole. Wolf stared at them with eyes still glazed and confused for only a few minutes before his natural instincts took over again and he started to pull himself up on his feet. His efforts only increased the flow of blood, causing all three women to plead with him to lie still. But the only thought in his mind was to retreat to his camp in the mountains as any wounded animal would do.

"Please don't try to get up," Rose pleaded.

A little more gruffly, Lorena demanded, "Whaddaya tryin' to do, drag yourself off in the woods somewhere to die? Sit still, dammit!"

Giving in to their insistence, he sank back to a sitting position, oblivious of all the activity in the saloon as patrons set tables upright again, picked up glasses from the floor, and gawked at the dead man. A circle of spectators gathered around the three whores trying to tend to the wounded man. One of them was Marvin Sloan, who was anxious to get his saloon back in order. "Who was he?" Wolf finally managed to ask.

"He said his name was Boyd Dawson," Rose replied, her face reflecting the deep concern she felt for the wounded man.

"Why did he shoot me?" Wolf asked when there was no recollection of anyone by that name.

"I don't know," she said. "I don't know. He just went crazy."

"Well, we need to get him someplace where we can see to that wound," Lorena said. "And send somebody down to the barbershop to get Doc."

"We can take him to my room," Rose volunteered.

"You need to take him someplace else," Marvin interjected. "He told me him and his two brothers just got in town. It's gonna get ugly when they find out he's dead. They'll be sure as hell lookin' for your half-wild friend there, and I don't want it to be in my saloon."

"I swear, you're all heart, Marvin," Lorena remarked sarcastically. "The man needs a doctor."

"I don't wish him no harm," Marvin insisted. "But I've got my business and my customers to think about, and I can't take a chance on that man's brothers comin' in here shootin' up the place and maybe killin' who knows how many innocent folks." He looked down at Wolf as if apologetic. "If we had a real sheriff, it might be different, but honest folks are up against the out-laws and murderers." Looking back at Lorena then, he said, "If you don't get him outta here right now, I'm kickin' you and your two friends outta my business. If he goes, you can stay."

"I ain't stayin'," Wolf forced out between clenched teeth, trying to bite off the pain. His instinct told him that he would be an easy kill if he remained in town. He had no idea what the brothers looked like, and he knew he would stand a better chance if the meeting with them was on his terms, in the mountains where he was at home. Although his wound was serious and painful, he felt that it was not a mortal wound. However, he feared it would hamper his ability to fight, so his one thought was to escape this town and find a place to heal before the reckoning. He tried to rise, but found he was already weakening. Rose and Lorena grabbed him and pulled him up to his feet. "Help me get on my horse," Wolf said. "I'll be better off away from here."

"He's right," Marvin said. "He knows what I'm sayin' is the best thing for him. He'll be a lot better off outta here. That fellow's brothers will be lookin' for him for sure."

"I think they were already lookin' for him," one of the spectators remarked as he stepped back to give them room to pass. "There was a feller at the poker table last night that said him and his two brothers were in town lookin' for somebody. I asked him if it was family he was lookin' for, and he just laughed and said, 'Not hardly.'"

Rose and Lorena exchanged concerned glances. "Why would someone be looking for you?" Rose asked as she struggled to keep Wolf upright when they got him out the door.

"I don't know," Wolf replied painfully. "Just get me on my horse."

"They're right," Lorena suddenly decided, now that she had more of the story. "He's got a better chance out where he knows what to do. Let's set him down in this chair while we tie up that wound." Turning to Marvin then, she said, "Get me some of those bar towels you've got under the counter—clean ones. Don't give me any you've cleaned the bar with, and bring me a bottle of whiskey."

"Those towels cost me money," Marvin complained. "Whiskey ain't free, either. Who's gonna pay for all that?"

Lorena paused long enough to send him a scathing glare. "I know you're fixin' to volunteer," she said sarcastically, "but I'll pay for the damn stuff. Now go get it." He went without further complaint while Lorena resumed her control of the situation. She pulled her skirt up again and finished ripping the skirt of her petticoat all the way around. Starting a tear with her teeth, she then ripped the skirt into strips to tie the bandage on.

Worried about the time wasted, Billie Jean spoke just above a whisper to Lorena. "He needs to be outta here before somebody gets the word to that bastard's brothers."

"I know it," Lorena replied, "but we need to slap a bandage on that wound that'll stop some of that bleedin'."

Billie Jean understood what Lorena was saying, but she didn't have much confidence in Wolf's chances. "He ain't gonna make it on his own. I don't care if he is part wolf."

"I'm going with him," Rose announced. "Billie Jean's right. He needs somebody to take care of him."

Lorena turned to give the young girl a skeptical stare. "I don't think you know what you're takin' on."

"I'm going with him," she repeated.

Both Lorena and Billie Jean looked hard at the girl. It was obvious to both that it was going to be wasted breath to try to talk her out of it. "Well, I reckon you're old enough to know what you wanna do," Lorena said. Marvin arrived then with the bar towels and the whiskey. "We've got to hurry. If you're goin' with Wolf, you'd better run get some more clothes and whatever else you think you'll need." She didn't have to say it twice.

As anxious as he was to escape to the wilds, he knew that he needed the care they could give him at this moment, for he was already fighting to keep his wits about him. Although he kept telling himself that it was just a slug buried deep in his side, he was feeling weaker by the moment, and he knew that flight was his only defense against these strangers who had come to kill him. So he sat quietly while Lorena and Billie Jean removed his shirt, only flinching slightly when a generous slug of whiskey was poured over the wound. By the time they had tied the bandage around him, Rose was back with a cloth bag that held her belongings. She had changed to the trousers and coat she had worn during their journey from Fort Laramie. He would have protested against her accompanying him, but he didn't feel like making the argument. The bandaging done, they got him on his feet again and walked him out to his horses.

"Try not to pull on that bandage too much," Lorena advised as she and Billie Jean helped him get a foot up in the stirrup. The bay horse, suspicious of the party of people approaching him, sidestepped away from them at first, but settled down when Wolf scolded him. "Ready?" Lorena asked when he got a hand on the saddle horn. He said he was, so all three women got up under his behind and pushed him up in the saddle. "You all right?" Lorena asked. "You gonna be able to stay on?" He nodded. "Well, move your foot outta the stirrup for a minute till we get Rose up behind you." The slender young girl was a much easier task for the two buxom women, and Rose was settled up behind the saddle. She put her arms around him. Lorena placed her hand on Rose's leg. "Honey, I know you're doin' what you think you should. You just be careful. You hear?"

"I will, Lorena. I'll take care of him. Then I'll come back when he gets well—unless he wants me to stay with him."

The two prostitutes stepped back up on the short strip of boardwalk to watch the two young people ride away toward the lower end of the gulch. "I hope to hell she's doing the right thing," Billie Jean said. "I'm afraid there ain't nothing but a world of hurt with a man like that, living like he lives—like a damn Injun." She turned to face Lorena. "And what if he don't recover from that wound? What if he dies and leaves Rose out in some godforsaken wilderness?"

"That would be bad, all right," Lorena replied. "But I've got a lot of faith in that man, and I think he'll do whatever he can to protect Rose." She paused a moment. "As long as they can stay hid long enough for him to get well."

They remained there on the stoop, watching until the two horses and their riders disappeared in the growing darkness before returning to the noisy saloon to find Marvin spreading sawdust over the several puddles of blood on the floor. "It wouldn't hurt you to help clean up the mess your friend made," he said.

"It wasn't our friend that put that blood all over the floor," Billie Jean responded. "It was that fellow lying back there in the corner. Talk to him."

* * *

"Where the hell is Boyd?" Buck, obviously annoyed, asked Skinner. "I told him we were gonna head up the gulch this afternoon."

"The Star of Deadwood," Skinner announced grandly. "He's got an eye for that young little whore there, and you know how the women can work Brother Boyd for every cent he's got."

"That saloon's way down at the bottom of the gulch," Buck complained. "He'd better be on his way back here right now, 'cause I ain't plannin' on waitin' around here while he gets his tater cooked."

Skinner laughed. "That mighta been ol' Boyd shootin' up the place," he said, referring to the shots they had heard from that direction. "That gal mighta been busy, and you know how irritated Boyd gets if he don't get his way."

"I oughta bust a limb across his behind," Buck said. They had searched every store and saloon on that end of Deadwood, with no sign of the man called Wolf, and Buck was ready to move on up the gulch to the next little settlement. Their search had gone on for too long and had reached a point where Boyd was beginning to lose interest in the chase. With every passing day that yielded no progress in their hunt, Buck grew increasingly anxious to satisfy his desire for a kill, and he had no patience for Boyd's dallying. He stewed over the decision to wait for his brother or go on and leave it to Boyd to catch up as best he could. Finally he decided. "Let's go on back there and get him. The damn fool might not ever find us if we don't."

"I reckon," Skinner said, laughing again. He knew

Buck wouldn't leave without Boyd. He was just letting off steam. They stepped up in their saddles and turned back toward the Star of Deadwood.

Twenty minutes at a steady lope brought them to the busy collection of huts, tents, and rough buildings that made up the center of the town of Deadwood. Forced to slow their horses to a walk because of the congestion of horses, wagons, and a bull train, they continued on until within fifty yards of the Star. "Just like I figured," Buck said. "Yonder's Boyd's horse tied up at the hitchin' post, and us settin' up there waitin' on him. I'm gonna thump his ass for sure." He gave his horse a kick with his heels and hurried it along to the saloon, where he pulled in beside Boyd's sorrel and dismounted. Skinner guided his horse in on the other side of Boyd's and stepped down. The two of them were about to step up on the narrow stoop when the door opened and four men came out carrying a body.

"I reckon that's what them shots was about," Skinner commented with a grin as he and Buck stood aside to give the four men room. In the next instant, the two brothers froze when they gazed down at the corpse and recognized it as Boyd's.

Buck grabbed the arm of the man holding Boyd's left leg, almost causing him to lose his grip. "What the hell?" the man exclaimed as he scrambled to keep from dropping his share of the load. He had started to offer Buck a piece of his mind until he saw the unbridled fury in Buck's eyes and thought better of it.

"Who did this?" Buck demanded. All four men turned to look at Marvin Sloan, who had followed them out the door.

"Hold on, mister," Marvin exclaimed in reaction to

the accusing glare in Buck's eyes. "It ain't the fault of anybody here. The fellow that done this is long gone."

"Somebody better start tellin' me what happened to my brother," Skinner demanded, "and I mean right now."

With all eyes still focused upon him, Marvin hurried to assure the two sinister-looking strangers that he was in no way implicated. "We're all awful sorry for what happened to your brother, but it was between him and another fellow. Didn't nobody else have nothin' to do with it. And the fellow that done the shootin' took off."

"He had to sneak up on Boyd to put them two bullet holes in him," Buck said, his voice low and accusing as he suddenly cranked a cartridge into the chamber of the Winchester he was clutching tightly. "Who done it?"

"It was a fellow named Wolf," Marvin blurted, at once afraid Buck was going to start shooting indiscriminately to vent the anger obviously working up to a boiling point inside him. "And he's done gone, took off right after he shot him."

"The low-down son of a bitch," Skinner growled, almost beside himself when he heard the name of the killer. *Wolf*, the man they had searched for so long, and now they had to add the name of their own brother to the list of his victims. "He had to bushwhack Boyd, or he'da never got the jump on him," he said to Buck.

"Your brother got off a couple of shots," one of the men carrying the body offered in the hope of providing some consolation to the two irate strangers. "He was wounded pretty bad when he took off."

Over the initial shock that had paralyzed him for a

few moments, Buck began to think clearly. It couldn't have been much more than half an hour after they heard the shots when he and Skinner started back down the gulch heading to the Star. Wolf couldn't be that far ahead of them, and if he was wounded, he might not be in any shape for hard riding. "Which way did he head out of here?" Buck demanded.

"Yonder way," one of the men replied, pointing toward the lower end of the gulch.

Buck cocked his head toward the man and asked, "What kinda horse was he ridin'?"

"I don't know," the man said.

"He was ridin' a bay and leadin' a red roan," another man volunteered, eager to appear helpful, since both brothers were still threatening with rifles ready to fire at the first sign of hesitancy on the part of anyone questioned. "And there was a whore went with him."

"Ain't nobody mentioned the fact that your brother took the first shot." Standing in the doorway, watching the drama unfolding, Lorena wasn't going to let them omit that fact. "Your brother tried to shoot Wolf in the back, without no warnin' or nothin'—just out-and-out murder was what he was tryin' to do. But he got killed instead."

"Who the hell are you?" Buck asked.

"Somebody who saw the whole thing happen," Lorena replied. "And I know for a fact that Wolf didn't know your brother from Adam, and he sure as hell had no reason to shoot him except to defend himself."

"That son of a bitch is gonna know us before this is over," Buck snarled. "He'll learn the same lesson anybody else learns that messes with the Dawson family." He was in the process of getting worked up to administer a dose of punishment to the mettlesome whore when Skinner spoke to remind him that they were wasting time while Wolf was getting away. "Right," Buck responded. "Let's get goin'."

"What about Boyd?" Skinner asked. "Ain't we gonna take care of him?"

Concerned only with catching up with Wolf at that point, Buck paused to stare at the corpse of his late brother, which was still being held off the ground by the four men. "Boyd would want us to get the man that murdered him," he said. "There ain't nothin' we can do for him now." Thinking to appease Skinner, he asked Marvin, "Where were you takin' him?"

"To the undertaker for a decent burial," Marvin quickly replied, although his initial instructions to the four volunteers had been: "Haul his ass outta my place, and dump him somewhere far enough away so we don't smell the stink."

"All right," Buck said, satisfied. "When we get done with his killer, I'm comin' back to see that he's been took care of proper. If he ain't, I'll be takin' it outta your hide."

"Yes, sir," Marvin said. "We'll see that he's given a proper restin' place. Course, there'll be some expense involved that you may wanna settle with the undertaker." His remark caused Buck to glower menacingly in his direction, prompting Marvin to quickly retreat. "But that's somethin' for a later time." He took a step back. "We'll take good care of your brother." In the saddle then, the two Dawson brothers rode down the narrow street toward the lower end of the gulch, following the one road that led to the hills north of the town. Marvin watched them until sure they were gone for good, then instructed the four pallbearers to take Boyd's body to the barber, who was also the undertaker. "Tell him to bury him and put some kind of tombstone on the grave. Tell him his brothers will pay him when they return." He paused, then added, "And tell him I ain't got nothin' to do with it."

Chapter 12

Rose could feel the blood seeping through the layers of Lorena's petticoat bandage wrapped around Wolf's waist, and she was afraid the life was going to drain out of him before they could reach a place of safety. She had no experience in treating wounds, but she felt certain that he desperately needed to rest, to lie still, and maybe the blood would stop pumping from the wound. She pleaded with him to stop and let her make camp so she could try to do what she could to take care of him. But he continued on, refusing to stop until he found a place that suited him. He was not sure who was chasing him—even if they would be coming after him at all—but he knew he was in no condition to fight them. Someone had said the man he had killed had brothers and would be seeking revenge. It was all a mass confusion in his brain, helped not at all by the growing feeling of dizziness, probably from the loss of blood. The fact that Rose was riding in the saddle behind him was puzzling as well. He could not say why she had insisted upon coming with him, but he had not felt strong enough about it to resist, and he was convinced now that, without her, he might not have been able to remain upright in the saddle.

Rose could not understand why he would not stop to let her tend his wound. They had crossed several streams that looked to be suitable places to camp since leaving the road that led to Spearfish and turning back into the heart of the mountains. Still Wolf pushed on. "What are you looking for?" Rose finally asked.

"I'll know it when I see it," Wolf answered weakly, not sure himself, and unable to explain the natural animal instincts that drove him to retreat to his den to heal. He wanted to reach his permanent camp deep in the mountains by the waterfall, but he knew he was not going to make it, for it was a day's ride from Deadwood, and he was already spent. Finally, when images before his eyes began to alter in their shapes, and the dark pines seemed to have developed fuzzy outlines, he knew there was little time left before he would be useless in selecting a camp. Moments later, when following a game trail, and coming to another sizable stream, he uttered one word, "Here," and turned the bay's head up the stream, even as he began to lean heavily in the saddle.

Not sure if he was dead or just unconscious, Rose held him tightly to prevent his falling from the saddle. Equally frightened and determined, she let the bay continue up the slope, following the stream, until she came to a small clearing about two hundred yards up the side of the mountain. "This will have to do," she announced, and drew back on the reins. While trying to steady Wolf in the saddle, she slid off the horse and prepared to help him down. Bracing herself to catch his weight, she gave a gentle pull on his arm. The weight was too much for her. She collapsed under his body, and they both went sprawling on the ground. The jolt seemed to revive him somewhat—enough to express concern for his horses. "Unsaddle the horses," he said feebly.

Pulling herself out from under him, she told him, "The horses can wait till I take care of you." Taking charge then, she paused a moment to evaluate the spot they had landed in, and decided it was as good a place as any to make his bed. He was too much for her to move without help, anyway, so the decision was not that difficult. Relieved to see that the bleeding appeared to have slowed down, she refolded the bandage to press a dry portion over the wound. "Do you have a blanket?" she asked then.

"Pack," he answered.

She waited a moment to see if he was going to say more. When he did not elaborate, she went to the packhorse and looked through the packs without success before realizing that his one blanket was rolled and tied behind the packsaddle. She untied it and spread it over him. "That'll help you till I can find something to make a fire," she told him. "When I unsaddle your horse, I'll put the saddle blanket under you." He placed his hand on the small deerskin pouch on his belt. Understanding, she untied the pouch and found flint and steel among the items inside. She had seen him build enough fires to know what they were

for. Glancing back at the packhorse, she was at once
thankful for the quantity of smoked venison Brownie
was carrying, for she was not confident of her ability to
hunt for food—and he was going to need plenty of
good meat to build up his blood.

When she had searched through his packs for the
blanket, she had found no pots or pans for cooking,
so she took the hand axe she had employed to chop
limbs for the fire and fashioned a spit to roast some of
the deer meat. Resting a little easier at that point, Wolf
was reluctant to eat, but she insisted and badgered him
until he finally downed a small quantity to pacify her.
"You've got to build your strength back," she lectured
him. "I'm not going to let you lie around and die
on me."

"I don't plan to," he said weakly. It was enough to
encourage her. She gave him a firm nod to let him
know that she meant business, and left him to take
care of the horses. When she returned to his side, it
appeared that he was asleep, so she placed some more
limbs on the fire and sat down beside him. Without
opening his eyes, he said, "Bring me my rifle, the Winchester, off my saddle." He paused then as if talking
exhausted him, then said, "That Henry on the packhorse is loaded if you wanna hold on to it." She did as
he said, although she feared that if they were attacked,
he would be of little use, as weak as he appeared to be.

In a short time, night descended upon the rugged
mountains, filling the canyons and valleys with a deep
stillness that seemed to give weight to the darkness
that closed in around the little stream and the two
souls close by the tiny fire. The wounded man slept,
having given in to the weariness caused by his loss of

blood. Helpless against any who might seek him out, he lay defenseless. Knowing this, Rose sat beside him, holding the Henry rifle, determined to remain alert and to watch over him. She shivered in the chill night air and tried to draw warmth from the dying fire. There was only the one blanket, so she laid the rifle down after a while and hugged herself against the cold. Another hour passed and the last of the limbs she had been able to find before darkness set in were reduced to glowing ashes. Finally she gave in and crawled under the blanket with him, pressing close to his body. *I can still remain alert,* she told herself. *And the horses will help me listen and warn me if anyone comes near.*

When the first needles of morning light found their way through the thick dark branches of the pines that covered the slope, Wolf woke to find Rose fast asleep, her body tightly pressed against his, her arm around him. The fire had long since gone out, but the slight girl's body seemed to generate enough heat to keep both of them warm. At first alarmed that he had been so vulnerable to any trouble that might have found them in the night, he tried to rise to look around him. The pain that immediately shot through his side forced him to lie back. The movement was enough to awaken the sleeping girl.

"Oh!" she exclaimed when she realized she had fallen asleep, and she scrambled out from under the blanket. "I was cold," she rushed to explain. "I was gonna keep watch. I didn't mean to fall asleep."

"Well, we're still here," he responded, "so I reckon it don't matter. I'm still in bad shape, and I'm hungry." He considered that an encouraging sign. "Maybe you can get the fire built up again, and we'll see how bad that wound is." He paused to think the situation over. "I think you might have to see if you can cut that bullet outta me." When he saw the immediate look of despair on her face, he said, "I might be able to do it myself, but you'll have to help me." He forced himself to roll over on his good side, but not without considerable discomfort. "First thing, though, I need to get to the bushes."

Puzzled at first, she realized then that he meant he had to answer a call of nature. "I need to pee, myself," she said. "Here, I'll help you." She took his arm and prepared to help him up. With her assistance, he was able to get to his feet. "You can go right there by that bush," she suggested, pointing to a serviceberry bush a few yards away.

A look of despair quickly spread across his face. "I reckon I need to go by myself."

"You don't look like you can make it by yourself," she said, but his frown of concern remained firmly in place. "Don't be silly," she chided. "I'm a prostitute, for goodness' sake. Don't you think I've seen a few tally-whackers before?"

"You ain't ever seen this one," he insisted defiantly.

"Come on before you fall down," she goaded impatiently, took his elbow, and began walking him toward the stand of berry bushes. When they reached them, however, he refused to take care of business until she left him and returned to revive the fire.

The realization that he managed to stagger back by the fire was further encouragement that his wound was not debilitating and that if the bullet was removed, he might heal more quickly. "I'm gonna cut that bullet outta me," he told her.

Regaining her resolve, she bravely insisted, "I can

do it, but I don't have anything to kill the pain. I didn't even see any whiskey in your packs."

"We don't need anythin'. It's bleedin' enough to clean the wound. There's a whetstone in one of the packs. Take my knife and put a keen edge on it. Then I'll dig around and see if I can work that bullet loose." He grunted in pain when he tried to shift his body to make it easier for her to draw his skinning knife from his belt.

Pulling the knife free, she looked at it with apparent disdain. The long, cruel blade had been used to skin and gut animals of all kinds as well as any number of other tasks calling for a sharp tool. Reading her thoughts, he said, "After you put a good edge on it, you can hold it over the fire till it kills whatever's on it."

The surgery was not without difficulty. Wolf insisted upon doing the probing for the bullet himself, but because of the flooding of the wound with blood, he could not really see what he was doing, so Rose took over the job. With his encouragement, she overcame her reluctance to hurt him and began to dig deeper until she was finally successful in feeling the tick of the metal slug with the tip of her blade. During the entire procedure, he made no sound with the exception of a grunt and a deep drawing of breath when she cauterized the wound with the red-hot knife blade. When it was over, however, she saw that he was exhausted. As he lay back on his blanket, she watched him until he closed his eyes to sleep, and she prayed to God that she had not killed him.

"Dammit!" Skinner cursed. "If you think you can do any better, you can do the damn trackin'. There ain't no way I can pick out their tracks from anybody else's on this trail. I ain't got no way of knowin' what tracks to look for."

Buck Dawson made no response to his brother's outburst, knowing it was useless complaining on his part to expect Skinner to know one horse's hoofprint from another. It was the utter frustration of being so close to his prey, yet with no notion where he might have gone, that drove him to complain. With nothing more to go on than reports from those at the saloon that Wolf and the woman had ridden a common trail out of the gulch, he and Skinner could only surmise that they were heading toward Spearfish. The rapidly approaching darkness of the night before had caused them to decide it best to wait for morning before trying to overtake Wolf and Rose.

At a point now where the trail veered from a heading due north to turn more to the west toward the little settlement of Spearfish, the two brothers paused to consider the state of the man they pursued. "You know," Skinner suggested, "if that bastard is hurt as bad as they said he was, he might be too bad off to try to get to that little town this trail is leadin' to. He mighta crawled off in one of these canyons to try to lie up for a spell till he heals up some." The thought was inspired by a distinct set of fresh tracks left by two horses leading away from the trail, one shod and one not. The fact that there were no tracks of other horses made it even more easily followed.

"He might have at that," Buck allowed. In fact, it seemed more logical the more thought he gave it. He dismounted to give the tracks a closer look, as if they might tell him something to confirm the idea. His trigger finger began to itch as he continued to stare at the two distinct sets of hoofprints, and he decided they had to be the same tracks they had started out following before losing them at the onset of winter.

"Course, it could be some damn Injun that crossed over here," Skinner suggested. "Might just be an Injun with a horse he stole."

Buck considered that possibility before commenting, "They keep sayin' that feller is wild as an Injun, and he's ridin' an Injun pony. We'll follow 'em," he decided. "They'd better be the tracks of that murderin' son of a bitch, because I'm gonna shoot whoever's at the other end of 'em."

Skinner rose to his feet and looked toward a narrow ravine leading down to a canyon formed by two steep slopes. "They look to be headin' down to that bottom yonder," he declared.

"Well, let's get after 'em," Buck said, and they mounted up. He held back to let Skinner take the lead, knowing he had the sharper eyes.

The trail proved easy enough to follow for the first mile or so, but after coming to a series of small streams, it appeared that the man they followed had begun to take some measures to cover his tracks. Skinner lost them altogether a couple of times when the tracks entered a stream and failed to come out on the other side. Both times they spent some time scouting up and down the streams until finding the exit tracks, which led them back to the general path first started upon. "He knows we're on his trail," Buck said. "He's wantin' us to think he's changin' directions, but he keeps comin' back to the same line down the middle of this canyon." It only made him more anxious to track him down. They continued on until losing the trail again after crossing a sizable stream.

"Dammit!" Skinner swore. "There he goes again. You go upstream. I'll go downstream." They parted then and rode up and down the stream, moving slowly, studying the banks carefully for signs of tracks leaving the water. Skinner continued following the stream as it led him higher up the mountainside. He stopped after going approximately one hundred yards, and paused to listen for any signal from Buck, but there was none. "I mighta missed it, but I don't see how I coulda," he mumbled, and decided to keep going. Remaining in the stream, he pushed on until he stopped abruptly at a small clearing in the pines. He cupped his hands around his mouth and turned to call out, "Buck," repeating it several times until he heard a response from his brother, who had already reversed his search and was on his way to join him.

After a few moments passed, Buck appeared, walking his horse up the middle of the stream to find Skinner on one knee, examining a patch of grass near the bank. "Take a look at this," Skinner said. Buck stepped down and knelt beside his brother. "It's him, all right," Skinner went on, "and it looks like he might be hurtin' pretty bad. Lotta blood on the grass." He nodded toward the remains of a small fire. "They spent the night here, ain't no doubt about that." He rose to his feet then and walked over to some berry bushes a short distance away. "Had the horses tied here," he observed aloud.

"Question is, which way'd they head out?" Buck said. "And how long ago?" He was hoping that Wolf was hurt so bad that he wasn't able to get an early start.

"Hard to say," Skinner answered, looking around him on the bank for some sign that might enable him to make a guess. "His damn horses ain't et enough to make a turd."

"Dammit!" Buck swore, his impatience growing by the second. "That boy is hurtin'. They can't be makin' much time. We need to get movin'." He led his horse in a circle around the camp and it didn't take long before he found what he was looking for. "Ha, I thought so," he crowed. "He didn't go back down that stream. He cut across and headed right back to the bottom of this canyon. He ain't just lookin' for a place to hide. He's got a permanent camp someplace and that's what he's tryin' to get to." He peered down the slope, following the direction of the tracks and the occasional broken branch through a thick pine belt. He had a feeling the man they tracked was close, even though there was no physical evidence to substantiate it.

The object of their search was closer than Buck thought. About one hundred feet above him, near the top of the mountain, the wounded man and the young prostitute lay on a rocky ledge, watching their pursuers. Wolf was tempted to touch off a couple of shots, but there was no clear line of sight to ensure his accuracy, and a miss might put Rose and him in a position hard to defend. Something he was forced to consider as well was his still-weakened state. His aim was not as steady as he would have liked, and the recently cauterized wound greatly hampered his ability to move freely. Added to that was a heightened sense of responsibility for Rose's safety, so he decided to sit tight and hope the two men would move off down the mountain and follow the obvious trail he had purposefully left for them.

Ignoring a great deal of pain, he had led Rose down the slope, angling back toward the bottom of the canyon, making no effort to hide their trail. After reaching the bottom, he took pains to avoid leaving tracks then as he led the horses back up the slope to a place where the pines were thickest. Counting on his pursuers' eagerness to overtake him, he hoped they would not notice that he had doubled back through the forest of pines to return to the stream once again. After climbing back up the stream to their camp of the night before, he had continued past until reaching a rocky ledge. The entire effort was enough to exhaust him, so he positioned himself where he could see their camp below them and instructed Rose to take the horses back farther around the crown of the mountain, where, hopefully, they would give no announcement of their pursuers' horses. All this was a precaution in case they were, in fact, being followed. And now, watching the two men below them, he had proof that his precautions had been worthwhile. In no condition to fight, he had to satisfy himself with at least the opportunity to get as good a look at his two stalkers as he could from that distance. He felt certain that there would be a day of reckoning between them. His foremost hope was that it would not come before he had been able to regain some of his strength.

"They've gone," Rose whispered when Buck discovered the obvious trail down through the trees, and was quick to alert Skinner. The tone of her voice betrayed the bravado she was trying to display. "We'll be all right now."

He nodded slowly to reassure her but kept his eyes on the little clearing below and made no move to pull back from the ledge. "We'd best wait here awhile longer, in case they found where we doubled back and figured out where we're hidin'."

An hour passed, and then another. Still there was no sign of the two men who hunted him. Finally, when his weary eyes threatened to close on him, he decided they had successfully evaded their pursuers. "It's time to go now," he said, and struggled to get to his feet.

She was there immediately to help lift him. "Lean on me," she insisted. "I may not be big, but I'm strong." She slipped under his arm and strained to shoulder his weight. His weakened condition would not allow him to puzzle over the girl's eagerness to help him. For now, his only concern was to reach his camp by the waterfall where he felt they would be safe.

With Rose to help support him, he walked to the horses and managed to climb aboard the bay. Instead of returning to the canyon they had ridden the day before, he continued around the crown of the mountain and descended the other side to what appeared to be a box canyon. He had killed an elk in the canyon before the passes had been closed last winter and knew there was a narrow passage at the end that led to a long valley. Once they reached the valley, they would be less than half a day's ride from the cross canyon where he had made his camp. Upon reaching the valley, however, he found he was too weary to continue on that day, so Rose was called upon once again to make their camp, a chore she eagerly accepted. After the horses were cared for, and a fire showed a healthy blaze, she carved off more of the smoked venison to roast for him. Feeling that there was no more immediate danger from the two men who had been trailing them, Wolf found it easier to relax and accept the nourishment his wounded body needed. On this night, Rose made no pretense of remaining on guard. Instead, she slid under the blanket beside him and snuggled close to his body. Although weak and exhausted, he was sharply aware of her slender warm body next to his. He was not certain how to interpret his feelings.

He awoke the next morning feeling a little steadier, and even though any twisting motion he made brought a stabbing pain in his side, he was convinced that he was beginning to heal. Rose, too, noticed the signs of improvement, and she went about making his breakfast in a more cheerful mood, even to the point of chiding him about his meager supplies. "The first chance we get, I'm going to buy some coffee," she said. "I need coffee to get my day started." She pretended to scold. "Maybe you are used to living like an Indian, but I'm not."

He shrugged, then winced when it caused a sharp pain in his side. "I have coffee beans in my camp," he said. "You can have coffee tonight."

"It's a good thing," she joked, "because I might be too cross to live with unless I get some." She smiled then in case he didn't realize she spoke in jest. She was almost lighthearted with the new sense of safety since losing those who had pursued them.

With plenty of time to reach his camp, they saddled up and moved off down the valley. It was early afternoon when they came to the cross canyon he had told her about. Though uncomfortable sitting up in the saddle, he felt well enough to make the ride with no stops to rest. Entering the cross canyon, they rode only a little over one hundred yards before coming to a notch in the mountain on their right. Looking toward a hole in the thick forest above when he pointed, she saw the falls created by a sheer drop in the rushing stream from a ledge about seventy-five feet above the canyon floor. As a precaution, he hesitated before riding through the narrow opening in the rocky face of the mountain base while he scanned the trees, then checked the ground to make sure there were no fresh tracks to indicate anyone had visited his camp while he was gone. Satisfied then, they rode in.

"By God," Buck swore. "Them Injuns mighta thought this son of a bitch was a spirit or somethin', but nobody said he could take off and fly." His frustration was growing by the moment, and he had to vent his anger on someone. "Where the hell did he go? You're supposed to be so damn good at trackin'."

"Don't get your back up at me," Skinner retorted. "I don't know how he done it, but he ain't left no tracks up this canyon, else I'da found 'em." He knelt down again to reexamine the game trail down the middle of the narrow valley. It appeared to be an often-used path and there should have been tracks on the bare ground. "He musta rode on the grass beside the trail," he speculated, although he could find no evidence of hoofprints to substantiate the thought. He got to his feet then and gazed along the path toward the mountains ahead. "Well, there ain't no tracks headin' back the

way he came," he announced. "He's headin' for someplace he's got in them mountains at the end of this canyon. He's been headin' for it ever since he doubled back
offa that road outta town."

"So we'd best quit wastin' time and get on up this
trail," Buck finished for him. "He's good, but there's
bound to be someplace up ahead where he ain't gonna
be able to hide his tracks." His irritation was such that
he wanted to make some move that might allow them
to catch Wolf, even though there was no visible evidence that the man had actually gone past this point in
the valley. Skinner had no alternative plan to suggest,
so he stepped up in the saddle and followed his
brother, who was already moving away at a fast lope.

Adding to their frustration, the valley ended at a
rocky pass between two more mountains, the floor of
which was almost solid rock. Skinner cursed the luck.
"There ain't no way I can find a track across this stuff,"
he complained as he dismounted to closely examine
the rock for signs of a scar left by a horseshoe, or damage to the grass growing in the cracks here and there.
He looked up at Buck, still in the saddle. "I ain't got no
idea in hell which way he went." He stood up then and
considered their options. There were two. At the end
of the short pass, there were two canyons, one on either
side of a steep mountain. He waited for Buck to decide
which one they would follow.

"It don't make no sense," Buck complained as he
considered his choices. "The man couldn't just fly
away—two horses to boot." After a long moment, he
picked one of the canyons and said, "You just keep
your eyes peeled. He's gonna slip up somewhere."

"What if that ain't the one he took?" Skinner asked.

"Then, by God, we'll come on back and go up the other one." He whipped his horse then and continued on. Skinner mounted and followed and both men went unknowingly farther and farther from the object of their hunt.

Chapter 13

Another night served to improve Wolf's condition noticeably, no doubt aided by the peace of mind and sense of security he felt in returning to the seclusion of his camp. His wound seemed to be healing as well as could be expected, and there was no lack of attention from Rose, who strived to anticipate his every need—even to the point where he had to insist that he didn't require all the care she offered. By the end of the second day in camp, he was able to move around enough to take care of the horses. Luckily, food was no problem, for he had plenty of meat cached in addition to the remainder of the venison he had planned to give Billie Jean. Even though he felt confident that they had lost the two men seeking to overtake them, he would have avoided using his rifle had they needed food in case their pursuers might be close enough to hear the shots. To Rose's disappointment, Wolf felt it was time to talk about her return to Deadwood, thinking she must surely be anxious to rejoin her friends.

"You're not really well yet," she argued. "You still need someone to help you."

"I'm all right now," he assured her, astonished that she could not see that he was getting around on his own with a great deal less pain. "I'm healin' up fine." Then remembering, he added, "Thanks to your help." He was not oblivious of the degree of help she had provided. Although his initial thought after first being shot was to escape to the mountains and hole up to heal, he had to admit now that it would have been a difficult time for him without her. "I wanna thank you for takin' care of me," he said then, realizing that he had not really shown his gratitude for her sacrifice. After all, she had placed herself in harm's way when she really had no obligation to do so.

She smiled at him and said, "I could take care of you all the time." The puzzled expression on his face told her that he didn't understand what she was hinting at. "Don't you ever get lonely out here in the mountains by yourself?" she asked.

"No," he replied. The thought had never crossed his mind. He had always been alone since he was a boy, except for the time spent in the Crow village. It was a natural state of being for him, and the few times he had complaints were the occasions when he had come into contact with other human beings.

"I don't guess a man would be interested in me 'cause of what I've been doing up to now," she suggested wistfully. "But I could change that in a second. I would make some man a good wife. I know I would."

Slow to realize the implication of her comments, he was suddenly hit with the impact of what she was leading up to. He shrugged and thought a few moments before he responded, "I don't see any reason why you wouldn't make a good wife if you set your mind to it," he said.

"Are you saying that you could forget about what I've been doing and start all over?" Her pleading eyes told him what he feared she was suggesting.

"I'm sayin' that what you've done in the past shouldn't be held against you—that a man would be lucky to have you as a wife." Before she had time to jump to the wrong conclusion, he was quick to add, "I think it'll happen for you someday when the right feller comes along. I hope it does, and I hope it ain't a man like me, so you won't have to live like a coyote on the run."

She bit her lip, trying to hide the disappointment on her face, but he had definitely given her his answer. She should have known better, she told herself. He had never shown the slightest interest in her, and she felt like scolding herself for being interested in a man who was little more than a wild animal. She was a whore, and she would die a whore, although she had thought there might be a chance that two misfits might make a strong union. "Well," she said, anxious to change the subject, "I think I'll finish the last bit of coffee in that pot. You want any more?"

He shook his head, knowing he had disappointed her, but in all honesty, any thoughts of a union with the young prostitute had never taken root in his mind. The idea of taking any mate had never struck him, and he felt bad about rejecting her. "Rose," he said, looking directly into her eyes, "if I was lookin' to take a wife, I'd be askin' you," he lied. "But I care too much to have you, or any woman, in danger from the likes of those two that was followin' us. And they're gone right now, but they'll be lookin' for me, so that's the reason I'm takin' you back to Deadwood, where you'll be safe—just as soon as I'm well enough to ride."

She smiled and nodded her understanding of what he was trying to put in as charitable terms as possible. "I didn't mean to scare you," she said. "I think you misunderstood what I was saying. I don't regret living with Lorena and Billie Jean. It's better than being tied down to some man." It was a subject best dropped, so they both sought to busy themselves with something else. For the next two days, they pretended the conversation had never occurred, and when Wolf told her that he was ready to take her back to Deadwood, she made no attempt to dissuade him.

While Wolf's gunshot wound was rapidly healing, the nagging wound that was Buck Dawson's frustration continued to fester, leaving him in a constant state of bitterness and impatience with every blind canyon they searched. His obsession with seeking vengeance for the deaths of his brother and cousins had even caused friction between him and Skinner, for he blamed Skinner for failing to track the wild man called Wolf. Reining his horse up at the boxed end of another narrow gulch, he complained yet again, "This ain't gettin' us one damn foot closer to that bastard. We've rode everywhere a man could ride a horse in these hills, and you ain't found nary a track. I reckon you've met your match when it comes to followin' a trail."

Skinner turned his horse's head, preparing to go back the way they had just come. "So you're blamin' me for there not being no tracks to follow, I reckon," he responded with undisguised irritation. "I swear, I'm about to believe the son of a bitch is a ghost. If there were tracks, I'da found 'em. So don't be jawin' at me about it no more, 'cause I'm sick of hearin' it."

"Don't go gettin' your back up," Buck said, realizing that Skinner was close to a boiling point. He knew he could whip his brother in a fistfight, and he knew Skinner knew it. But he also knew that Skinner would see to it that he got his share of licks in, so he backed down. "If there ain't no tracks, there just ain't no tracks, and we could hunt these mountains till hell freezes over and we ain't liable to stumble on that bastard's camp."

"You sayin' we oughta quit?" Skinner responded, ready to express his disapproval.

"No," Buck replied before Skinner had a chance to get wound up. "I'm sayin' it's time we played it smart instead of running around in these canyons, waitin' for him to wave and holler, 'Here I am, fellers. Come and get me.'" As he thought about what he was saying, it made even more sense to him. "Look at us. We're about slap out of supplies," he went on. "He's bound to run out, too, most likely. And he must be pretty close with them whores in the Star saloon in Deadwood for one of 'em to defend him and another'n to run off with him. I'm thinkin' that he's gonna be back there to see 'em sooner or later. He mighta gone back there already while we're out here chasin' our tails." Skinner nodded thoughtfully, thinking Buck might be making sense. Buck continued. "I'll bet that whore ain't likin' livin' out here in the woods."

"You might be right," Skinner said. As determined as Buck to track Wolf down, he was nevertheless ready to give up the fruitless search in the mountains and wait for the wild son of a bitch in town. "We're just wastin' time."

Their decision made, they turned around and headed back to the valley trail they had first started out on. "Just one thing, though," Skinner said. "When we get back to that place where they came down off that mountain, I wanna have another look at that trail."

It took a full day's ride to return to the spot where Wolf and Rose had ridden down through the pines, leaving an easy trail to follow. They stopped there to rest the horses while Skinner searched the hard dirt of the game trail that led down the middle of the valley. After a thorough examination by both men, the only tracks they could find were their own. It was only after Skinner had climbed up the side of the mountain where Wolf had come down that he stumbled upon the tracks leading back to the stream. "Damn," he swore, realizing then that Wolf had doubled back on them. "Here's why there ain't no tracks down there," he called to Buck. "The son of a bitch never rode down that valley. He musta went right back to that camp at the top of the trail, and if he ain't there, then I'll bet he headed back to take that whore home." It made sense to them both, so they hurried to get back to the stream and climb back up to the little clearing where the pair they were hunting had camped. Finding no one there, they headed straight back to Deadwood.

I hope to hell that ain't some fool looking for a ride this early in the morning, Lorena thought as she closed her robe and tied the belt around her waist. At her age, she could no longer be choosy about her customers, but it took her a little longer to get herself ready in the morning. "All right, I'm comin'," she called out when the tapping on her door continued. "Well, for goodness' sake!" she exclaimed when she opened the door to find Rose and Wolf standing there in the hall. Holding the door open wide then, she stepped back and said, "Come on in." When they were inside, she closed the door and took a good look at Wolf. "You look a little better than the last time I saw you. I never woulda thought you'd be on your feet again this soon."

"He's strong as an ox," Rose answered for him.

Lorena gazed at Rose for a long moment before stepping up to give her a hug. She knew what the young girl had been hoping for, and from the lack of a joyous expression on her face, she guessed that it had not happened. She wished that she could convince Rose that a future with Wolf was not in the cards. Releasing her then, she said cheerfully, "I'll put on some coffee, and maybe we can find somethin' to eat around here. I wish I had known you were comin'. I woulda had somethin' cooked. I'll go tell Billie Jean you're back, maybe borrow a little flour from her to at least fry up some bread." She took a dipper and filled her coffeepot with water from a bucket on the table. "Well, tell me what's happened," she demanded impatiently. "What about those two hooligans who were

lookin' for you?" She was accustomed to the stony
reaction typical of Wolf, but she expected some indication of urgency from Rose.

"We lost them," Rose replied, "back in the mountains." She went on to relate what had happened since
she and Wolf had fled from Deadwood.

"But why did you come back here so soon?" Lorena
asked, unable to understand the reason. "If they didn't
find you out there, you know they're still gonna be
lookin' for you. It don't seem like the smart thing to do
to come back here."

Finally Wolf spoke. "It'll be safer for Rose here with
you and Billie Jean. I don't want to take a chance on her
gettin' hurt with me. I'll be leavin' right away."

That figures, Lorena thought. *And that will probably be
the last Rose or anyone of us will ever see of you.* With the
coffeepot charged up and on the stove, she said, "I'll go
get Billie Jean."

"I'll do it," Rose volunteered, and headed for the
door, leaving Lorena time to talk to Wolf alone.

"How well are you?" Lorena wanted to know. "You
look a little peaked." When Wolf shrugged indifferently, she said, "Those two fellers looked mean enough
to cause you some real harm, and if you ain't up to a
run-in with 'em, I think you're takin' a helluva chance
comin' back here. You know, that was their brother you
killed."

"I didn't have no choice," Wolf replied. "I reckon if
they catch up with me, it'll just depend on which
one of us is the luckiest. But I didn't want her in the
middle of it, if they do catch up with me, and like I
said, I ain't plannin' to stay around here long. I'm goin'

back to my camp and waiting for them to come lookin' for me." It was his intention to wait only until he regained his full strength. Then he planned to go in search of them. He realized at this point that he was at war with an entire family, and he feared it were not going to be over until he or all of that family were dead. Since he did not know how many men were in the family, it was a strong possibility that he might be hunted from now on. Further discussion was interrupted by the arrival of Rose with an excited Billie Jean, who was carrying a sack.

As surprised as Lorena had been to find Wolf back in Deadwood, Billie Jean wanted to know all the details of his and Rose's flight to escape an encounter with the two outlaw brothers. As she was never one to beat around the bush on any subject, her next comment caused some discomfort for Lorena as well as Rose and Wolf. "I sure wasn't looking for you two to be coming back here. To tell you the truth, when you left here that evening, I kinda figured you'd probably hook up together for good—maybe head for some other part of the territory, find you a place to set down some roots."

Lorena rolled her eyes toward the ceiling in disbelief, while Rose flushed, visibly embarrassed. Of the four, Wolf had no expression beyond a frown, although the comment caused a feeling of guilt, for which he had no explanation. He shifted his gaze to Rose, but she immediately looked away to avoid it. Seeking to change the subject, Lorena said to Wolf, "I don't reckon ol' Marvin will be happy to see you. He's still complainin' about the bloodstains on his floor."

"Hell," Billie Jean said, "I told him they add a touch of color to the place—gives his customers something to talk about while they're swilling down his whiskey."

"I won't give him the chance to complain," Wolf said. "I'm fixin' to leave."

"I reckon you can stay long enough to drink a cup of coffee," Lorena said. "Set yourself down at the table." He didn't argue.

Shifting her attention to Rose again, Billie Jean said, "There's been a couple of fellows asking about you. I expect they'll be glad to see you back." She grunted then when Lorena jabbed her sharply in the side with her elbow.

"I'm not doing that anymore," Rose said softly.

Astonished, Billie Jean started to respond, but Lorena interrupted. "Shut up, Billie Jean. Rose is tired right now. She don't wanna talk about it." She gave Billie Jean a scorching look.

"Ohhh . . . ," Billie Jean responded apologetically as enlightenment finally penetrated her brain. She looked quickly at Wolf, then back at Rose. "Right, no time to talk about that now."

Lorena's heart went out to the young woman, for she remembered when she was a young girl, and the dreams she had once dared to dream. It was a long time ago, but she could recall the sorrow and disappointment caused by misplaced faith. "Let's see if we can rustle you up somethin' to fill your belly before you ride off again," she said to Wolf, attempting to get past the awkward topic of conversation that Billie Jean had unconsciously introduced.

"I brought the flour you said you needed," Billie Jean said. "I brought some bacon, too, in case you didn't have any of that."

Before long, there was bacon frying in a pan on the small stove in Lorena's room. With no time to prepare a proper breakfast, Lorena added flour to the bacon grease and rolled the strips in it. "Not fancy, but fillin'," she announced when she served it to Wolf and filled his cup with coffee.

"Much obliged," he replied. "I wasn't countin' on gettin' fed. I reckon I oughta apologize for not leavin' the deer meat I brought you, but me and Rose ate it up."

"It was a good thing we had it," Rose said. "We'd have both starved if we'd had to count on me to do the hunting."

"She took care of me, and I don't reckon I've thanked her enough for that," Wolf said in an attempt to express his appreciation for Rose's sacrifice. He was about to say more when he was interrupted by a knock on the door. Without having to think about it, he picked up his rifle from the floor.

"Who is it?" Lorena asked.

"It's me, Marvin," came the answer. "Open the door."

Lorena got up from the table and went to the door. "Whaddaya want?" she asked as Marvin stepped inside.

His eyes reflected the displeasure he felt upon seeing the gathering in Lorena's room. "I saw the horses tied up behind the building, and I was wonderin' if you had some early visitors," he said. He didn't have to express the disappointment he felt when he found out who they were. He stood there a few moments, trying to decide whether to risk triggering the violence he had witnessed before in the man called Wolf by asking him to leave. One violent shooting was enough in his saloon. He didn't relish the possibility of another, and Wolf seemed to be the kind that attracted trouble.

"Don't worry," Wolf said, reading the obvious message in the man's face. "I'm fixin' to leave right now. I just had to bring Rose back."

The worried frown on Marvin's face relaxed in relief. "You know best," he said, then backed toward the door. "I'll get back to the saloon, then. I was just stoppin' by to see if Lorena was comin' in this mornin'."

"I'll be in directly," Lorena said as she closed the door behind him. "Like I do every damn mornin'," she said to those left in the room. "I swear, it's gettin' to where he can't get started in the mornin's without me there to help him." She didn't feel it necessary to admit that her assistance in operating Marvin's business was by design. She hadn't even told Billie Jean of her plans to work her way into a partnership with Marvin, the result being to eventually take over the saloon entirely. She had to think about the future, and she did not have to be told that her body, the only asset at present for her support, was already approaching retirement. Her original plans to be the first of her profession to establish herself in Deadwood had not been entirely successful. Already she found herself behind in that endeavor with madames like Dora DuFran and Mollie Johnson enjoying unlimited success. But Lorena knew that the demand for women in the towns along the gulch was great enough for all competition. Her plans might take a little longer, but she was confident that she could manipulate Marvin Sloan into a partnership to her liking.

Wolf got to his feet, drained the last swallow of coffee from his cup, and placed it on the table. "I best get in the saddle," he announced. "Much obliged," he said to Lorena. After a nod to Billie Jean, he turned to Rose. "I ain't got words good enough to thank you for takin' care of me."

She avoided meeting his gaze. "It wasn't much trouble," she said. "No more than I would have done for anybody." She stepped deliberately away from him then as if to let him pass.

Only Lorena saw her gesture as symbolic in releasing him from her heart. It might take a little time before she got over this disappointment, Lorena thought. But every whore Lorena ever knew was scarred from some disappointment in her life. After a while Rose would change her mind about getting out of the profession, and be back to work. What choice did she have? *In the meantime, I'll take care of her until she returns to pull her weight.* Then her practical mind came back to remind her. *She's got a lot of good years left in that young body.*

Outside, Wolf slipped his rifle back in the saddle sling, then took a few moments to check his horses. He remembered to say a few words to Brownie, since the gelding no longer had Ned to speak to him. The thought filled him with a moment of regret. He hadn't thought about the big deputy marshal for a while. *Too bad*, he thought. *Ned might have been a good friend.* He untied the bay's reins and said, "Well, your load's gonna be a little lighter without Rose behind the saddle." He pictured the slender girl then, and added, "But not a helluva lot." He patted the horse's neck for a few moments before stepping up in the saddle, wincing a little when the motion caused a stinging sensation in his side. He glanced down to make sure the minor pain was not a signal that something had torn loose and made it bleed again. When he found no evidence of it, he swung the horses away from the corner of the building where they had been tied. He was in a melancholy mood, and he couldn't explain why. Shaking his head in an attempt to rid it of meaningless thoughts, he nudged the bay and started back on the trail he had just ridden in on. Behind him, in the saloon, Marvin glanced up from behind the bar when a couple of early customers walked in the front door.

Too startled to speak, Marvin stared wide-eyed at the two rough-looking men walking toward the counter. He had truly hoped that he would never see them again. Hearing the door to the back hallway open, he glanced briefly in that direction to see Lorena standing in the doorway, frozen speechless as well. His next thought was to hope that Wolf had gone. "Good mornin'," he heard himself say, when he finally found his voice. "What can I get for you gentlemen?"

"You know who we're lookin' for," Buck growled, then turned and pointed in Lorena's direction. Wiggling his index finger, he summoned her to him. "Best check them back rooms, Skinner, see if they've got any company."

It took a moment for Lorena to recover her usual bravado, but she did as she was told, stepping aside as

Skinner brushed rudely past her. "He ain't here," she told Buck as she walked up to face him. "You oughta know he ain't. You took off after him when he left here. Hell, we need to ask *you* where he is."

"You know, that mouth of yours is liable to get your face busted up," Buck threatened. He was about to say more when Skinner called out from the back door.

"Lookee here what I found," he announced, herding Billie Jean and Rose into the saloon ahead of him.

"Well, now," Buck crowed smugly. "All three of them whores is here. There weren't but two of 'em here that night, 'cause one of 'em went with him—that little young one, I bet, 'cause I ain't ever seen her before. You ever seen her before, Skinner?"

"Nope," Skinner replied.

"So that looks to me like that murderin' bastard came back here," Buck went on. "And that means you all have been lyin' about it." He pulled his pistol and stuck it in Marvin's face. "And I don't like bein' lied to." Terrified, Marvin clutched the bar to keep from collapsing.

"He ain't got nothin' to do with the man you're lookin' for," Lorena insisted angrily. "He doesn't know where Wolf is."

Buck cocked his head to gaze at her. A smug smile spread slowly across his rough features. "Maybe you're right. Maybe he don't know where Wolf is. I'm askin' the wrong person. Bring that one over here, Skinner." He pointed to Rose. Skinner grabbed her by the back of her neck and pushed her over to face Buck. Buck took hold of her throat and pulled her up close against him. "Now, here's the way we're gonna play this game," he said, glaring deeply into her terrified eyes. "I ain't gonna ask you but once, and you're gonna tell me where your boyfriend, Wolf, is. 'Cause if you don't, I'm gonna put a bullet right between your eyes. And then I'm gonna ask the same question to the next one, and the next one, till somebody tells me what I need to know." He clamped down hard on Rose's throat. "Now, what about it, missy? Is he worth dyin' for?"

"You lookin' for me?"

The voice came from the front door of the saloon and startled everyone. Buck reacted quickly, shoving Rose out of the way and swinging his .44 around to aim at Wolf, but his pistol fell from his hand to clatter loudly against the floor. Then he dropped to the floor beside it, an ugly hole in the side of his head. Skinner managed to fire once, but not before Wolf ducked behind the door frame, where he dropped to one knee, swung his rifle around the frame, and fired a second shot. This one, because of his haste to fire, was not a killing shot, only hitting Skinner in the lower leg, but it was enough to cause him to panic, and he dived back through the doorway into the hall. He attempted to peek around the door to take another shot at Wolf, but the angry avenger was now walking across the bar-room floor toward him, firing one shot after another as fast as he could pull the trigger and chamber another round. The one-man volley was tearing the door and its frame to pieces as chunks of wood flew in every direction. Fearing his life was about to end, Skinner scrambled to his feet and ran for the door at the end of the hallway, ignoring the bullet wound in his lower leg. Wolf reached the hallway in time to see the frantic outlaw as he neared the outside door. He raised his Winchester with time to place the front sight squarely between Skinner's shoulder blades and pulled the trigger, only to hear the metallic click of the hammer falling on an empty chamber. A second later Skinner was gone. Wolf started to give chase, anxious to end his war with the Dawson brothers, but he felt compelled to make sure Rose and the others were all right and no one had been hit by a stray bullet. He could not explain what had caused him to return to the saloon: instinct, gut reaction, or something else. He just knew that he had felt that something was wrong. Whatever the reason, it had been a critical decision.

Reloading the magazine in his rifle as he went back into the saloon, he looked at Rose first. She was shaken, sitting on the floor by the bar where she had fallen when Buck had shoved her, but otherwise appeared to be unharmed. Marvin, his face still ashen with fright, exclaimed, "Somebody go find the sheriff!"

"What for?" Lorena responded. "He won't come." A sheriff had recently been appointed by a committee of business owners in the gulch, but fighting and shootings went pretty much unpunished in the wild boomtown.

His rifle fully loaded again, Wolf looked around the room once more before declaring, "I reckon everybody's all right. I'll be going after the other one." He turned and went out the door. Rose scrambled to her feet and ran to the door to watch him leave. He untied Brownie's lead rope from his saddle and retied it on the hitching post, then turned to a wide-eyed miner who was one of a dozen spectators drawn to the sound of the gunshots. "A man just rode outta here—" Wolf started to ask.

That was as far as he got before the man blurted excitedly, "That way! Ridin' hell-for-leather!"

All thoughts of a tender wound in his side gone from his mind, Wolf jumped aboard the bay and was off at a gallop down the narrow street toward the north end of the gulch. Rose turned back to find Lorena watching her. "He'll be coming back," Rose told her, a hopeful look upon her face. "He left his packhorse here."

Lorena did not comment, but to herself she thought, *She ain't learned her lesson yet.* She shook her head sadly and went to help Marvin clean up another puddle of blood. "Tell that undertaker it might be to his advantage to have an office here."

Marvin didn't appreciate the joke.

It was not difficult to follow Skinner's wild flight down the middle of the busy street, for the people were still parted after their attempts to avoid being run over or, in the case of wagons, a head-on collision. Near the end of the street, the parting of the crowd ended, causing Wolf to pull back on the reins and scan the alleys between the buildings. Then a lone horseman climbing up the side of the mountain caught his eye, just as he disappeared into a stand of pines near the top. Wolf swung the bay's head toward the mountain and was immediately off again, his horse laboring up the steep slope.

Confident that the bay could match the horse Skinner rode, Wolf encouraged him on until reaching the pine belt near the top of the mountain. Then judging from the condition of the gelding, he figured that Skinner's horse would be no better off, and Skinner would be forced to rest it or face the possibility of being on foot. That increased the high possibility that Skinner had positioned himself for an ambush, so Wolf dismounted and left his horse behind while he continued on foot.

By God, Skinner told himself, in an attempt to bolster his courage, *let him come on.* He was aware that Wolf was close on his trail. He had seen him take to the hill behind him, so he had whipped his horse mercilessly until coming to a narrow ravine that led to the crown of the mountain. It was deep enough to hide him and his horse, so he hurriedly dismounted and left the horse to stand with its head drooping, trying to recover its wind. Skinner, his rifle loaded and cocked, his left boot filled with blood from the slug that had torn through his calf, burrowed into the side of the ravine and waited for the man chasing him. While he waited, lying flat against the hard ground, he thought of the image of his brother's head as it was suddenly slammed to one side with the impact of the rifle slug. He could not rid his mind of that horrible image as he stared back along the path he had taken to the ravine. It was combined with frequent flashes of the determined countenance of the hunter stalking him now. He had killed Buck! And that was something Skinner had thought could never happen, and it was a crushing blow to his confidence. Always before, no one had stood up to the Dawsons, especially Buck, and he thought again about running but knew that his horse was spent. These thoughts were causing havoc in Skinner's brain, and he tried to calm himself. *He ain't nothing but a man. He ain't no spirit. He just got lucky with that shot that killed Buck, and he's got to come up through those trees to get me. And when he does, he's a dead man.* His attempted reasoning did little to steady nerves already frayed with fear.

With his eyes riveted on the pines below him, he shifted his rifle to his other hand and wiped the sweat from his palm on his trouser leg, quickly returning the weapon to a ready position to fire. Minutes passed with no sign of his pursuer. He should have been there by this time. *Where the hell is he?* he thought, and turned his head to one side and then the other, scanning a wide swath of the forest before him. There was nothing. The forest seemed to have gone deathly silent. Still he waited. Finally he had to assume that Wolf had broken off the chase for some reason. He had gotten away! *Time to get the hell out of this place,* he told himself, and turned to hurry back to his horse. He didn't see him right away, and he had taken half a dozen steps toward the bottom of the ravine when he suddenly discovered the pitiless form standing on the opposite side of the ravine, patiently awaiting him. In his panic, Skinner dropped his rifle when he tried to raise it to shoot, and watched in horror as it slid down the gravel side of the gully. He cried out his terror until silenced forever by the rifle slug that struck his chest.

It was over then. Wolf ejected the spent cartridge, chambered another, and took careful aim before making sure the man was dead with one more shot. Suddenly he was overcome with a feeling of weariness, as if his body had released all the tension built up during the heat of battle. Standing now, gazing down at the body of one who had come to kill him, he took a moment to consider the rage with which he had attacked the two brothers. Unlike the coolness typical of his actions in times of combat, his passion for vengeance had increased when going after Ned Bull's killer. Ned was his friend. The passion he felt to kill Buck and Skinner must have been created by the threat to Rose's life, and the rage that he had felt was another result. These thoughts were troublesome, and he decided it best to clear his mind of them.

A twinge of pain in his side reminded him that he was still not totally healed, but now that the threat to his life was over, he could take more time to recover. He made his way down to the bottom of the ravine to strip Skinner's body of weapons and ammunition, then took his horse's reins and led the weary animal back down through the pines to the place where he had left the bay. Like his brother Buck, Skinner had carried a '73 model Winchester. It would be worth a great deal in trade.

After a leisurely ride back to Marvin Sloan's saloon, Wolf dismounted and tied the horses beside Brownie at the hitching rail. Although it was still early in the day, there was a noisy crowd inside, generated by the shooting that morning. About to enter the saloon, Wolf paused, then stepped back when the undertaker and his helper came through the door carrying Buck Dawson's body. "I reckon we'll plant him beside that other fellow that got shot here," Wolf heard the undertaker say to his assistant. "Somebody said they were brothers." The assistant replied, "The two of 'em might turn the soil sour."

Inside, Marvin appeared to be selling a lot at the bar. *Gunfights must be good for business,* Wolf thought. He glanced around the room, looking for the women, and spotted Lorena standing over a table of four miners. A second later, he heard Billie Jean's raucous laugh from a table in the back, but there was no sign of Rose, and the thought entered his mind that she might be entertaining a customer in her room. *It's no concern of mine,* he told himself, and walked over to the end of the bar. Two men who were standing there took one look and moved away to give him room. Their movement happened to catch Lorena's eye, and she came to join him.

"You came back," she announced, primarily to herself. "Did you catch up with the other one?" she then asked.

"Yep," he answered.

"And I reckon he's dead," she said.

"He is," Wolf replied.

"What are you gonna do now? Off in the mountains to your camp, I reckon."

"Maybe, I don't know," he answered honestly, for his mind was a little mixed with emotions he wasn't sure of.

It was an unusual answer coming from the man she had come to know. He always knew what he was going to do. She watched him closely for a few moments, noticing his gaze constantly sweeping the crowded room. "She's in her room," she said, studying his reaction. When the look in his eye confirmed her speculation, she added, "Alone." Still watching his eyes, she suggested, "Why don't you go see her? I know she'll be glad to know that this whole terrible mess is over with."

"I reckon I could," he replied hesitantly. "But I reckon she'll find out soon enough."

"Why don't you go tell her?" Lorena insisted.

He shrugged, unable to think of a reason not to, then finally said, "I reckon she'll wanna know she don't have to be afraid no more."

She watched him move through the crowded saloon and hesitate at the door to the back hall for a long moment. *Go on, you dumb bastard,* she urged silently, *open the door.* Just when it appeared he was going to turn around and come back to the bar, he suddenly grabbed the knob and opened the door. *Well, congratulations, Lorena, you just lost the best chance you had to expand your business. You'd better start looking for a replacement.*

"Who is it?" Rose called out from behind the closed door.

"It's me, Wolf," he replied. "If you're busy, I can come back later."

She opened the door at once. "Come in, Wolf," she said politely while studying his face much the same as Lorena had before. "Are you all right? Did you—"

"He's dead," he replied without waiting for her to finish. "They're all dead, so I just wanted to let you know you don't have to worry about them no more."

"I'm really glad to know that," she said, finding their conversation stiff. "And I appreciate you coming to tell me." There was an awkward lapse of silence then when it appeared he had nothing more to say. "How is your wound?" she asked to break the impasse. "Has it started to bleed again?"

"No." He looked down at a stain on his shirt. "That's just an old one. It's holdin' up just fine."

"That's good. I guess you can pretty much take care of it now. You don't need anybody to take care of you."

"I reckon not," he muttered. They stood there for a long moment more in the cumbersome silence. Finally he grasped the doorknob as if to leave, but hesitated, and the faltering words spilled out. "I might need somebody to take care of me. I mean, if somebody wanted to. I mean, I'd do my best to take care of them, too." He suddenly felt as if he had plunged into a bottomless pool and he was struggling to reach the surface for air. But the smile that lit up her face encouraged him to say, "I've got an extra horse now, and a saddle, so you wouldn't have to ride behind me."

She stepped up to him and put her arms around his neck, hugging him tightly, her head nestled against his chest. "I'm not really sure if you're asking or not," she said, "but my answer is yes." She pulled back then to peer straight into his eyes. "I'll be the best thing that ever happened to you."

His grin spread all the way across his face. It was the first time she had witnessed such emotion on the habitually stony countenance. "We can even get married if you want to," he suggested.

"Whatever you want," she replied, then pulled back again. "But if we do, I'll not be Mrs. Wolf. What is your proper name? You must have one."

He had to think for a moment before saying, "Tom Logan."

She smiled, pleased. "That sounds a lot more respectable—Mrs. Thomas Logan. Come on! Let's go tell Lorena."

"I think she's already figured it out," he replied sheepishly.

Chapter 14

Walter Hoffman, undertaker and barber, directed his assistant, Harvey, to dig a little more dirt out of the fresh grave just dug at the edge of Mt. Moriah Cemetery. "We wanna make sure he don't come back up," he joked. The grave was located next to another recent one on which the dirt was still settling. He turned then when he heard a horse snort and discovered a rider approaching from the other side of the cemetery. "Howdy," Walt greeted the stranger when he rode up and stopped beside the grave.

"Howdy," the rider returned. "A feller in town told me you was fixin' to bury somebody today. I thought maybe I'd take a look at the body."

His request struck Walt and Harvey as strange. "The lid's already nailed on the coffin," Walt said. "Did you think you knew the feller?"

"I might. That's why I wanna take a look."

"Maybe I can save you the trouble," Walt said, not

wishing to open the coffin. "The feller in the box is supposed to be the brother of the one in that grave," he said, and nodded toward the other grave. "And they were both killers and outlaws. Ain't likely it's anybody you know."

"Open it up," Nate Dawson demanded softly as his hand dropped to rest on the butt of his rifle.

Walt had no further thoughts of objecting. There was no room for argument in the tone of the stranger's voice. "Yes, sir," he said. "Harvey, get that claw-hammer off the buckboard." Nate remained in the saddle, watching Harvey until he returned with the hammer and handed it to Walt. Without hesitation, Walt went around the edge of the pine box, prying the nails out. When he had removed enough to lift one side of the coffin about eight inches, he said, "That'll give you enough room to take a look inside. Is that all right?" Nate didn't answer but dismounted, grabbed the lid, and forced it a little farther. "You know him?" Walt asked.

"Yeah, I know him," Nate muttered, barely above a whisper as he stared at the ghastly image of his older brother. No attempt had been made to dignify Buck's remains. The body had simply been loaded into the wooden box. Nate felt the muscles in his arms tighten as a result of the white-hot anger that raced through his veins. "Yeah, I know him," he repeated. "I know both of them." He glanced at the grave next to the open one. "They're my brothers." His calm announcement conveyed the promise of something sinister to follow, causing both Walt and Harvey to take a step backward in case a violent storm was about to occur. Instead, Nate simply said, "Close it up."

Relieved to see there was no intent to take his anger out on him, Walt was quick to comply. "I'm real sorry about your brothers," he offered as he quickly drove the nails back into the coffin. "I'm just the undertaker. I didn't have nothing to do with their deaths. Would you need to spend some time with the deceased before we bury him?" When Nate shook his head, still calm, Walt decided it was safe to make an attempt for additional profit. He had claimed the weapons and the little bit of gold dust that was left on the bodies as his payment, but he thought it worth a try to take advantage of the brother's grief. "I was wondering if you might wanna reimburse me for my expenses in burying your brothers. I'm out quite a bit on the coffins and the burial itself."

He was answered with a stare as cold as ice and the only vocal response was a question. "Who killed my brothers?"

Wishing desperately not to be a part of the violence that was sure to follow, but afraid not to answer the stranger's question, Walt stammered, "Fellow name of Wolf."

"He killed both of 'em," Harvey offered.

"Where can I find him?"

"He's a friend of them whores at the Star of Deadwood," Harvey blurted.

Nate stepped back up in the saddle and pulled his horse's head around toward town. "Cover him up proper," he instructed Walt.

"You didn't say if you wanted to help with my expenses," Walt said.

Ignoring the undertaker's solicitation, Nate kicked his horse into a lope, heading for town. *Wolf*, he thought. *The same man Boyd had said was Mace Taggart's killer. And now he's killed Buck and either Skinner or Boyd. I don't know which.* What kind of man was panther enough to kill his brothers? And where was the surviving brother? If he knew his brothers as well as he thought, either Skinner or Boyd was searching for this wild man, Wolf, just as he was. He only hoped that he found him first.

Walt and Harvey stood for a moment, watching Nate ride off toward town, still amazed by what had just taken place. "Let's hurry up and cover this one up," Walt said, anxious to get back to town. "I believe there's gonna be some more business coming our way pretty damn quick." They hurriedly picked up the coffin and dropped it unceremoniously into the bottom of the grave.

"Uh-oh," Harvey blurted when one side of the flimsy box split upon impact.

"Don't make no difference," Walt said, already shoveling dirt on top of it.

She had guessed right. Lorena shook her head, still finding it hard to believe nonetheless. She couldn't help feeling joyous on Rose's account, since the young girl had wanted it so badly. But she had to also feel concern for the success of a union between Rose and the, frankly, uncivilized man of the mountains. Where would they go? How would they live? Like Indians? For Wolf, or Tom Logan, according to Rose, knew little about anything other than hunting. When she and Billie Jean asked the couple about their plans, they were answered with the honest confession that they didn't know. "I reckon I can feed us, no matter where we go,"

Wolf told them. "Ned Bull thought I oughta scout for the army. I'm pretty good with horses. Maybe I could raise 'em, or maybe I can learn to farm."

"That'll be the day," Billie Jean scoffed, unable to picture him in any of those roles.

"It doesn't matter if we don't make it but one day," Rose replied joyously. "At least we'll have that day."

Looking at the lean, powerfully built specimen of feral man, Billie Jean grunted, amused by the thought. "One day of the wolf," she said, "might be worth it at that." She picked up one of two bags that Rose had packed to take with her, and she and Lorena followed the couple out to the horses. They were going to Wolf's camp in the mountains now to decide where they were going from there. It was understandable to both of her friends that she wanted to leave Deadwood behind immediately, as well as the life she had known there. "Going on your honeymoon, huh, stud?" Billie Jean teased, amused by the flush of embarrassment on Wolf's face.

He placed his rifle in the saddle sling, then helped Rose up in Skinner's saddle. "I'll need to take these up some," he said, and started to adjust her stirrups. He heard the slug impact against Rose's shoulder at almost the same time he heard the gunshot, and he caught her in his arms when she fell from the saddle. He staggered back a step to catch his balance and saw the gunman standing near the saloon door, his rifle trained on him. Caught with Rose in his arms, and his rifle in his saddle sling, he was helpless to defend her or himself. He braced himself for the shot that had to come, but his assailant paused, with his rifle still trained on him. "Just so you know who killed you, my name's Nate Dawson, and I'm fixin' to send you to hell for killin' my

brothers." Then he suddenly jerked to one side as first
one bullet and then a second ripped into his ribs, dropping him in a heap on the ground.

"We'll see about that," Billie Jean said as she held
her double-barreled derringer up as if to examine it.
Standing only a couple of feet from Nate when he fired
the shot that hit Rose, Billie Jean had shoved her derringer into his side and fired both barrels. The last of
the evil clan of brothers was dead seconds after he hit
the ground.

The next moments were chaotic as Wolf carried
Rose back into the saloon with Lorena and Billie Jean
running to help him. "Take her in my room," Lorena
ordered. "Billie Jean, go get the doctor." She talked to
the wounded girl as Wolf swept through the barroom to the hallway door. "Rose, can you hear me?"
Although she did not answer, Rose nodded. "You're
gonna be all right," Lorena said. "Billie Jean's gone to
get the doctor. It don't look like it hit anythin' serious—
just your shoulder." They took her inside, where Wolf
laid her gently down on Lorena's bed. She stared up at
them, trembling, unable to figure out what had happened. Lorena kept assuring her that she was going to
be all right, but she was obviously in shock.

Though it seemed an eternity, it was only a matter
of minutes before Billie Jean returned with the doctor
in tow. He soon confirmed what Lorena had told Rose
over and over: she was going to be all right. "Nothing
to worry about," he assured her after he had dressed
the wound. "The bullet went through clean as a whistle. You'll be up and around in a couple of days."
Lorena paid him after he rejected her proposal to take
his bill out in trade. Then she walked him to the door.

Turning back to Rose then, she said, "See, I told you you'd be up and around in a day or so."

Perhaps the one more perplexed than the others was the man standing bewildered in the corner, watching the drama surrounding the girl he had just decided to spend the rest of his life with. How many more brothers were there to worry about? And if this was to be a never-ending line of avengers, was he wrong to subject Rose to such a life? It was Rose who eased his concern. Feeling stronger since the doctor reassured her, she was better able to talk about the incident, her fear having been quelled. When Wolf spoke of his concern for the other members of the family who still might be coming after him, she told him that there were no more. She was reluctant to remind Wolf of her prior life before she quit prostitution for good, but she thought it important to tell him that Boyd Dawson had told her that he was one of four brothers. "There aren't any more," she told him. "This doesn't change anything, does it? We're still going to your camp, aren't we?" She didn't know why, but she worried that he might have changed his mind.

"Nothin's changed," he assured her, "but we're gonna wait a couple of days till you're in a little better shape to ride." At peace then, she lay back and relaxed.

Since Wolf had no love for the beehive that was Deadwood, it was a long couple of days for him before everyone decided it was all right for Rose to travel—including the doctor—but mostly the decision was made by Lorena. With her okay, they packed up Rose's things on the horses again, and Billie Jean and Lorena stood in front of the saloon, along with Marvin Sloan, to watch their departure. As Lorena gave Rose a warm embrace, she slipped a small sack with several gold coins in her hand. "That's just a little gettin'-started money," she whispered. "Remember, if things don't go the way you hope, I'll always have a place for you." She stepped back then, almost trampling on the feet of an elderly lady who had come to see what the parting was about. "I'm sorry, honey," Lorena said. "I almost stomped your feet, didn't I?"

"No, no," the lady replied. "I should oughta watch where I'm going. Is that a wedding party?"

"You could say that, I guess," Lorena replied.

"The man in buckskins, is his name Wolf?"

Lorena smiled. "That man is Mr. Thomas Logan," she said. "And that respectable lady with him is Mrs. Rose Logan."

"Oh," Mavis Dawson Taggart replied, removing her hand from the pistol in her skirt pocket. "Well, I hope they make it all right. Times are hard on families these days." She turned and walked back up the street again.

Please read on for an excerpt from
another exciting historical novel
from Charles G. West

WAY OF THE GUN

Available July 2021 from Berkley.

Looks like I might have company, young Carson Ryan thought as he watched the two riders approaching the North Platte River. Always one to exercise caution, he remained in the cover of the cottonwoods on the north bank until he could see what they were about. *Cow-punchers from the look of them,* he thought, no packhorses that would indicate it was just the two of them on their way somewhere—maybe scouts for a wagon train of some kind. As he watched, the two separated to inspect the banks up and down the river, almost to the point of Carson's camp. It was obvious to him then that they were selecting a crossing. Unable to contain his curiosity any longer, he led his horse over beside a tall cottonwood and pulled off his boots. Then he stood on the buckskin's back to reach a stout limb. Climbing up in the tree, he looked back to the south and soon got the answer to his question. A faint cloud of brown dust in the distance announced the approach of a cattle herd. He remained up in the tree until he saw the first steers. With no further concern for caution, he descended from the tree to drop down on the ground. When the two point men rode back to meet the herd, he sat down and pulled his boots back on.

It was getting a little late in the day to cross the river, he thought. They'd most likely hold them on the other side tonight and cross them over in the morning. He knew from experience that cows weren't fond of river crossings. Although only seventeen years of age, he had worked with cattle for most of those years, so he guessed it would always be in his blood. He was hoping to catch on with a herd heading for Montana where there were already some big outfits grazing their cattle on the vast open bunchgrass prairies. He had come up from Texas with a herd of twenty-five hundred head belonging to Mr. Bob Patterson. Starting on the Western Trail at Doan's Crossing near Vernon, Texas, they went only as far as Ogallala. Mr. Patterson tried to persuade him to return to Texas with him to pick up another herd, but Carson wanted to see Montana. Patterson wished him well, and Carson set out for Fort Laramie, thinking it a possibility to catch a herd stopping there for supplies. It was a long shot, but at seventeen, a boy can wait out the winter and hope for something in the spring.

Carson was thinking now that he must have luck riding with him, because he had decided to make camp earlier than usual—and along comes a herd right where he camped. Maybe they could use another hand. One thing for sure, they weren't looking to buy any supplies at Fort Laramie, because if they were, they missed the fort by a good forty miles. "We'll just sit right here and see what kinda outfit they are," he told the buckskin gelding. On second thought, he decided it would be better to cross over to the south side, since that was more likely to be where the herd would be bedded down for the night. While he waited, he decided he would inspect the river to find the place he would pick to cross a herd.

"Well, now, who the hell is that?" Duke Slayton asked when he sighted the lone rider waiting by the river.

Johnny Briggs turned in the saddle and looked where Duke pointed. "Damned if I know," he replied. "He weren't there when me and Marvin scouted the banks."

"Well, he's sure as hell there now," Duke came back. "You and Marvin go on up ahead and make sure he ain't got no friends lyin' below that riverbank, waitin' to pop up, too."

Johnny wheeled his horse around a couple of times, straining to get a better look at the man before he complied with Duke's order. He had his suspicions the same as Duke, and he wasn't anxious to become the sacrificial lamb in the event that there might be a welcoming party waiting to gain a herd of cattle. "He don't look to be much more'n a kid," he finally decided. "He might just be a stray, lookin' for a job," he said. "And we're damn sure short of men," he added.

"Or lookin' for a meal," Duke said, although he noticed that the young man was riding a stout-looking buckskin and was leading a packhorse. "You goin' or not?"

"I'm goin'," Johnny replied, and wheeled his horse once again. "Come on, Marvin." The two of them were off at a fast lope while Duke turned back to meet Rufus Jones, who was riding forward to meet him.

"I'm thinkin' 'bout beddin' 'em down in the mouth of this shallow valley, where they can get to the water and there's plenty of good grass," Rufus called out as he pulled his horse to a stop. "That all right with you?"

"Yeah, hell, I don't see why not. I ain't wantin' to try to push 'em across tonight, and that's a fact," Duke replied. They were driving close to two thousand head of cattle, and by the time the boys riding drag caught up, it would most likely be approaching dusk. The herd had been strung out for about two miles since the noontime rest.

Up ahead, Johnny and Marvin slowed their horses to a walk while both men scanned the brush and trees behind the lone stranger, alert to anything that didn't look right. With nothing to suggest foul play afoot, they walked their horses up to the rider awaiting them. Johnny was the first to speak. "Well, young feller, what are you doin' out here all by your lonesome?"

"I was campin' down the river a ways," Carson replied, "and I saw you ride up. So I thought I'd say howdy—maybe visit awhile if you're fixin' to bed that herd down here."

Johnny studied the young man carefully. He was young right enough, but he was a husky fellow, and fairly tall, judging by the length of his stirrups. He could see no deceit in the deep blue eyes that gazed out at him. "Why, sure," Johnny responded. "Right, Marvin?" He didn't wait for Marvin's answer. "We're always glad to share our campfire with strangers. Where you headed, anyway?"

"Well, I was thinkin' about ridin' up to Fort Laramie and maybe catchin' on with a herd movin' on through to Montana Territory."

"Is that a fact?" Marvin asked. "Maybe you should

talk to the boss." He nodded toward Duke Slayton, who was riding up behind them now. "'Cause that's where we're pushin' this herd—up Montana way."

Maybe Lady Luck *was* following Luke, Carson thought, as a sturdy-looking man with a full face of gray whiskers rode up to join them. Like the two before him, he cast a sharp eye back and forth along the line of the bank behind Carson. Figuring that if there was any funny business planned, it would already have been happening, he nodded to the young man. "Howdy, young feller," he remarked. "Where are you headed?"

Marvin answered before Carson had a chance. "He's on his way to Fort Laramie, lookin' to catch on with a herd goin' to Montana."

That brought a look of interest to Duke's face. "Well, now, is that so? You ever work cattle before?"

"Yes, sir. I just came up from Texas with a herd that belonged to Mr. Bob Patterson, but he only took 'em as far as Ogallala."

"How come you wanna go to Montana?" Duke asked.

"'Cause I ain't ever been there," Carson replied.

Duke grinned. "I reckon that's reason enough. Reminds me of myself when I was about your age." He paused to think about it a moment longer before deciding. "We are short a man." He glanced at Johnny and shrugged. "Hell, we could use about two more men than we've got, but one more would make a heap of difference. Wouldn't it, Johnny?"

Johnny responded with a grin of his own, "I reckon that's the truth, all right."

"I guess we could give you a try," Duke went on. "This feller, Patterson, I reckon he was payin' you about twenty dollars a month. Right?"

"No, sir," Carson replied. "He was payin' me thirty dollars."

"That's the goin' rate for an experienced cowhand," Duke came back. "And right now you're a pig in a poke." Carson shrugged indifferently, and Duke continued. "I'll tell you what I'll do. I'll give you a try at twenty until you show me you can cowboy with the rest of us. Whaddaya say?" Carson started to reply, but Duke interrupted when a thought occurred. "You ain't wanted by the law, are you?"

"No, sir," Carson answered. "I ain't." He hesitated for a moment, then said, "I reckon I'll go to Montana with you." He knew he was worth more than the twenty dollars offered, but he didn't blame the man. Besides, he figured, he was bound for Montana one way or another, so he might as well go with this outfit. It might be a better bet than looking for one passing near Fort Laramie this late in the summer. He didn't know where in Montana they were taking the cattle, but if he had to guess, he'd say they had over three hundred miles to go. So they were cutting it close as far as the weather was concerned. It was going to get pretty cold in a month or so.

"Fine," Duke said. "My name's Duke Slayton. This is Johnny Briggs and Marvin Snead. What's your name?"

"Carson Ryan."

"All right, Carson, you can meet the rest of the boys at supper. Might as well just wait around till the drags come in and we settle the herd in this valley. You can dump your bedroll and other stuff in the chuck wagon and talk to Skinny Willis—he's the wrangler—about a string of horses." He turned to Johnny then. "You and Marvin pick the best place to cross in the mornin'?"

"Right here where we're settin' is about as good as

any, I reckon," Johnny said. "There ain't much bank to climb on the other side."

Duke turned to Carson then in a spirit to playfully test the new man. "What do you say, Carson? This look like a good place to push 'em across?"

"No, sir," Carson replied stoically. "If it was me, I'd try it upstream a couple hundred feet, maybe on the other side of that tallest cottonwood." He pointed to the tree.

All three men looked genuinely surprised to hear his reply. "Is that so?" Duke responded. "And why would you do that? The banks are good and low on both sides right here."

"Quicksand," Carson answered, matter-of-factly.

"Quicksand?" Johnny exclaimed. "How do you know that?"

Carson shrugged. "Well, I don't know for sure, but I noticed a couple of places toward the other side where the water looked like it was makin' little whirlpools. And it wasn't flowin' around any tree roots or rocks or anything, and that's what the water looks like when there's quicksand under it."

Duke couldn't contain the laugh. He threw his head back and roared. "Whaddaya think, Johnny? Maybe we oughta go ahead and give him the thirty dollars."

"I'm just sayin' that's what the water looked like when we got into some quicksand on a drive two years ago crossin' the Red River," Carson quickly offered, afraid he might have made an enemy of Johnny. "Might not be quicksand here at all."

"Ain't worth takin' the chance," Johnny said, apparently not offended. "That stuff can cause a lot of trouble that I'd just as soon be without."

"All right, we'll cross 'em up above the big cottonwood," Duke said cheerfully. "And if we get into any quicksand, we'll hang Carson in the damn tree. Does that suit everybody?" Everyone grunted in approval, including the new hire. "Now, let's get them cows watered. Come on, Carson, I'll take you to see Bad Eye—he's the cook."

Supper that night consisted of sourdough biscuits, white gravy, and sowbelly, washed down with black coffee. Bad Eye, so named because he had only one eye, wore a patch over the empty socket where his right eye had once resided. The loss of his eye had evidently occurred quite a few years back, because the rawhide cord holding the patch in place had worn a permanent furrow around the sides of his head. A heavy man, he perspired a great deal while he was fixing the vittles, causing Carson to wonder how much of his sweat had dropped into the gravy. It didn't seem to affect the taste of the food, however, other than perhaps adding a little more salt. The appearance of the cook seemed to have no adverse effect on the appetites of those lined up to fill their plates, and this included Carson. It seemed to him that the cook on every cattle drive he had ridden with was the last man to take a bath whenever there was an opportunity to do so.

The rest of the crew were naturally surprised to see a stranger at the cook fire when they had all gathered to eat supper, but all seemed friendly enough after Duke informed them that Carson was a new hire who was on his way to Montana. It was a rough-looking crew of men, but most drovers were, so Carson felt right at home. When Marvin sat down beside him with a plate of food, Carson asked, "Is Duke the owner of the herd, or is he just the trail boss?"

"Duke's the trail boss," Marvin replied after a gulp of black coffee. "There ain't no owner. What I mean is, we're all kinda partners in the herd. We own it."

"Oh," Carson said, "so I reckon I'm workin' for all of you."

"That's right," Marvin said, then chuckled. "Kinda makes you feel like the low man on the totem pole, don't it?"

"Well, it ain't like I never been there before."

Marvin laughed again. "You'll do all right as long as you pull your share of the load."

Their conversation was interrupted then when a tall heavyset man, who had been introduced as Jack Varner, knelt down to speak. "Duke says you know how to run cattle. Maybe you'll be ridin' swing with me," he said facetiously. We've been short a man, but Duke might want you to ride drag instead, and put one of the other boys with me."

"Makes no difference to me," Carson said. "I'll do whatever job you fellers think best."

Jack winked at Marvin and chuckled. "That's the spirit, boy. Whaddaya think, Marvin? The new man always rides nighthawk, don't he?"

"Maybe so," Marvin replied. He gave a nod of his head toward the sky. "I don't know, though. The way them clouds look, we might come us up a thunderstorm later tonight."

"Nighthawk's fine with me," Carson quickly interjected. He didn't express it, but he had always enjoyed riding nighthawk.

"Good," Marvin remarked, "'cause it was supposed to be my turn." He yelled over to Duke on the other side of the fire, "Hey, Duke, Carson says he'll ride nighthawk with me tonight."

"Is that so?" Duke called back. "He'll most likely do a better job than you. Maybe he'll stay awake." He yelled to Carson then, "You're still a pig in a poke, so there better not be any of our cows missin' come mornin'.'"

"I've rode night herd before," Carson responded.

"All right, then, you've got the job tonight," Duke said.

Jack got up to leave then, but made one more comment to the new man. "You'd best listen to what Duke told you. If there's any cows missin' in the mornin', he'll probably shoot you." Then he laughed when he recalled Duke's comment. "Pig in a poke, that's a good name for you—Pig, that sounds better'n Carson." He walked away then, laughing at the joke he had made.

"Don't pay no attention to that big blowhard," Marvin said. "He just farts outta the wrong end." He leaned over closer to Carson then as if what he was going to say next was confidential. "If you get hungry ridin' the herd tonight, sometimes you can sneak a cold biscuit outta that big drawer on this side of the chuck wagon. That's where Bad Eye keeps 'em when there's leftovers. He don't want nobody to get 'em, 'cause he mixes 'em up in the gravy in the mornin'. He sleeps right under that side of the tailgate, so make sure that eye patch is over his left eye. That's his good eye. He shifts the patch over it when he goes to bed." He snickered then. "Hell, if you're quiet enough, you can sneak a hot biscuit when he's fixin' supper if you sneak up on his blind side. But you'll likely get a thump on the head with an iron skillet if he catches you."

Ready to find
your next great read?

Let us help.

Visit prh.com/nextread

Penguin
Random
House